Kissing The Enemy

Scandals and Spies
Book 1

Leighann Dobbs
Harmony Williams

This is a work of fiction.

None of it is real. All names, places, and events are products of the author's imagination. Any resemblance to real names, places, or events are purely coincidental, and should not be construed as being real.

KISSING THE ENEMY
Copyright © 2016
Leighann Dobbs
All Rights Reserved.

No part of this work may be used or reproduced in any manner, except as allowable under "fair use," without the express written permission of the author.

Chapter One

London, England
April 1806

There was no one in all of London that Miss Frederica Vale disliked more than Lord Elias Harker.

Oh, she knew she *should* like him, and not only because he was a distant relative on her father's side. Thanks to his so-called generosity, she, her mother and her sister Charlotte hadn't been turned out into the streets after her father had squandered their money and then had the bad manners to die.

But she just couldn't bring herself to like Harker. In fact, she would rather stick a fork in her eye than be in the same room with him.

My eyes are several inches higher, you bounder. Freddie wrapped the shawl sewn into the shoulders of her beige walking dress across her upper chest, left bare by the modest curve of the neckline. Harker's hairy eyebrows waved like little pennants as he craned his neck to leer at the shadow of her cleavage.

With a sigh, he daubed at the sweat on his bald forehead with a monogrammed handkerchief. A glimpse of the embroidered letters made Freddie's stomach pitch. *LV*. Louisa Vale. It belonged to her mother! Freddie didn't want to contemplate how the linen had found its way into Harker's possession.

Tucking the handkerchief into the pocket of his waistcoat, Harker leaned forward. When his paunch brushed against her arm, Freddie took a healthy step away. Her back collided with the door frame. She knocked her head.

Ouch! She pursed her lips together to keep from making a sound.

"Freddie, are you all right?" From her position in the sun pooling from the wide window facing the cobblestone street, Charlotte lowered her embroidery into her lap. Unlike Freddie, Charlie wore a patterned pink-and-white placket-front dress in the newest style. With the blond ringlet falling from her pinned hair to caress her cheek, she looked the picture of London beauty. A diamond of the first water.

Harker's attention wavered as he glanced into the ostentatiously-decorated sitting room.

Don't you dare look at her, swine. Is my mother not enough for you?

Freddie cleared her throat. "I'm fine." Her voice emerged as a thin whine, but it did the trick. Harker turned back to her.

His beady eyes narrowed as he lowered his voice.

"I've secured an invitation to the Tenwick Abbey house party for your mother, you and Charlotte." He leaned in so close, she caught a whiff of stale cigar smoke and foul breath.

"Impossible." Freddie clamped her lips shut before she said something else incriminating.

The party at the unmarried Duke of Tenwick's ancestral estate was the highlight of the season. Hosted by one of the oldest, richest and most influential families of the *ton*, the party attracted the richest and most powerful eligible bachelors in Britain—including the duke and his younger brothers. Even for the elite, securing an invitation was quite the coup.

The Vales were pale shadows of the *ton*'s splendor. Ever since her father had left them with nothing, they'd survived on the fringes of Society. The small annuity her mother earned from an inheritance could not support the lifestyle of the fashionable *ton*. Harker, for all that he welcomed them into his home, refused to spend a penny to keep up their appearance. Even living in his house came at a dear cost.

Freddie glanced into the sitting room. Charlie hunched over her embroidery hoop, her clear blue eyes squinting as she focused on the fine details of a flower petal. Thank Jove Charlie didn't take after Freddie. If Freddie tried to sew, she'd probably wind up as bloody as if she'd fought Napoleon. Charlie's accomplishments with the feminine arts, paired with her beauty and vivacious wit, would be the key to landing her a rich husband and removing them all from beneath Harker's thumb. In fact, it had probably been what had earned them an invitation to the Tenwick party. That, and Charlie's friendship with the Duke's sister, Lady Lucy Graylocke.

Harker followed Freddie's gaze, a smug smirk teasing the corners of his lips. "This will be a good opportunity for her to make a match. Even better, with a dowry."

Freddie wrapped her arms around her middle to hide a twinge of regret. "She has no dowry." Their father hadn't left them any advantage.

Harker's eyebrows danced a cotillion as he waggled them. "Not at the moment. But she could."

Freddie held her breath. Her arms tightened reflexively around her waist. What was he saying?

What was the cost?

Freddie chanced a glance at her sister again. Only seventeen, her first Season out in Society. With her blond-haired, blue-eyed beauty, she was their only chance at marrying well. Freddie's brown hair, hazel eyes, and dusting of freckles certainly wouldn't attract a rich man. Or any man, come to think of it. Without a fortune, she had no allure.

But, of course, it wasn't only about money. Since the untimely death of her father, Freddie had seen it as her duty to watch over and protect her sister and their mother. She intended to insure Charlie married a good man, a man who would love and cherish her, even if he didn't have the means to lift Freddie and her mother from Harker's company.

The odious man leaned closer. "I will give your sister that dowry...*if* you do something for me." Once again, his gaze drifted down the front of her old dress, which had become uncomfortably tight around her increasing chest size of late. He wore the same leer as when he stared at her mother. It was not at all the way a gentleman should look at a gently-bred woman, especially one young enough to be his daughter.

Freddie's stomach threatened to turn itself inside out. What would she do to give Charlie a good life?

Heaven help her, but she would do anything.

She licked her cracked lips. "What would you have me do?" She rasped, her throat as dry as if she'd swallowed ashes.

Her stomach turned a somersault as she backed into the room. Her leg stung as she bumped into a table. It teetered. She lunged for it, and put it between her and Harker as she righted it. Thankfully the table had been divested of any curios years ago due to Freddie's wretched clumsiness.

Across the room, Charlie shifted in spot, cocking one ear toward the conversation. Harker turned his back to her, shutting her out.

"I need you to find something for me in Tenwick Abbey," he whispered. "Something important."

That's all? Freddie breathed a sigh of relief. *Wait...why can't he procure this thing of importance himself?*

She narrowed her eyes. "Do you intend to tell me what this important item is, or must I guess?"

He peered over his shoulder toward Charlotte, presumably to ensure she couldn't overhear, then glanced toward the stairs. Not a soul lingered, not even the servants.

"You mustn't tell anyone about this." His whisper was so low that Freddie had to lean toward him to hear. "I need a book. A code book."

"Code book?"

"Shhh!" Harker stepped around the table to hiss in her ear. He didn't have to lean down much to do it—they were almost the same height. She cringed as drops of spittle fell on her earlobe. "Yes, a code book. For spying."

"Spying." Freddie couldn't keep the disbelief from her voice, though this time she matched his pitch.

"Yes. One of my contacts assures me that it is ensconced in Tenwick Abbey." At her blank look, he added with an impatient look, "I'm a spy for Britain, of course."

"You. A spy."

"Yes." The wrinkles around his nose and mouth deepened as he sneered. "Are you bird-witted? I thought I spoke with the more intelligent sister."

Freddie curled her fists. *Simply because Charlie prefers balls and shopping to reading books does not make her stupid.*

Harker added, "If I was wrong..." He took a step away, half-turning toward Charlotte.

"No." Freddie almost grabbed his sleeve before she stopped herself. "Forgive me. I just...never thought of you as a spy."

A pig would make a better spy than Harker. If Harker's indolent, self-indulgent manner was an indication of the types of spies Britain employed, then it was a wonder Napoleon hadn't overrun them already.

"I am. You mustn't tell a soul."

Freddie nodded. "Of course."

Harker's eyes narrowed, his eyelashes sticking straight out like little daggers. He must have decided to trust her because he continued. "The two eldest Graylocke brothers are French spies."

Freddie's mouth dropped open. "Not the Duke of Tenwick!" Why would one of the oldest and most powerful in Britain turn his back on his country?

Harker's glare convinced her to hold her tongue.

"Yes, him. His brother, Tristan, too. I need you to get a book in Tristan Graylocke's possession before he passes it on to the French military. The book is coded with Britain's strategy for winning the war with France. If Napoleon gets his hands on it, it could be the end of Britain as we know it."

Freddie shook her head. "The Graylockes are one of the oldest and most trusted families in Britain! Is the entire family involved?"

"Apparently, they are not above the lure of money. I'm sure Napoleon is paying them very well. And I'm not certain about the rest of the family. Tristan and Morgan are undoubtedly the enemy."

"But why me? I don't know anything about spies or books...or the Graylockes."

Can't Harker find someone more experienced to ferret out the book?

"My movements will be limited at the party. The Graylockes already suspect I might be working against them so they'll be watching me. But they won't suspect someone like you. You're the perfect candidate to find the book."

Freddie narrowed her eyes at him. He did have a point. No one ever paid any attention to plain Miss Frederica Vale.

Since attending the soirees this year for her first Season, she'd felt invisible. Not that she minded. In fact, she liked it that way. She could probably scour the entire abbey from top to bottom, looking in every nook and cranny, even under the Graylockes' very beds and no one would notice.

"Will you do it?" Harker's eyes bored into hers.

Freddie furrowed her brow. "What you're asking sounds dangerous." She fought a tingle of excitement. Balls and soirees usually bored her to tears. For the first time since her late come out this year at age nineteen, she looked forward to a two-week-long party.

Still, it could be dangerous—what would the spies to do her if she were caught?

Harker must have sensed her hesitation. "I'll make it worth your while."

"Oh?"

Harker nodded anxiously. "If you succeed in bringing me the book, not only will I see your sister gets a decent dowry, but I'll deed a small cottage in the country to you and your mother. You'll be able to live there forever—rent free."

Freddie's heart raced.

A dowry and a cottage?

A cottage to live in meant Freddie and her mother would be able to live comfortably on their small annuity. Charlie wouldn't have to marry for money—she could marry for love. They'd be free of Harker.

"How will I know what this book looks like?"

"It's very distinctive. Red leather, about so big." Harker motioned with his hands to indicate the size of a small pocket book. "Inside, there will be handwritten text in code. Oh, and there is a gold seal on the front."

Freddie sucked on her bottom lip. She didn't relish the idea of being hanged as a spy, but, since she would be working to uncover French spies *for* Britain, that hardly seemed likely to happen. The promise of the dowry and cottage more than made up for the risk she would be taking.

"I'll do it."

"Excellent." Harker bowed slightly. "This is very important and you'll be doing your country a great service...but you mustn't tell anyone. Not even your sister."

Freddie felt a swell of pride. She'd never done anything important before. If she discounted the possibility of being at the mercy of French spies, it sounded like a fun adventure. She nodded her agreement. "I won't tell a soul."

Harker motioned for Freddie to follow him into the hall. He accepted his topper from the stoic butler by the front door and turned toward Freddie as the butler opened the door, letting in a gust of the cool April air.

In a dismissive tone, Harker said, "I'm off to the club. I'll arrange for the carriage to await you tomorrow at nine of the morning to collect the three of you and take you to Tenwick Abbey. I'll travel separately and meet you on the road."

At least she wouldn't have to suffer the stench of his breath throughout the two-day drive.

The butler shut the door behind Harker with a note of finality. Freddie's ears rang. Had she really just agreed to steal a spy book from the brother of one of the most influential men in Britain?

***

Freddie stared at the door for what seemed like an eternity, her thoughts awhirl.

"Was that Lord Harker leaving just now?" Her mother's voice from the top of the stairs pulled Freddie out of her daze.

When she turned, she found her mother staring at the door with a worried expression pulling at her face. Curving locks of her pale hair—as much blond as gray—framed her face. In coloring and stature, Mama most resembled Charlotte, though she and Freddie had the same oval-shaped face.

Freddie forced a smile. She didn't want to worry her mother. "Yes. He informed me that he secured us invitations to the house party at Tenwick Abbey."

Mama broke into a smile. "Isn't it exciting?" The weight on her shoulders didn't quite lift as she gracefully descended the stairs. Her back was perpetually bowed with it, these days.

"It is." Excitement warred with anxiety in her stomach.

"Have you taken ill? You look pale." Mama reached up to touch her warm hand to Freddie's forehead. "You don't feel hot. Was it something Lord Harker said...or did?"

Worry infused her voice. Freddie had a good idea of why Mama was concerned. Over the past four years, the way Harker leered at her and the look of despair on her face when they retired to a locked room to 'go over the family budget' had been impossible to miss.

Freddie was nineteen, old enough to know what that 'budget meeting' really entailed. Though she didn't know the specifics, she knew her mother was submitting to Harker's advances in order to keep the three of them living in the manner they were. It broke her heart to see the life draining out of her beautiful, vivacious mother each time Harker descended on her.

She was certain Mama was worried Harker would soon turn his attentions to Freddie in the same manner—or worse, Charlie. Freddie, herself, feared it was only a matter of time before he did. What would she do then?

You won't have to find out. Now that she had a way out from under Harker's thumb, she was determined to take it. As soon as she delivered the book, they would be free.

But she couldn't tell her mother. Not only because Harker had warned her to keep silent but because Mama might try to do something drastic to keep Freddie from delivering on the agreement. She might even try to do it herself. When Freddie's father had left them in the cold, Freddie had been the one to hold the family together. Freddie had met with and accepted Harker's generous offer to stay with him when the creditors had ejected her family from their home. Freddie had consoled her mother and sister through countless tears and a year of official mourning. Freddie had ensured that her sister received a proper education in the maidenly arts, even though that left Freddie with little time to practice. Through it all, Freddie hadn't cried. She'd remained strong, for them all.

And she would do it all again, if need be.

Freddie put on her most dazzling smile. "I'm not ill. It must be the excitement about the party."

"What party?" Charlie poked her head in from the sitting room door. She left her embroidery in the room.

Mama beamed. "We're attending the spring party at Tenwick Abbey."

Charlie's pale blue eyes grew even bigger. She gaped as she glided closer. "We are? But that's *the* party of the Season. You have to have a special invite."

"We have one." Mama reached over to tuck a corn-silk blond curl behind Charlotte's ear. "We leave tomorrow morning, which means we'd all better get upstairs and start packing."

Charlotte squealed. She bounced up and down in excitement, then grabbed Freddie's hand and pulled her toward the stairs. "Oh, Freddie, it'll be so much fun. All the most handsome bachelors of the *ton* will be there. I just know you'll find your true love!"

Freddie's chest warmed. Trust Charlie to care more about Freddie's matrimonial prospects than her own. She had a heart of gold.

Gently, Freddie said, "Charlie, you know I don't care to marry."

Charlotte stopped on the stair above Freddie. She frowned at her sister, her eyes on the same level as Freddie's. Charlie's gaze swept down the plain, outdated gown that Freddie wore.

"No one will offer for you if you keep dressing like a nun." Charlie met Mama's gaze over Freddie's shoulder. "Mama, can we alter some of my dresses for Freddie? I don't know why she refused to accompany me to the modiste at the beginning of the Season for new gowns."

Freddie knew why. Their annuity could support only one new wardrobe. In fact, only one Season between them. It had to be Charlotte's.

Charlie, of course, had no idea of the state of their funds. Freddie was determined that she never find out.

She swallowed, her throat suddenly thick. It was hard to be cheerful with the black cloud of what she must do hanging over her head. *Think of the reward.*

Freddie forced a smile. "Lud, I hardly think that will work. Your head is barely past my chin.

"So?"

"So," Freddie said, drawing out the word. "The dresses would be too short. No, I'm quite happy with the gowns I have."

Charlie caught and squeezed Freddie's hand. "Please let us try. My pale green gown would be gorgeous on you. It's all wrong for my complexion anyway. We can have Lisane add some lace to the bottom."

"A dress won't make much difference. No one notices me. Compared to beauties like you, I'm plain and uninteresting. Besides, Lisane will be much too busy getting us all ready for the parties," Freddie lied. The three of them shared an abigail,

Lisane. Even so, none of them required much fussing over and Lisane often found herself with spare time.

"Fiddlesticks!" Charlie turned, pulling Freddie once again upstairs. "I insist. You're beautiful *and* intelligent. That's a rare combination. Any man will be happy to have you. You only need to present yourself better. Besides, if you don't have a beautiful dress, it will spoil all my fun."

Freddie sighed. She didn't want to take a dress from Charlotte, but she didn't want to ruin the event for her sister, either. Freddie glanced to her mother for support.

"Just *one* dress won't hurt, Freddie," Mama said as she followed the girls upstairs. A fond smile curved her lips.

Freddie sighed. "Very well. If you can find the time to alter it before we leave for the party tomorrow morning."

Charlie bared her teeth in a grin. "I'll stay awake all night if I must. You'll see, Freddie. You'll be a smashing hit."

Freddie didn't want to attract a man to marry. She was too busy taking care of her family. Besides, she'd learned a keen lesson in marriage by watching her father hurt her mother over and over again as he gambled away the family money without a fig of a care for the three of them. If that was what marriage was about, she wanted no part of it.

Not to mention, given the task Harker had set her, it was better to be invisible.

She decided not to argue about it for the moment.

Mama shooed both girls up the stairs with flaps of her hands. "Get a move on, you two. It will be a long trip tomorrow and you girls need to finish packing before the clock strikes midnight."

Charlotte released Freddie's hand and all but skipped up the stairs. As Freddie followed, tripping over the next stair, an ominous rip of the stitches in her hem raised the hairs on the back of her neck. She pin-wheeled her arms to keep from losing her balance. When she righted herself, she found the butler staring at her. She gave a little flourish of her hand, as if she'd put on a show, but didn't dare chance a curtsey while on a staircase. If she did, she would end up in a heap at the bottom.

With a smile, Mama shook her head at the sight. She, like Freddie, was used to Freddie's abominable clumsiness.

As Freddie faced forward, she watched one of Charlotte's long curls swing jauntily with her movements. For once, Freddie wished she could share her sister's excitement. But instead of the carefree happiness her sister enjoyed, Freddie felt a pressing weight of foreboding.

The future of her family, and possibly all of Britain, rested in her hands. How far would she have to go to secure it?

Chapter Two

Tristan Graylocke flattened his palms on the smooth mahogany railing of the second floor balcony overlooking the front hall at Tenwick Abbey.

A sigh escaped his lips as his eyes grazed over the throng of people in the entryway below him. "I can't think of a single thing I hate more than these parties."

Next to him, his older brother smirked. "Prinny?"

Tristan grimaced. Heaven help Britain, because the indolent, self-indulgent heir to the throne, and his senile father certainly wouldn't. It was a wonder the country hadn't gone up in flames the moment Pitt had died three months ago.

Tristan ran a hand through the longer forelock of his hair. "Prinny has never tried to marry me off."

Morgan's chiseled face and square jaw, almost an exact replica of Tristan's, hardened as he watched the crowd. His gray eyes showed no sign of emotion. The only indications of the pressures of being a duke were the slight tic in his cheek and the streak of silver in his hair.

Tristan shot his older brother a grin. "Luckily, I have you to distract Mother. She'll likely try to marry you off to any lady healthy enough to produce an heir." Tristan laughed. "Once again, I'm happy I didn't inherit."

It was Morgan's turn to sigh. He had been only twenty when their father passed, leaving him with the title and responsibility of a duke. Early on, their mother and grandmother hadn't pressured him about marrying, but now that he neared thirty years of age, that changed with remarkable quickness.

The only pressure Tristan received from Mother was to stop his carousing. Impossible. He couldn't exactly say, *I'm a spy, Mama. I get my best information that way.* No, in the *ton*'s eyes, his gambling and carousing labeled him a degenerate. To the families with the bluest blood—in other words, almost everyone Mother had invited to this charade—it made him unmarriageable. A relief, to be honest. Tristan preferred to spend his money on investments of his choosing, not on feminine fripperies.

"If I'm lucky, she'll focus her efforts on Lucy." Morgan nodded toward the entry where their younger sister, Lucy, stood next to Mother as they greeted the new arrivals. Compared with mother's steely gray and brown hair, Lucy's jet black hair—the same color as all the Graylocke siblings—provided a stark contrast. Lucy wore her hair in an elaborate coil around her head, threaded through with creamy pearls that matched her dress. Though he was too far to see from his vantage point, Tristan imagined her dark brown eyes, the exact same color as his, sparkling with delight. This was Lucy's first Season and she thrived beneath the attention heaped on her.

"Does she have that confounded journal sticking out of her dress again?" Morgan asked as he squinted across the room.

Yes, there it was. The brown leather corner of the journal his sister carried everywhere stuck out of the bulging reticule hanging from her wrist. Lucy fancied herself to be a novelist. The notebook, she insisted on keeping on hand to record various moments of inspiration as they came to her.

"She does," Tristan confirmed.

"Well, at least she isn't sequestering herself away from everyone like Gideon."

Tristan scanned the room for their youngest brother. The tallest of the Graylockes, he should have been easy to pick out from the crowd. If he was there. Which he wasn't.

"I suppose we'll have to drag him out of the orangery again."

Upon completing his education, Gideon had foregone his Grand Tour and shut himself in their orangery instead to put his extensive knowledge of botany to good use by inventing a new species of orchid. He barely thought of anything that didn't have roots and the brothers often had to remind him to eat and bathe.

"Mother will be livid if he doesn't make an appearance," Morgan agreed.

Their mother, Evelyn Graylocke, hosted the annual house party at Tenwick Abbey for one reason: to show off her children to advantage. Along with the rest of his brothers, Tristan would rather have been in the middle of a battlefield between Napoleon and the Third Coalition. However, none of the Graylocke brothers had the heart to disappoint her. Since the death of their father, the party had been one of the few things that brought her joy.

Tristan's heart warmed as he watched his mother greet the newly arrived guests, a wide smile of genuine happiness on her face. She chatted with each new arrival before sending them off to mingle with the other guests or turning them over to one of the many footmen who would lead them to their rooms.

The whole of Tenwick Abbey, the expansive, centuries-old monastery that the Graylockes had called home for nearly twelve generations, had been aired out for the party. The granite stones scrubbed, the carved mahogany polished, the twenty fireplaces cleaned and stocked with wood. The maids had laundered enough linens and towels to paper the walls of the abbey from floor to ceiling twice over. Under his mother's supervision, the entire east wing had been reorganized into comfortable accommodations for the two-week-long affair.

"Operating with all these guests underfoot will be a nightmare." Tristan gritted his teeth to keep from making a face at the thought.

Even if all parties in the war had entered into a shaky truce or fled home to lick their wounds, in the case of the Russians, the war was far from over. Britain and France had entered into an economic stalemate. Britain held command of the trade routes by sea; Napoleon held most of the continent. Times like these, in the lull between battles, was when Tristan's job was most important.

Morgan's, too, though Tristan was loathe to admit it. The one thing Tristan could do that Morgan couldn't was enter the field to spy. Tristan could afford to take risks. Morgan, as Duke, could not. But, with so much information to comb through, his contribution to the spying network was invaluable. Without Morgan, Tristan wouldn't be in possession of the book he was tasked with passing along.

Morgan ran his hand over the railing, his face impassive. "Mother will expect us to attend most of the activities."

Games, contests, dinners, and balls. And all while under the scrutiny of vicious *ton* gossips and matchmaking mamas. *Oh, joy.*

"We can't let that deter us."

Morgan nodded, shifting his gaze to Tristan's face.

"Where is the book now?" Although they stood alone on the balcony to the family's private wing, he whispered.

Tristan rolled his eyes. "Safe."

"We must get it into the right hands before the war turns." Morgan pressed his lips together.

"Passing it off beneath the noses of the most meddlesome matrons in the *ton* is a foolhardy plan."

"To the contrary. This party provides us the perfect cover." Morgan's voice was hard, steely to match his eyes.

Tristan thrust his shoulders back. He met his brother's gaze, unflinching. "If the wrong person happens across it..."

"It's your duty to protect it." Morgan spoke in his ducal voice, a voice sharp enough to chip ice.

"And I will." Tristan bit off his words. He turned away. "But once I pass it off, it will be someone else's responsibility."

"Our agents are trained well."

Morgan should know. He trained most of them.

A rotund gentleman in a brown redingote and topper swaggered into the foyer. Tristan swore.

"Harker!" Morgan clenched his fist as he turned. "Who invited him?"

"Mother must have."

"*Why?*"

Tristan wondered the same thing. Even though Mother had no idea about the brothers' spying efforts—and therefore no knowledge of the fact that Harker was an enemy spy, albeit one labeled untouchable by Tristan's superiors—Harker was no better than swine. The mystery of his invitation dissolved as a joyous squeal lit the air. Lucy embraced one of the three women Harker escorted, a blond girl about her age.

Tristan sighed. "On a guess, I would say that Lucy begged her to."

"Who is that with him?"

Tristan leaned forward on the balcony. Aside from the blond and a pale-haired older woman who must be her mother, Harker stood next to a plainly-dressed young woman. Her brown hair was coiled and pinned without flourish. She wore a brown spencer that rose to her chin, coupled with a faded blue dress. Her bonnet, which she held in her hand, was equally drab. She couldn't possibly be related to the striking blond beauty. A companion, perhaps?

"That must be Miss Charlotte Vale, the beauty everyone is talking about." Tristan nudged his brother. "Perhaps Mother thinks she'd make you a good wife."

Morgan snorted. "I don't think so. I usually find the beautiful ones to be rather dim-witted. Besides, I'm not ready to settle down yet."

"What about your heir and a spare?"

Morgan's gaze turned piercing. "I'm not dead yet. I have time."

Tristan chuckled. "Less of it than you think, if this year's guest list is any indication." Almost every family invited included one or more unwed daughters. With the way Mother waged war, Morgan ought to recruit her into his spy network.

His smile fading, Tristan turned to study Harker and his companions once more. That scoundrel's presence complicated his mission. He would have to be even more discreet than usual.

As for his companions... The blonde was pretty enough. In comparison, her companion should have faded into the background. Tristan found himself studying the curve of her cheek, the way she carried herself, and her protective manner toward the blonde. A beam of sunlight filtered in through the open door, highlighting rich chestnut hues in her hair.

"Sisters, do you think?" Morgan asked.

Tristan shook his head. "Too plain. My money is on companion."

"Can the Vales afford to hire a companion?"

"Harker can."

As if his name carried weight, Harker lifted his beady gaze to the balcony. He leaned close to whisper in the brunette's ear. Slowly, like clouds parting after a rainstorm, she turned her face up. Toward Tristan.

Their eyes locked. A strange tightness clamped over Tristan's chest. He couldn't look away. From this distance, he couldn't make out the color of her eyes. At that moment, he'd never wanted to know such a banal piece of information more.

"What are they whispering about, do you think?"

Morgan's voice pierced Tristan's strange daze, but he still couldn't summon the will to look away. "I haven't the faintest. Do you suppose Harker has put her in place to spy on us?" The vise around his chest tightened, rebelling at the notion.

"An interesting thought." Morgan drew out the words, as though tasting them while he spoke. "Perhaps Harker has outfitted himself with reinforcements...I say we might be well served by keeping an eye on that one."

"That won't be a problem," Tristan replied. He broke his gaze in order to follow his brother toward the stairs leading to the hall below.

***

Freddie's heart skipped a beat as the cold, dark eyes pierced into hers. Traitor's eyes. A tingle traversed her spine—a chill of foreboding. Strangely enough, it wasn't an altogether unpleasant sensation.

"Don't stare at them," Harker hissed, low enough so only she could hear. "You'll give yourself away."

Ripping her gaze away, she returned her attention to the people in front of her. Mama watched with narrowed eyes, her gaze flitting between Freddie and Harker.

"Do you two have a secret?" She smiled, but Freddie noticed the concern in her eyes.

Freddie laughed to lighten the moment. "Of course not, Mama. Lord Harker was just pointing out the architectural details on the banister above."

When they glanced at the railing again, the balcony was empty. Freddie's heartbeat quickened. Where had the brothers gone? She bit her lip. *Hurry up, Charlie.* Never before had Freddie felt such a keen urgency to retire to her room to freshen up.

Beside her, Lucy and Charlotte pulled away from their embrace in order to link arms. Both wore broad smiles. From the moment they'd been introduced earlier in the Season, they'd formed an instant friendship.

"I'm so happy you could come. We'll have a smashing time!" Lucy leaned her head so close to Charlie's that the curls at their temples brushed. She lowered her voice. "The other girls are so boring, only interested in sizing up the peers for marriage."

Charlotte laughed. "I have no such aspirations for myself, though I will be looking for Freddie."

Freddie found herself pinned beneath Lucy's shrewd brown gaze. *Lud, Charlie. Why did you have to say that?* She forced a smile.

In answer, a sly look crossed Lucy's face. "Between the two of us, I think we should be able to find someone who will suit her. Will the two of you join me later? I'll give you a tour of the abbey and we can discuss our plan."

A plan for marriage? Freddie's cheeks heated. They spoke about her as if she wasn't there! *I don't want your help.* The last thing she wanted was a husband, a man who believed himself better than her.

She stiffened her back. "I hardly think—"

"Ladies."

A frisson of awareness leaped up her spine at the deep, male baritone. Freddie spun. Her breath caught in her throat as she came face to face with the man responsible.

Tristan Graylocke.

Like most men, he ignored her. He peered straight over her shoulder as he addressed his sister. "It looks like you're having a grand time."

Did Lucy know her brother was a traitor? From her sunny smile, Freddie guessed not.

"I am. Have you met the Vales?" Lucy released Charlie's arm in order to gesture at the group.

"I don't believe we've had the pleasure." The low, controlled voice drifted from Freddie's left. A glance confirmed that the other Graylocke brother—the duke—stood on her other side. They'd cornered her.

Lucy glanced to each of them in turn, ignoring Harker, who had taken a healthy step back. "Mrs. Vale." Mama inclined her head. "Miss Charlotte."

Technically, Lucy should have introduced Freddie first, but she couldn't begrudge Charlie the chance to shine.

"Miss Vale."

Oh. That's me. Gathering her skirts, Freddie dipped in a curtsey. Her toe slipped on the polished floor and she nearly introduced herself to the floor. She clenched her fists as she righted herself. From the corner of her eye, she noticed Lord Graylocke raise his eyebrows as he exchanged a glance with the duke. Blast! He'd noticed her clumsiness.

Lucy, to her credit, pretended Freddie didn't resemble a Fanny Royds doll. She nudged Freddie forward as she said, "May I introduce my brothers, the Duke of Tenwick and Lord Graylocke?"

A round of curtseys and a chorus of 'Your Grace' and 'my lord' ensued. This time, Freddie managed to do it without drawing attention to herself.

When she straightened, she found herself pinned beneath Lord Graylocke's stare. His gaze flitted between herself and Charlie. "Sisters?"

She didn't take offense at his incredulous tone. Most people were surprised to find that the plain Frederica Vale was related to the beautiful Charlotte.

Freddie raised her chin. "Indeed." She took a small step to the right to shield Charlie from his interest. With any other man, she would have done the opposite, but she didn't want that traitor to bat an eyelash in her sister's direction.

Without Charlie to lavish with attention, Lord Graylocke caught Freddie's gloved hand. He raised it between them. "It is my pleasure to welcome two such lovely sisters into our home." He bent, ghosting his lips across Freddie's knuckles. An antiquated gesture. One that made her hand tingle as if she'd stuck it in a bush full of nettles.

He lifted his gaze to find hers. His eyes weren't black, as she'd originally thought, but a deep velvety brown. Her heartbeat stuttered. The world spun around them, Lord Graylocke—Tristan—her only anchor.

She had agreed to steal a book from *him?* Impossible. At the moment, she couldn't even reclaim her hand. If she did, the spinning world might induce a swoon.

Every muscle in her body urged her to flee. At that moment, Tristan Graylocke wasn't staring at her as if she were another debutante arriving to the house party. He stared at her as if he knew *exactly* what she meant to do—with a fierce determination to stop her.

Chapter Three

"Isn't this room magnificent?" Charlie straightened from the task of transferring her dresses from her trunk to the bed. She twirled, her sunny yellow skirts whipping around her as she drew attention to the lavish surroundings.

Royal blue velvet curtains—the color matching that of the yellow and blue toile wallpaper—framed the large French windows. The two beds, set on either side of a carved granite fireplace, were loaded with thick blue and yellow quilts. The room surely was much more splendid than their room in Harker's townhouse.

And this was only the guest room.

"It is," Freddie agreed. She perched on the edge of her bed. With a teasing smile, she added, "Imagine, if you marry a duke, you'll have a house full of rooms this luxurious."

But not the Duke of Tenwick.

Charlie wrinkled her nose. "Marry a Duke? I don't intend to marry this Season...maybe not even next. I'm much too young. I want to have some fun."

Freddie's heart clenched. "And you should." She swallowed heavily, trying not to think of the fact that they couldn't afford to give Charlie another Season. She might yet change her mind before the *ton* retired to the country this summer. More bizarre things had happened. "Marry someone you love no matter what his title or how much money he has."

The excitement drained from Charlie's face. Softly, she admitted, "If I marry a man with money, I can make life easier for you and Mama."

Freddie stood. She found her sister's hand and squeezed it. "Why do we need life to be easier? Everything is fine as it is."

"Is it?" Charlie's blue eyes hardened. "Sometimes I wonder about mother and Lord Harker."

No. Freddie had worked so hard to try to hide that from her. She smiled, but it felt forced. "Lord Harker has been very kind to us. Mother helps him with his accounts, is all."

Charlie tugged free and crossed her arms. "I'm not a child. Don't lie to me."

I don't want to. The words stuck in Freddie's throat. She couldn't venture into this conversation with her sister. If she did, it would inevitably turn to the fact that Harker's eye seemed to be wandering away from Mama, of late. If Freddie wasn't careful, she—or her dear sister—might be the next recipient of his unwanted attentions.

She changed the subject. "Why don't we meet Lucy? We don't want to keep her waiting."

Charlotte's expression lightened. She straightened her dress, then peeked in the mirror to make sure every curl was in place. "I'm ready."

In the hall, Freddie rapped on the door next to theirs, the one given to Mama. When she opened the door, she found the room inside as opulent as the one Freddie and Charlie shared, though Mama's was decorated in emerald green. Mama sat next to a small vanity, wringing a handkerchief. Was she nervous about something? When Freddie cleared her throat, Mama glanced up in surprise. She must not have heard the knock.

"Charlie and I are meeting Lucy for a tour of the abbey."

"Of course." Mama batted at a lock of hair that had strayed from her coiffure. She managed a tight smile. "Have a nice time. Shall we go down to dinner together?"

"Yes. We'll meet you here at half five this afternoon?"

"Absolutely. Have fun, dear."

Her voice was strained. Tight, like the muscles in her cheeks.

Freddie frowned. "Would you like to come with us?"

"No, of course not. I have some...business to attend."

"We'll see you later, then." With a troupe of acrobats doing flips in her stomach, Freddie shut the door. What business could Mama possibly have in the middle of a house party?

"There you are!" Lucy's excited voice pierced the air along with her clipped steps. Her expression was radiant as she bustled down the hall. The contrast of her inky black hair against her porcelain skin was stunning. Her deep brown eyes sparkled, alight from within as she stepped abreast of Freddie.

She has her brother's eyes. Freddie pressed her lips together at the uncomfortable reminder of Lord Graylocke. Whereas Lucy's eyes shone with exuberance, his were dark with danger.

Deftly, Lucy wedged her way between Freddie and Charlie, linking one arm in each of theirs.

"Your mother doesn't care to join us?" Lucy tugged them toward the end of the hall toward the staircase as she spoke.

Freddie shook her head. "She begged leave to rest after our long journey."

Charlie, who hadn't stood close enough to hear what Mama had really said, didn't contradict.

As they reached the staircase, they passed Lord Harker. Lucy's expression turned icy. Harker inclined his head toward them and stood to the side to let them pass. When Freddie glanced over her shoulder, she watched him turn right instead of left. Toward the women's guest quarters, rather than the men's. She stiffened. Could he not leave her mother alone even at a house party? Tongues would wag. The gossip would cripple Charlie's chances of a match.

As he peeked over his shoulder, he gave Freddie a pointed look. A spark of disgust flared in her belly. It fueled her determination to find the code book. With luck, the tour would provide a clue as to where that book might be.

***

Lucy took them through the kitchen, dining hall, four salons, and a ballroom while she explained the history of the abbey. Once a monastery, it had been acquired by the family in the 1400s. Her ancestors had lived there ever since. Freddie marveled at the carved marble and wood fixtures, the rich tapestries and opulent furnishings.

They left the ballroom and Lucy led them down a dark hall. At the end stood a wooden door with gigantic scrolled iron hinges, ancient if the streaks of discoloration along the boards were any indication.

Lucy confirmed Freddie's suspicions as she said, "This is one of the original doors of the abbey." She reached for the handle. "Over the years, most of the abbey was modernized, but this section has been kept intact. I like to use it as a secret passage because it leads back around to the west wing."

The door opened to reveal a long, narrow room with walls of gray stone. The ceiling towered two or three stories over their heads. Enormous cathedral-shaped windows marched along the tops of the walls, their bottoms starting high above Freddie's head.

"This was one of the original cathedrals when this was a monastery in the middle ages. Now it's my second favorite room in all of Tenwick Abbey —a wonderful place to absorb the energy of the past and use it in my writing." Lucy tapped the notebook in her reticule. "You might think all the dead ancestors a bit eerie, but I find them inspiring."

Portraits lined the wall opposite the windows. Each frame must have been as tall as Freddie, if not larger. The light shining through the windows illuminated painting upon painting, all of which depicted the strong Graylocke chin, chiseled cheekbones, and black hair. Several past dukes even had a white streak, like the current one.

Lucy pointed to an oak door set into the stone wall between two portraits, a smaller version of the one they'd entered by. It blended with the frames so completely, Freddie almost didn't notice it.

"This door is the secret passage to our private quarters."

"How intriguing," Charlotte exclaimed. "But what is all this?" She waved her arm to indicate the opposite side of the hall, beneath the windows, where various artifacts were on display.

"Oh, these are old family heirlooms. Things nobody cares to keep around, anymore." Lucy stepped over to a suit of armor that stood in the corner and rapped on its chest. The hollow ring echoed in the lofty room. "This is the armor my great-great-great-grandfather wore when he fought in the Thirty Years' War."

Lucy rambled on about the various artifacts. Her voice faded into the background as Freddie's attention turned to the door leading to the family's private quarters. Did Tristan Graylocke keep the code book in his bedchamber?

Freddie bit her lip. She stepped back, as if by distancing herself from that door she could deny the need to infiltrate his private abode. She gasped as she bumped something solid and cold.

She swung around in time to watch the Neoclassical pedestal rock on its foundation. As it righted itself, the bust of a Graylocke ancestor tipped toward Freddie's chest. She yelped as the aristocratic nose of the sculpture buried itself in her bosom. Blast! It was too heavy. She couldn't hold it!

A pair of strong, male arms snatched the bust from her grip and righted it. Freddie sighed in relief. Opening her mouth to express her thanks, she raised her gaze from the large, tanned hands to their owner. The words caught in her throat.

Lord Graylocke.

He braced a palm on the pedestal to ensure it wouldn't tip before he released the bust. When he turned to her, his eyes were dark with accusation.

"Miss Vale."

I didn't mean to.

"Lord G-graylocke." Freddie chided herself for stammering. *He's only a man.*

A traitor and a spy, but a man.

If she was going to divest him of that book, she had best get her reaction to him under control.

For once, her invisibility worked to her advantage as he turned to his sister. His eyebrows dipped in a disapproving V. "Lucy, what brings you to this section of the abbey?"

Undaunted, Lucy smiled. "I was showing my favorite guests around the abbey. You know this is my inspiration room."

Tristan's laugh startled Freddie. It had a deep, pleasant timbre—not the evil cackle she expect from a traitor. Perhaps she spent too much time reading fanciful novels.

"Is it? I would never have known." His gaze, so disapproving a moment before, danced as he teased his sister. "Somehow, I doubt these young ladies have any interest in dead dukes and old armor."

Lucy shrugged. "I think the room is fascinating."

"And I think you need to remember what we talked about when it comes to your novel writing." Tristan shot Lucy a look of warning as he expertly herded all three ladies through the open door by which they'd entered.

Lucy shot him a sweet smile as she stepped past him. "Would I ever disobey your wishes, brother dear?"

His expression soured.

With a skip in her step, Lucy left the room. "Come now, I saved the best part of the house for last."

Charlotte dipped a small curtsey to Lord Graylocke before she followed in Lucy's wake. Reluctantly, Freddie followed suit. As she left, her shoulder blades tingled with the weight of Lord Graylocke's gaze. *It's your imagination.* She willed herself not to look back.

But it clearly wasn't her imagination that Tristan Graylocke had very much wanted them to stay away from the family's private quarters. Did he insist due to privacy—or because he kept something in there he didn't want anyone to find?

***

The moment they turned the corner, leaving Lord Graylocke far behind, Charlie danced closer to Lucy. "Don't your brothers want you to write?"

Lucy pursed her lips, as though searching for the right words. "They encourage my writing, but take quarrel with my method of research. A good novelist needs to experience things before they write them and, well, that can be a bit dangerous. My brothers tend be overprotective."

A traitor, overprotective? Freddie pressed her lips together at the incongruent image. She didn't trust herself to speak a word.

Meanwhile, Charlie's eyes sparkled with interest as she linked arms with Lucy. "Dangerous? How so?"

"One time, I climbed out on the ledge of the turret so I could experience the vertigo. Another time, I dressed as a boy and walked the streets of London at night. I got into quite a bit of trouble when my brothers found me out." Lucy stopped at a large, round-topped door. Shaking her head, she added, "How do they expect me to write with authority if I haven't experienced the same things as my characters?" She pulled the door open. "Enough about me. What do you like to do, Frederica?"

"Call me Freddie, please."

Lucy pinned her beneath a sunny smile. "Of course." Lucy guided them down a grand hallway, one side a wall of marble bricks, the other a wall of glassed in windows.

To answer her question, Freddie said, "I suppose I like reading and learning, mostly."

"Then you'll love the last stop we make—the family library." With her free arm, Lucy gestured to the windows. "These windows used to be open archways when this was an abbey. The room ahead was constructed later to match, then glassed in to be used as an orangery."

She pulled open a foggy glass door at the end of the hall. The moment she entered, Freddie was bombarded with a wave of warm, moist air. Inside the room on long tables and planted in the mounds of dirt heaped between a narrow stone walkway was an array of tropical plants the likes of which she had never seen before. The humidity was so thick, Freddie felt her hair battle its pins. She held out her hand, palm up half, expecting to feel raindrops.

The afternoon sun filtered in through the glass walls and ceiling. Somewhere in the distance came the soft murmur of trickling water. A black-haired man stood on the other side of a potting table in the middle of the room. He was bent over a plant, his hair sticking up in disarray. His greatcoat had been tossed carelessly on the table and his white shirtsleeves were pushed up to the elbows.

"Giddy, I brought some guests," Lucy called.

The man's head jerked up.

"What?" His eyes narrowed with confusion for a moment, before clearing. "Oh, right. Mother is having another one of her infernal parties. I forgot."

"This is Miss Charlotte and Miss Vale." Lucy linked her arm through Freddie's and drew her forward. "My brother, the Honorable Lord Gideon Graylocke."

He was younger than Tristan, if the honorary title and the youthful softness to his cheeks was any indication. Unlike the two eldest Graylocke brothers, Lord Gideon wore at least a day's worth of dark stubble on his jaw. A hank of his hair dropped limp onto his forehead as he nodded.

Freddie and Charlotte curtsied. For once, Freddie managed it gracefully.

Wresting her arm from Lucy's hold, Charlie approached the potting table. "What have you got there?" She leaned over the table to get a better look.

Lord Gideon stared at her warily, as though she might bite. "It's an orchid. An exotic species. My friend Catt and I are trying to cultivate different variations of it."

"Don't orchids have green leaves?"

He ran his hand through his hair, causing it to stand up even more. "It will, as it matures. It's a very young plant."

Beaming, Lucy stepped closer to draw Charlie away. "Gideon is quite the botanist, you know." Her voice radiated pride in her brother. "We'll leave you to your work, Giddy. Shall I see you at dinner?"

"Huh? Oh, yes. I suppose I don't have much of a choice. Join in the festivities or suffer Mother's wrath."

The women drifted away. Lord Gideon returned his focus to the flower before they so much as turned their backs. On the way to the door, they stopped to admire an assortment of tropical plants and flowers.

"So, you have three brothers?" Charlotte asked as they stepped into the same windowed hallway they had passed through earlier.

"Four," Lucy said. "Anthony is away in the Royal Navy. He's a captain, now."

"Oh, how patriotic." Charlotte smiled.

Bizarre, in Freddie's opinion. One brother in the navy, but two others spies for France?

Charlie continued. "I always wanted a brother, but I wouldn't trade Freddie for anything."

Freddie's chest warmed. She exchanged a smile with Charlie. *I wouldn't trade you, either.*

"I always wanted a sister," Lucy exclaimed. Her exuberance dimmed as a cloud crossed her face. "My cousin Cecily was close, but since she married, we never see her."

They reached the round-topped door to the main house. Lucy opened it and led the way through. The instant she stepped foot in the adjoining hall, she turned with a pained look on her face.

A second later, a sharp, nasally voice pierced the air. "Lady Lucy, whatever are you doing out here?" Mrs. Theodosia Biddleford stepped abreast of Lucy and blinked several times. Behind her round spectacles, her eyes appeared owlish. "Is that Miss Charlotte and Miss Vale?"

Forcing a smile, Freddie said, "Nice to see you, Mrs. Biddleford."

The notorious gossip straightened to her full height, an inch taller than Freddie. She leered down her thin nose, turned up at the tip. "Should you ladies be out unescorted?"

"We haven't left the house," Lucy pointed out. "I should think I'm perfectly safe to walk around my own house without a chaperone."

Mrs. Biddleford adjusted the fichu around her neck. "You're far from the main section of the house."

So are you. Freddie bit her tongue to keep from speaking the words aloud.

As her companion, a short spinster of the same advanced years as Mrs. Biddleford, stepped forward, the tall busybody added, "Aren't they, Hester?"

"Yes." Hester Maize squinted at them. In her round face, it made her eyes look as though they'd been swallowed by the wrinkles framing her plump cheeks. "What are you girls up to?"

"Nothing at all," Freddie answered, her voice as poised and graceful as she aspired to be in person. "Lady Lucy kindly offered us a tour of the house."

The two older women frowned their disapproval. Likely, they had to scare up some gossip to pass on.

Luckily, Lucy remained undaunted. Coolly, she asked, "Are you lost?"

"Uh, well..." Mrs. Biddleford glanced at the stone walls of the hallway. They offered no excuses ripe to be plucked. "Yes, I suppose we are. We were searching for the back terrace."

Lucy smiled sweetly. "I'm afraid that's back down the way you came, then through the blue salon. You'll see the French doors."

"Thank you." Miss Maize's voice was thin. With nods to Lucy, the two women shuffled down the hall.

The moment they stepped out of earshot, Lucy turned to Freddie and her sister. Lucy wrinkled her nose. "Forgive me. I usually try to avoid those two."

"So do we," Freddie said. She didn't need to stir up gossip and risk Charlie's chances at a respectable marriage.

"They're probably out looking to unearth the latest *on-dit*," Charlotte added.

"No doubt." Lucy turned in the opposite direction. "Thankfully, our destination is the other way."

She led them down the hall, then through a large oak door with intricately carved moldings and into another imposing room, this one with floor to ceiling bookshelves lining all four walls.

"And here is my favorite room." Lucy spread her arms. "The family library."

Freddie and Charlotte stared at the room in awe. The ceiling was a good two stories in the air. An upper loft area covered half of the room like an open-air second story with a balcony and spiral staircase. Oriental carpets cover the floor, and overstuffed leather settees ringed a fireplace big enough to stand in.

And the books! They were stacked neatly, their leather spines stamped with gold lettering facing out. Some of them looked to be from two hundred years prior. Others, more recent.

"Look at all these books," Charlotte said. Although she didn't read much, even she sounded in awe.

"Yes." Lucy ran her fingertips lovingly over a set of tan leather books. "You can see why this room is my favorite. I get a lot of the inspiration for my novels in here. Tristan and Morgan love this room, too. In fact, they spend more time in here than I do."

"Do they, now?" With the door shut, the room would be perfect for spies to plot and scheme in. It was private. Only one entrance and the books would make a good insulation to keep the room soundproofed.

"Goodness, look at the time." Lucy nodded at a pendulum clock that stood in the corner, ticking away the seconds. "We'd better hurry to get ready for dinner."

The girls' chatter as Lucy herded them out of the room washed over Freddie. She left reluctantly, scanning those books once again. Hundreds upon hundreds of books. *If I were to hide a code book, I would do it in plain sight.* In a library, where the book would blend with everything else. Her stomach dropped. How would she find it?

She gritted her teeth. *I will. I have to.*

Freddie took one last glance into the library as Lucy shut the door. Suddenly, she couldn't wait for dinner to come and go. She had a sneaking suspicion she was going to need a good book to read right before bed.

Chapter Four

"I don't know why Lucy insists on showing the ancestors' hall to everyone." Morgan stretched his legs out in front of him, a half-empty glass of amontillado dangling loosely in his right hand.

"I wouldn't be surprised if Miss Vale somehow finagled the tour," Tristan said as he leaned against the mahogany sideboard in Morgan's office and drained the remains of his own glass.

Turning, he grabbed the crystal decanter and poured another half-glass of the amber liquid. Pausing with the tumbler halfway to his mouth, he glanced at the painting of a centuries-old fox hunt on the wall above the sideboard. The hunt reminded him of the spy game in which he was currently entrenched. Was he the fox or the hunter? He didn't know.

When he turned back, Morgan looked at him quizzically. "Why would Miss Vale do that?"

"I found her staring at the door to the private family quarters. If she is Harker's spy—"

Morgan set his tumbler on the desk with an audible *click*. "We don't know that she *is*." He stood. Although Tristan was broader in the shoulders, his brother stood an inch taller. He used that height to his advantage as he stepped closer to Tristan. "You're jumping to conclusions. I haven't heard anything about her from our contacts and besides, she seems awfully young...and looks very innocent."

Tristan stiffened. "We've seen younger and more innocent-looking spies. You've trained women to act that way to mislead people." He set his glass on the sideboard and crossed his arms, refusing to move away from his brother and show that Morgan had the upper hand. Morgan might be a duke, but Tristan was the man out in the field. "Miss Vale may be slyer than she lets on. You, yourself said we should watch her."

Morgan's left eyebrow twitched, a sign of irritation. "I didn't mean for you to harass Mother's guests."

"I wasn't harassing her. I happened upon her and Lucy in the ancestors' hall."

"Precisely," Morgan snapped. "It may be coincidence. You know how Lucy loves to dramatize, and she's fixated on that old passage. Let's not antagonize anyone until we're certain of their allegiance."

"You mean like Harker?"

Morgan made a face. "The decision not to touch him comes from a higher authority than me, you know that."

"I don't like sleeping under the same roof as him."

Morgan sighed. He raised his hand to toy with the white streak of hair at his temple. "Neither do I, but I can't very well lock him in the stables. My assistant is keeping an eye on him."

Tristan's boots thudded on the wooden floor as he paced the length of the room. "We have to rid ourselves of the book before Harker finds it. The sooner, the better."

As he turned back, he found Morgan seated in his desk chair once again. His brother liberated the sherry from its nest of papers. Tristan couldn't begin to guess which pile related to the various Tenwick estates and tenants, and their seat in Parliament, which Morgan sifted through as part of his contribution to the spy network, and which was correspondence. If Morgan died before he produced an heir, all that paperwork would fall into Tristan's lap.

He suppressed a shudder. One more reason why he was glad he was the one doing the fieldwork, whereas Morgan decoded and compiled reports.

After sipping from his glass, Morgan raised his eyebrows. "I won't argue with you."

Tristan clenched his fists. With a sigh, he retrieved his sherry from the sideboard. "If Miss Vale is his spy..."

The eyebrow started twitching again. "We don't know that she is a spy at all. Still, I do wonder about that business in the entry hall with Harker. They seemed...close." Morgan narrowed his eyes and looked up at Tristan. "Perhaps she is his mistress."

Tristan choked on his drink. The liquid stung as it shot up his nose. He sputtered as he cleared his airway. When his eyes stopped watering, he gasped, "Mistress to that old goat?" He made a face. "I can't imagine why she would. Unless she was somehow coerced."

Morgan's left brow raised a hair. "I've never heard you defend a woman before. I hope she isn't turning your head."

Tristan managed a thin smile. "You know me better than that."

Tristan's head wasn't turned easily by women. Not that he refused offers to warm his bed, but he always treated his bed partners kindly and never made any promises. His relationships were always short-lived. A long-term relationship meant he would be beholden to someone and *that* was something Tristan was definitely not interested in.

Finishing the last of his drink, Morgan stood. He grabbed his sapphire tailcoat from the back of his chair and slid it over his broad shoulders.

"I don't want to jump to conclusions about Miss Vale and I certainly don't want to antagonize her. If you want to keep an eye on her, by all means do, but don't make her feel unwelcome. Not until we know for sure what kind of woman she is."

Tristan gritted his teeth, but didn't want to get into another argument—even if he knew in his gut that his brother was wrong. He checked his pocket watch. "We'd best be getting down to dinner."

Morgan nodded. "I'll ask around discretely about Miss Vale. In the meantime, we'll be careful around her. At least, until we discover the *real* reason she seems to be so friendly with Elias Harker."

A strange pain squeezed Tristan's chest at the thought of Miss Vale with the lecherous old Harker. His hand closed into a fist. Harker had no charm to offer a woman like her. Any liaison between them would *have* to be forced on his part.

Ignoring that strange protective feeling, Tristan muttered, "We *will* discover the reason for their friendliness." And if the bounder was forcing himself on her, whether Tristan had orders not to lay a hand on the man or not, he was determined to stop it.

Oblivious to the dark turn of Tristan's thoughts, his brother grinned. He clapped Tristan on the shoulder. "Of course we will. You can't keep a secret from spies, can you?"

***

Freddie moved the boiled apple pudding around on her plate, willing her eyes to remain fixed on the dessert in front of her. She'd suffered through three torturous courses of dinner, each with over ten dishes served, but had hardly eaten a bite. She couldn't wait for the evening to end.

"You will sit with us after dinner won't you, Freddie?"

Charlie leaned forward, speaking around the uncomfortable young man seated between them. Throughout the course of the meal, he hadn't said a word. Every time Charlie had so much as glanced his way, he'd turned red in the face. Freddie pitied the poor man. He was clearly out of his depth. She knew exactly how that felt.

When she glanced toward her sister, her eyes slid like magnets farther up the long, narrow table to the far end, where the brothers Graylocke sat. Tristan turned his head so fast, the forelock of his fashionable Brutus haircut bounced onto his forehead.

Was he looking at me just now? It had to be her imagination. Freddie was easily overlooked. Forgettable.

"Freddie?"

She forced a smile and met her sister's insistent gaze. "Of course I will." Inwardly, she kicked herself. She would have to find a way to sneak off later.

The tinkling of silver on porcelain signaled the end of the meal. The diners finished their dessert and pushed themselves away from the table. Seated on a diagonal from her, Harker took the opportunity to cast a pointed look. Pressing her lips together, she nodded. *I didn't forget, you dimwit.* She hadn't gotten a chance to search for the book yet. She'd been engaged from the moment they arrived.

As the guests milled, the men retiring to drink port and smoke cigars with the duke, Lucy navigated the chaos to reach Freddie and Charlie. As she did, she linked arms with Charlotte. She tilted her head toward the door, choked with female bodies as they retired to one of the salons as directed by Lucy's mother.

Freddie followed Lucy as they crept along at a snail's pace.

"Charlie's shown me some of her embroidery. Beautiful detail work, better than I could ever do. Do you have a talent for embroidery too, Freddie?"

"I'm afraid not," Freddie said as she followed the two younger women.

"Freddie is the smart one," Charlotte said proudly. "She likes to read, and she's always outdoors in fine weather."

Lucy smiled. "Then you'll delight in tomorrow's events," she exclaimed. "Mother has planned a variety of outdoor activities and games all week."

They turned into a large room furnished in pale blue and gold. Above a dado, a panoramic Neoclassical scene was papered on the walls. It depicted a blue sky, greenery, the ocean, a mountain, and Greek men and women entwined in a dance. The detail work was exquisite. Tufted sofas and upholstered chairs ringed the room. Some of the ladies were already seated and starting to work on their embroidery, tatting or crochet. Freddie recognized Charlie's embroidery hoop set in a plain basket. Lisane must have brought it down. In one corner of the room rested a vacant pianoforte. For the moment, the ladies ignored it.

Freddie felt as out of place as a circus bear. Her needlework was beyond abysmal. She shifted from foot to foot. "Maybe I ought to go to the library to fetch a book."

"You can't," Lucy said, her eyes widening. "The men are in there with my brothers."

Drat!

"It's fine. We'll sit over here in the corner. No one will notice you haven't got any sewing."

From the hawkish gazes of some of the women, including Mrs. Biddleford and Miss Maize, they had already noticed. Freddie stiffened her spine and followed as Lucy claimed a trio of chairs in the corner. With difficulty, she hauled one so the occupant's back would be partially toward the group. Freddie gave in to the weakness flirting with her knees and dropped into that chair. A moment later, Charlie joined them with her basket of embroidery. Lucy plucked the notebook and a stubby graphite pencil from her reticule. At least Freddie wouldn't be the only one without needlework.

Charlie hummed a cheery tune under her breath as she picked up exactly where she left off. Within moments, soft chatter filled the room.

Lucy tapped a page riddled with indecipherable scrawl with the butt of her pencil. Was Freddie certain that *she* wasn't the one carrying the code book? It might as well be code, for all that Freddie could decipher it. After a moment, Lucy flipped the brown leather book shut. She held it on her lap.

Turning to Freddie, she asked, "Have you met all the guests?"

Freddie twisted in the armchair to scan the interior of the room. Most of the faces she recognized, though some were obscured by the angle. "I think so. I'm sure we've crossed paths once or twice in London."

"What of the men?"

Freddie shrugged, helpless. "I can't recall who is here."

"My brothers, of course."

When Lucy shot her an expectant look, Freddie nodded. "I've met the three in attendance, of course." Her stomach shrank at the thought of seeing Tristan again. Somehow, she had to separate him from a book he would most likely be set upon keeping. Even when not in the room, he sent a shiver up her spine. She didn't relish the thought of completing her task.

But she must, for Charlie's sake. For Mama's.

Lucy's face fell. "Giddy's friend Catt—Mr. Catterson—is also here. Have you met him?"

Freddie shook her head.

Encouraged, Lucy continued, "He doesn't have any notable fortune, but he's as smart as a steel trap."

Freddie smiled. "I wouldn't know."

"You will the moment you meet him," she said, gushing. "He's as intelligent as Giddy. A botanist, too, you know."

What could Freddie say to that?

"That's very impressive."

Seated across from her, Charlie had her head cocked to the side. A smile played around her mouth as she exchanged a glance with Lucy. "Intelligence is a *very* good quality in a match. Wouldn't you say, Freddie?"

Had she finally come to her senses? A weight melted off Freddie's shoulders. "Indeed it is," she said with an answering smile.

Lucy beamed. "If Catt doesn't come to snuff, I daresay one of the other gentlemen will. We have more than one scholar in attendance."

With that, Lucy launched into a dizzying list of titles, breeding, and intellectual pursuits. With each, Charlie praised the man's good qualities with more enthusiasm than Freddie had ever heard from her, barring her embroidery. Had she only needed to present Charlie with a scholarly candidate for marriage? Freddie hadn't expected Charlie to shine so much at the prospect of marrying a man whose interests deviated so far from her own. Freddie warmly encouraged the conversation, watching her sister's face light up.

When Lucy had finished with her list, Charlie leaned forward. She even set aside her embroidery.

"So, Freddie, which do you like best?"

Freddie frowned. "It doesn't matter what I think. Your happiness matters most to me."

Charlie batted her hands. "Nonsense. I'll be happy with whomever you choose. Though he should be good to Mama. I wouldn't like you to marry a man who would turn her out."

Me? Freddie's voice caught in her throat. The twin eager gazes of her companions bored into her, awaiting her verdict. "I thought we were discussing your candidates for marriage, not mine."

Charlie wrinkled her nose. "Why would I want a stuffy man who spends most of his time locked away with books? No offense meant."

Lucy laid her hand on Charlie's sleeve. "I don't know any of the others personally, but Catty I can vouch for as a respectful young man of good manners and good humor. Shall I introduce you?"

If Britain had had two such tenacious generals on the front lines, Napoleon would have already surrendered. Freddie flapped her mouth as she stared from one woman to the other.

At that moment, movement in the doorway saved her the need to answer. Freddie stifled a sigh of relief. She never thought she'd be so glad to see the gentlemen return.

Chapter Five

The moment Lord Graylocke stepped into the room, his gaze flew to the corner of the room where Freddie sat. Her mouth dried. He stepped toward her with purpose. She jumped to her feet, but she had nowhere to flee. Lucy had boxed the three of them into the corner quite effectively.

Her heart drummed like a racing carriage as Lord Graylocke stepped up to them. His other brothers, the duke and Lord Gideon, remained by the door. The duke was immediately beset upon by the nearest young ladies. Using his brother as a distraction, Lord Gideon inched toward the opposite corner. He hunched his shoulders, as if by doing so he would somehow make himself as short as the other gentlemen in attendance. Although he'd changed into eveningwear, his hair sported the same disarray as earlier in the orangery, a stark contrast to the duke's tailored appearance.

Lord Graylocke's appearance was somewhere in the middle. He dressed as if he intended to leave for a night of carousing. His black curls were fashionably tousled. His cheeks sported the hint of stubble, a shadow over his skin. He wore a black jacket over a gold-embroidered waistcoat, black breeches that tucked into his polished Hessians, and a snowy white cravat. Compared to the peacock colors of the other guests, he should have faded into the background. Instead, Freddie found it difficult to look away. The eveningwear made his eyes appear darker, deeper. Vertigo flirted with her stomach, as though she was on the cusp of falling into those eyes.

He held her gaze for a moment more before he turned to his sister. "Lucy. Good to see you here."

Lucy frowned. The expression emphasized her rouge-painted lips. "I was seated beside you at dinner. You didn't say a word to me."

"Didn't I? I'm sure I must have."

She crossed her arms. "No. You were much too busy staring down the length of the table."

A tingle swept over Freddie's skin. *At me?* When she glanced at Lord Graylocke, he avoided her gaze.

"I'm sure you are exaggerating."

"I was not. In fact—"

"Do I hear Mother calling?" Lord Graylocke slipped a finger beneath his throat and cravat, loosening it. When he turned, Lucy stepped forward. She latched onto his arm with the ferocity of a pouncing tiger.

A sly look crossed her face. "Freddie, did you know my brother plays chess?"

Freddie forced a smile. Heat crept up her neck as Lord Graylocke turned the full force of his attention on her. There was something accusing in his gaze. *He knows I'm tasked to steal his book.*

No. He couldn't possibly.

But he could—and likely did—suspect her of wrongdoing.

His smile, unlike hers, was dazzling with its charm. "I do," he admitted, "though I don't see what this has to do with dinner."

"Nothing, of course," Lucy said. She raised one hand from his sleeve long enough to wave it through the air, as though chasing away the idea.

Charlie smoothed her mauve skirts as she stood. "Freddie also plays chess." She leaned closer to Lucy with a twinkle in her eye. "I'll wager that my sister can trounce your brother."

Lucy took up the cause with an abundance of enthusiasm. "Oh, yes. Let's have a tournament and find out!"

A look of alarm crossed Lord Graylocke's face. Did he fear losing? "Now may not be the best time…"

Lucy bared her teeth in a predatory smile as she tipped her face up to his. "If not now, when?"

The very last thing Freddie wanted was to be trapped with him for an hour or more.

At that moment, the Dowager Duchess raised her voice, piercing the renewed babble of conversation. "Why, that's a splendid idea! A bit of music sounds like just the thing. Who would like to play first?"

"Freddie will play!"

Wait. I will do what?

Frantically, Freddie swatted her hands at her sister, trying to stop her from saying more. Instead, she latched onto Freddie's hand and towed her away from the Graylocke siblings.

"Charlie, I don't play."

"You learned, the same as I did. I remember, you were the one who oversaw all my practices."

And never practiced, myself.

The blood rushed to her cheeks. She shielded her face behind her hand. If the *ton* learned she couldn't perform any of the feminine arts—that she preferred to expand her mind through reading books—she and her sister would be shunned. She couldn't let that happen.

At least, not until she found the code book for Harker and secured her future.

On the other end of the room, next to the pianoforte, a young woman raised her arm. "I'd love to play."

"Wonderful," Lady Graylocke exclaimed.

Freddie breathed a sigh of relief. The young woman brushed a curl out of her face, cast the duke a coy look, and slid into place behind the pianoforte. Apparently, she didn't know his true colors. Considering that his smile turned pained, Freddie considered the poor young woman seated at the instrument to be safe from his advances.

Narrowing her eyes, Charlie muttered, "You're next."

I hardly think so.

"Where did Lucy run off to?" Freddie asked, pretending to scan the room.

Charlie loosened her hold long enough for Freddie to pull away. "She's right over there—"

Freddie took advantage of her distraction to slip into the crowd. She found a vacant spot by the mantle and leaned her back against the wall. Safe, for the moment. The music began, a light, cheerful tune, adeptly played.

Charlie whirled, glaring at the guests until she found Freddie's position. Although Freddie expected her sister to rejoin her, she stormed off toward where Lucy and her brother still stood.

Wait. Where had Lord Graylocke gone?

Freddie noticed him when he was nearly upon her. His eyes were narrowed, his expression determined. A lump formed in her throat, hot and painful.

He knew. He had to know about her arrangement with Harker. There was no other explanation for why he would single her out. No man noticed her, not with her sister nearby.

Suddenly, Lord Graylocke stopped in place. His posture stiffened. His expression darkened. He turned on his heel. Why?

"You shouldn't be hiding. You should be searching."

Freddie jumped at Harker's accusatory tone. It was far too close—in fact, right beside her ear. She turned, but she was pressed against the corner of the mantle. She had no place to run.

Harker's eyebrows sank over his eyes like hawks swooping in for the kill. His expression was disapproving.

Freddie clenched her fists. "I will search, just as soon as I can leave without arousing suspicion."

"Leave now. No one notices you here."

Oh, if that were only true. Lord Graylocke stood with his brother, the duke, now, but his attention remained fixed on Freddie. She couldn't bat an eyelash without him noticing.

"I think Tristan Graylocke suspects me."

"Poppycock."

It was clear from Harker's tone that he thought her a paranoid fool. Maybe she was. She'd never ventured into spying before, let alone against so formidable an opponent as Lord Graylocke. His reputation for being a rascal clearly masked his shrewdness. Did he cultivate the rumors about his exploits on purpose?

Harker added, "I've never seen any person less likely to draw attention to herself. The Graylockes can't possibly suspect you."

And if they do?

"I'll slip away and find the book as soon as may be."

"Good." Harker's voice turned venomous. "I'm sure you'll prefer to earn the reward I promised than the alternative."

He didn't have the opportunity to elaborate. At that moment, Mrs. Biddleford and Miss Maize stepped up to either side of him with wide smiles.

"Lord Harker!" Mrs. Biddleford greeted him with more enthusiasm than Freddie would likely be able to muster, though her wide smile couldn't precisely be called friendly. Without her spectacles, her eyes looked small and sharp. She clasped her hands in front of her dusky blue gown. A fichu around her throat hid her neck and upper chest.

The moment Harker turned his attention to her, Miss Maize piped up on his other side. "We old birds need to stick together." Tonight, she presented herself as Mrs. Biddleford's very opposite: short where she was tall, plump where she was thin, hair light whereas hers was a steely gray, and dressed in a low-cut paler dress that might once have been purple. Now, it had faded to the point that it looked almost gray.

Looking harried, Harker coughed into his fist. "Actually, um, ladies, I believe I left my snuffbox in the library. If you'll excuse me." With more grace than Freddie would have expected from a man of his bulk, he wove through the guests and out the door.

Beside Freddie, Miss Maize snorted. "Idiot."

Her voice wasn't quite as low as she likely believed.

Mrs. Biddleford added, "Good riddance."

Freddie stifled a laugh. Under her breath, she said, "I couldn't agree with you more."

"What was that, Miss Vale?"

Both gossips turned the full force of their attention on Freddie. She blinked beneath their unwavering stares. "Oh, um, nothing. I said thank you for joining me."

Miss Maize nodded. This close, Freddie noticed a sparse scattering of pale hairs where her eyebrows should be. It seemed she didn't care to use kohl to draw them in.

Looming over Miss Maize, Mrs. Biddleford's nostrils flared as she studied Freddie. "Don't you live with Lord Harker?"

Not for much longer.

Freddie forced a smile. "I do. He was very kind, taking my mother, myself, and my sister in when we had no place else to go."

Her gracious words seemed to have no effect on Mrs. Biddleford's sour mood.

"'Kind' sounds out of character to me."

Freddie swallowed hard. "Do you know him well?"

The busybodies exchanged a look before reluctantly shaking their heads. Freddie couldn't quite bring herself to sing Harker's praises, so she pressed her lips together.

After a moment, Miss Maize ventured, "Your sister is rather lovely."

Freddie fastened her gaze on where Charlie laughed next to a tall, thin man with blond hair that looked red in comparison to hers. Lucy stood on the man's other side.

"Charlotte is lovely," Freddie said, her voice vehement. "In soul as well as body."

That, she meant with all her heart.

"She'll do just fine for herself."

Was it Freddie's imagination, or did Mrs. Biddleford's voice sound almost fond?

Miss Maize leaned forward, squinting. "With whom is she speaking?"

Mrs. Biddleford's eyes narrowed to slits. "I can't tell. You know I left my spectacles in my room before dinner."

Miss Maize turned to Freddie. "Do you know him?"

She forced a smile. "I don't. But I'm sure I can finagle an introduction. If you'll excuse me."

Without waiting for a response, Freddie hurried away from the wall. She smashed her shin on the carved wooden leg of a settee and pressed her lips together to keep from voicing her pain. She limped toward the door in time to the throb in her leg.

This was her chance. With the guests occupied by another pianoforte performance—this one not as impeccable as the first, but passable—she could slip away unnoticed. She must find that book for Harker at all costs.

"Freddie!"

She cursed under her breath. Pretending not to hear her sister, she quickened her stride to the door. Her shin only smarted now. She would have a bruise, no more.

In a feat worthy of a footrace, Lucy dashed into Freddie's path. Freddie stumbled. Lucy caught her by the arm. The fabric of Freddie's diamond-patterned gown stretched tight. For a moment, she feared that her detachable sleeves would rip free. When she righted herself and checked the basted stitches mooring the sleeves to her dress, only one had torn.

Lucy still remained squarely in her path, beckoning to someone behind Freddie. A heartbeat later, Charlie dragged the bewildered young gentleman who she had been speaking to Freddie and Lucy.

With the way his reddish-blond hair seemed to have been combed through with his fingers, he reminded Freddie of Lord Gideon. He was thinner than the Graylocke brothers and not quite as tall, though he topped Freddie by three or four inches. He wore a burgundy tailcoat that brought out the freckles across his nose, a cream waistcoat, tan breeches tucked into brown leather boots, and a cravat that was tied slightly crooked. As Charlie dropped his arm, he snagged one of the flutes of champagne circulating on a servant's tray, and glanced questioningly at the women.

"Would you like one?"

"How can you think of drinking at a time like this?" Lucy spread her arms akimbo. "I'm trying to introduce you to Miss Vale."

Frankly, Freddie didn't blame him. Any man would need fortification when faced with the fierce expressions on Lucy and Charlie's faces.

She mustered a thin smile. "I'm fine, thank you."

An excuse rose to her lips as she glanced to the door, but Charlie was too quick. She wrangled her way onto Freddie's other side and nudged her closer to the young man, who Freddie guessed to be no older than twenty-five.

Beaming, Lucy said, "Catty, I'd like to introduce Miss Frederica Vale. Freddie, this is Mr. Catterson, my brother's associate. You can call him Catty. We all do."

The young man grimaced. "Please don't. Catt or Mr. Catterson will do."

Charlie leaned forward, batting her eyelashes at Freddie. "Why don't you tell Mr. Catterson about the book you were just reading? The one about botany."

"To which book are you referring?" Freddie didn't read about botany.

Her sister elbowed her in the side. "You know the one. The book you were talking about earlier."

I never talk to you about books. Freddie opened her mouth to inform her sister as much, but Charlie snagged Lucy's hand, and with a giggle they retreated closer to the pianoforte. A plump young woman with her mouth set in a determined slash began to play the first movement of Beethoven's *Sonata quasi una fantasia*. She did so flawlessly. Charlie would no doubt be disappointed if she planned to play; it was her favorite piece.

Beside her, Mr. Catterson took a sip from his flute. He scanned the interior of the room above Freddie's head. He didn't appear particularly interested in speaking with her.

The feeling was mutual. Her shoulder blades itched. She had to slip away before Charlie and Lucy found another man to throw into her path.

Mr. Catterson offered her a bland smile. "So, Miss Vale. You're interested in botany?"

Not at all. She gave him a thin smile. "Not to compare with you, I'm sure. I hear you and Lord Gideon are in the midst of developing a new species of orchid."

"A hybrid, yes."

His pale blue eyes lit up at the notion. It was a pity Charlie wasn't interested in him for marriage, because he was quite handsome when he didn't look harried.

"Have you seen drawings of the orchid found in Colonial Brazil?"

"I have not."

"Beautiful flower. No one in the Botanical Society has been able to grow it outside of its natural climate. Gideon and I are attempting to graft it onto a hardier orchid in the hope that it will take."

Freddie's head spun with his enthusiasm for the topic. What was grafting? If she asked, it would be tantamount to admitting that she didn't know anything about botany, after all.

"Fascinating."

A brown curl dropped in front of her eyes. As she reached up to bat it away, her hand jerked into his glass. Its contents tipped down his waistcoat, causing a wet splotch on the embroidered fabric.

"Oh, dear. Forgive me." When she reached forward to help him by reclaiming the glass, the slick surface slipped from her fingers. It shattered on the floor.

Several pairs of eyes turned in their direction. Horrified, Freddie took several steps back to make room for the servants descending to clean the glass and help Mr. Catterson with his appearance.

Everyone's attention was fixed on him as he swore under his breath. Of those who remained—several guests had left the room to seek other entertainment or their beds, thinning out the crowd—no one glanced in Freddie's direction.

Freddie turned on her heel and slipped into the hall, unimpeded. This might be her only chance to find the code book.

Chapter Six

In the evening, Tenwick Abbey glittered like it was lit from within by a thousand stars. The effect was performed through lit candelabras perched on narrow, Neoclassical pedestals set at intervals throughout the hall. Behind each pedestal, a small round mirror in a gilt frame reflected the light down the hall onto various other mirrors, large and small, oval and square, all in equally ornate frames. A vibrant, ruby runner down the center of the hall provided purchase and muffled Freddie's footsteps. The light shimmered across the marble floors on either side of the runner and illuminated paintings—old and contemporary, classical and romantic, long and rectangular murals and smaller portraits. Between the paintings stood other pieces of art—busts, statues of rearing horses and mythical figures—along with intricately-painted vases with fragrant cut flowers, likely from the orangery.

In short, the hallway was a nightmare to a lummox like her. It was a labyrinth of items waiting to be broken.

Holding her breath, she slipped among them, keeping to the center of the aisle. She pulled the train of her gown over one arm to keep her hands busy and well away from the priceless breakables.

As she navigated the manor, retracing the latter part of the tour Lucy had provided, she left the occupied portion of the manor behind. Chatter spilled out of a sitting room where someone had set up card tables, four guests to a table. The scattered servant passed her as she left the populated hall in her wake. Silence wrapped around her, a spell she was afraid to break. She tiptoed around the corner to the library.

This corridor was just as opulently decorated as the last. Flecks of gold in the paint of a vase reflected the light. The flowers smelled like the orangery—a thick, cheerful floral scent with a hint of citrus. The door to the library was shut, but light peeped through the crack between the door and the floor. Someone must have lit a fire inside.

When Freddie lifted her hand to the latch, she froze. Were those voices? The male baritones were muffled. She couldn't hear the words. Holding her breath, she pulled back the latch and eased the door open a crack.

"How are we supposed to deliver the book if we don't know who in bloody hell our contact is?"

Freddie's breath caught. That was Lord Graylocke's voice. Hadn't she left him in the sitting room? Come to think of it, she hadn't thought to double-check that he was there before she'd left.

His brother, the duke, answered him. "We pass it to whoever gives us the signal. Our contact must have been compromised. You know it happens."

Who was their contact? Did this coincide with their spying efforts for the French? Freddie's heartbeat drummed, but she leaned her ear closer to the door.

"I don't have to like it," Lord Graylocke groaned. "This makes our task more difficult. We're under enough scrutiny during this party as it is."

"I am," the duke corrected. "You aren't Duke. You can wander unimpeded."

Lord Graylocke's voice darkened. "Don't remind me."

The click of a booted footstep on the wood floor sounded overly loud and alarmingly close. Fiddlesticks! They were walking toward the door.

Freddie recoiled instinctively. Her hip banged the corner of the table. She hissed in a breath. The vase wobbled. She lunged for it, but the slick surface slipped out of her fingers and plummeted to the marble floor. It shattered, the sound ringing in the silence.

Lord Graylocke wrenched the door open. He'd removed his cravat and loosened the laces of his shirt, baring his throat. The buttons of his tailcoat were undone, displaying a waistcoat that molded to his lean abdomen. His gloves stuck out of his jacket pocket.

"What are you doing?" His dark eyebrows hooked over his eyes, menacing.

Freddie closed her gaping mouth. When she took a step back, he followed, advancing on her. She tripped over the train of her gown, nearly falling. He caught her by the arm above her gloves, holding her upright.

"I—I was looking for a book." She tried to back away, only to press against the wall.

Lord Graylocke splayed his hand on the wall beside her head. He narrowed his eyes. "Is that so?"

"Of course. What else would I be doing?"

Freddie's voice shrank the longer she spoke. Her pulse thumped like a scared rabbit. She was no short woman, but Lord Graylocke loomed around her. His broad shoulders cut off the reflected light along the hall, casting her in shadow. Warmth radiated from his frame. Her skin burned from his touch on her arm, which he still held. His touch was firm, but not painful.

He leaned even closer. He smelled of port with the smoky hint of cigars. When he tilted his head, light glinted off his irises.

Her gaze dropped to his mouth, a tight, disapproving line. As she watched, the set of his mouth softened. How rough would his stubble feel?

She clenched her jaw. What was wrong with her? He was the enemy, a traitor. She loathed everything about him. She jerked her arm out of his hold. In the wake of his touch, her skin tingled.

"Haven't you heard what happens to gently-bred young ladies when they meddle where they aren't wanted?"

Was he threatening her? An icy feeling spread through her body like ripples on a pond. Hot on its heels, her anger unfurled. She ratcheted her chin higher.

"I hear it's the same thing that happens to the sons of dukes who pretend to be gentlemen to hide their black hearts."

When she turned to leave, he dropped his arm from the wall next to her head. A shiver crawled down her spine as she felt his gaze like a tangible touch. The itch to look back nearly overwhelmed her.

She ignored it, and the instinct that she run. As she strode away from him at a sedate pace, she pretended she wasn't afraid of him.

Perhaps if she pretended long enough, the fantasy would replace her reality.

***

Tristan stared after Miss Vale. Her hips swayed in a decidedly feminine swagger. For a moment, he'd thought his warning would spook her away, but now, he didn't know. She didn't seem afraid of him. In fact, there had been venom in her voice. She hated him.

What had Harker told her about him? He shook his head. It didn't matter.

"What was that?" Morgan leaned against the door frame of the library.

Tristan dropped his gaze to his hand. His fingers ached from the memory of touching Miss Vale's soft, silky skin. Could she possibly be a threat to him? She hadn't seemed particularly frightening. If anything, she seemed innocent.

Too innocent.

Tristan gritted his teeth. "Miss Vale. She knocked over the vase." He clenched his fist. The door had been ajar when he'd reached it. She'd been spying on them. She had to have been.

The realization washed over him like an icy rain. How much had she heard?

Morgan didn't seem as concerned. He shrugged. "Did she? I thought we left her in the sitting room."

They had. When Tristan had slipped out, she'd been cornered by Theodosia Biddleford and Hester Maize, two old gossips with hawkish stares. Morgan, the more noticeable of the two of them, had escaped first. Tristan had waited to ensure his brother hadn't aroused suspicion before he followed. He'd timed his exit perfectly, so Miss Vale wouldn't be at liberty to follow.

He glanced down the hall, but she hadn't lingered. "She claimed to have come searching for a book." Despite her excuse, she hadn't so much as entered the library.

Morgan raised an eyebrow. "It is a library," he pointed out. "Lucy showed her the way during their tour this afternoon."

"Then why the secrecy? Why skulk about in the hall?"

Morgan's gaze lingered on the shards of pottery from the vase. "Maybe she heard voices and didn't want to interrupt."

Tristan grimaced. "Maybe she heard every word of our conversation."

Stepping forward, Morgan clapped his brother on the shoulder. Tristan twitched his shoulder, throwing off the touch. He didn't need his brother to brush away his concerns as if they didn't matter. Tristan was the one who went out into the field; a misstep would put his life in jeopardy, not his brother's.

"Even if she did," Morgan said, "we didn't admit to anything incriminating. Let her believe she caught us in something. If she's bumbling around shattering pottery, she isn't a very good spy to begin with."

That lightened Tristan's mood somewhat. Morgan was right. Miss Vale acted far from a seasoned spy. So what was she doing at this party? Had Harker tasked her to spy on Tristan and his brother?

Maybe she's been duped.

Tristan clenched his fist, trying to banish the memory of touching her. Maybe she was a very good actress, and he was the one being duped.

Chapter Seven

The farther Freddie strode from the library, the more her tremors dissipated. Why had she let Lord Graylocke intimidate her? He was a scoundrel, a traitor, but if he'd meant to hurt her, he would have done so. Could he have a shred of honorability in that muscular frame?

She paused as she reached a junction between two corridors. Straight ahead to the left were the broad marble stairs leading to the guest chambers on the floor above. To the right, the long hallway ended in the ancient door leading to the portrait hall. Long shadows stretched down that corridor, a product of the reflected light near where Freddie stood.

She glanced over her shoulder. The hallway was deserted. The silence weighed on her. From somewhere deeper in the abbey, she heard the distant *tick, tick, tick* of a pendulum clock. Her heartbeat matched the steady rhythm.

Lord Graylocke was in the library with the Duke. That meant he would certainly not be in his bedchamber. Had he hidden the book there?

Weariness swept through her at the thought of more subterfuge. She'd have to avoid the other members of the Graylocke family, along with any servants. If she was caught... She didn't know what punishment the duke would seek, but she didn't anticipate enjoying the outcome.

They are French filth.

Even that thought didn't motivate her to move.

But the thought of Charlie did. Of Freddie's mother, too. This was for their future, a future far away from Elias Harker. If she could free them from his influence, the threat of punishment paled in comparison with the reward.

Please let Lord Graylocke be stupid enough to keep the book in his room unguarded.

Freddie filched the nearest candelabra from a pedestal. The intricately-wrought, silver-coated metal imprinted into her palm through her silk glove. Taking a deep breath, she arrowed along the hall toward that heavy wooden door. The flames spluttered with her quick steps. She shielded them with her free hand as best she could.

When she reached the tall, forbidding door, she hauled it open only far enough to slip inside. It thunked shut. She flinched as the sound echoed and amplified along the vaulted ceiling of the room.

No light drifted through the windows this time. They yawned far above her, gigantic swathes of shadow perched high on the walls. The candelabra shed light in a yellowish ring, reflecting off the dulled metal of the suit of armor. The visor on the helmet glinted as though someone was watching her. The hooded gazes of Tenwick dukes long dead crawled across her skin.

"There are no such things as ghosts."

Could she be sure of that? She had to approach those disapproving faces in order to find the well-concealed door between them. Tentatively, she stepped forward, giving the other artifacts in the room a wide berth. She didn't want the bust of some ancestor sniffing her bosom again—or worse, shattering on the floor.

The heels of her evening slippers clicked on the floor as she stepped forward. The sound resonated, throwing itself back at her as if someone followed her. When she glanced behind, she saw no one.

Find the door and get out of here. Unease tickled the back of her throat. She swallowed hard, peering at the spaces between the overlarge paintings and trying to avoid the way the candlelight caught the flecks of paint in their expressions.

The door. *Finally.* It wasn't shut by a latch or lock, but rather with a large iron ring. The ring was hard and a bit rough, as though she felt the beginnings of rust beneath her gloves. When she tugged gently on the ring, the door stuck fast. Transferring the candelabra to her less dominant hand, she dug in her heels and yanked on the door. It pulled free of the frame with a groan that echoed in the darkness. Her pulse pounded as she slipped inside.

When she shut the door, the resulting gust of air kicked up a swirl of dust. It coated Freddie's throat. She coughed, making a face at the bitter taste.

The candlelight slid over drab stone covered in dust and cobwebs. Clearly, the servants didn't clean this portion of the abbey. A smudged trail down the center of the passageway indicated that it got some use, likely by Lucy. The air smelled musty and stale.

As Freddie continued down the passage, it narrowed. The walls seemed to close in on her, now barely wider than her shoulders. The ceiling passed no more than a foot over her head. Breathing in pants through her mouth, she followed the passage as it changed direction. The stone on either side of her muffled all sound, even that of her breathing. Her heartbeat sounded overly loud in her ears.

At last, the passage led directly to another wooden door. Like the first, this had no handle on the inside. She braced her palm against the wood and pushed. The door didn't stick as badly on this end, but there was something hampering its ability to open. When she slid through the gap, holding the candelabra away from her body, still in the passage, her questing fingers met heavy, embroidered cloth. A tapestry? She wrestled it over her head and pulled the candelabra through, hoping it wouldn't catch flame.

Instead, she managed to bang her wrist on the edge of the door. The candelabra fell from her fingers and landed on the floor with a clang. The light guttered out. Freddie swore beneath her breath. She knelt, scooping up the metal fixture and the warm wax candles that had fallen free of their holdings. When she entered the hall, it took a moment for her eyes to adjust. Light mirrored along the hall. She wouldn't need the candles. She thrust them into a corner and shut the door.

The tapestry was a deep, royal blue and silver, the Tenwick family crest of a stag rearing on its hind legs. It was massive, easily six feet wide and ten feet tall. No wonder it had been so heavy. When it settled against the wall, it concealed the door perfectly. The light in the corridor threw her shadow across the fabric.

She turned. Down the narrow corridor, closed wooden doors punctuated the walls. Between them were costly paintings and tables with statuettes or vases of flowers. Freddie counted ten doors. Which belonged to Lord Graylocke?

She started on the right. The first door, unlocked, swung inward to display a monstrously large room. Bed, settee, wardrobe, and various other pieces of furniture didn't seem to make a dent in the space. A fire burned in the grate, casting warmth and orange light across the room. Since the room was empty, Freddie slipped inside. Over the bed hung a large, detailed portrait of the current duke. She made a face. What kind of man wanted to sleep beneath his own portrait? This must be the Duke of Tenwick's room, for she couldn't imagine Lord Graylocke sleeping in the shadow of his brother's painted gaze.

She was about to leave when she recalled that Harker had named the duke a French spy as well. Could he have possession of the code book? Freddie may not get the opportunity to search unhindered again.

The room was neat, tidy. Everything had its place, which made her search both easier and more difficult. She removed items with precision and replaced them with care not to mix up the order. She started at the stand beside the bed, searching along its bottom for a hidden drawer or latch. Then she searched beneath the bed, ran her hands across the mattress, fluffed every pillow, checked his wardrobe, felt along the other furniture in the room, and approached the two closed doors. One led into a dressing room that was utterly plain. She couldn't have found a place to hide a book in there. The other door was locked. She searched, but couldn't find the key. When she turned, her heartbeat quickened as she stared into the benevolent painted gaze of the Duke of Tenwick. He couldn't have hidden the book behind the painting...could he have?

She had to check. With trepidation, she approached the bed and climbed atop it. The mattress was soft and gave easily beneath her slippers. Her knees wobbled as she tried to find her balance. She used the wall next to the painting as an anchor. When she found her footing, she hooked her fingers along the bottom of the portrait's gilt frame and pried it from the wall.

Her fingers screamed at the effort. Blast, but this thing was heavy! It must have taken four men just to mount it on the wall. She hissed in pain as the frame dug into her flesh. She used her other hand to stick her fist beneath, holding it away from the wall. The throbbing in her fingers dulled. She couldn't stand like this forever. The pressure soon mounted near to unbearable.

"He'd have to be mad to hide it behind this dratted thing." She peeked beneath, trying to discern any kind of shape. Of course, the light from the hearth didn't illuminate this far, and she saw nothing. She would have to feel her way along the edge, to see if it was mounted behind. The frame cut off her circulation as she felt. The tips of her fingers started to tingle. She moved quicker.

Nothing. Not a book, not even a mysterious letter from a paramour. She yanked her hands free. The motion sent her off-balance. She bit her lower lip as she careened back onto the bed. Pain jarred her mouth as she impacted and bounced. She breathed hard and pressed her glove to her mouth. No blood, but it stung.

She hurled herself off the bed and noticed that her impact had mussed the pristine coverlet. Drat! She hurried to right it. No sooner did she finish than she stepped back, noticing that the duke's portrait was crooked. Her fingers smarted, recalling the weight of the painting. She gritted her teeth. *Too damn bad.* With luck, he wouldn't notice. She was not fixing it. In fact, she was leaving this room posthaste.

She opened the door. Voices and figures from down the hall made her shut it reflexively. At the last moment, she pulled back and eased the door into its frame soundlessly.

Her heart pounded like a drum. What if it was the duke?

A woman's voice pierced the air. "Goodnight, my dear. Are you off to bed?"

That was the Dowager Duchess. Freddie's knees weakened with relief.

Until a man's voice answered. "Not quite yet. I must check on my night-blooming flowers in the orangery. I've only come to change out of my evening clothes."

"Don't stay up too late," the dowager chastened. "I have plenty of games planned for the morrow."

"Of course." The man sounded resigned. "Sleep well, Mama."

"You, too, dear."

A door opened and shut, far too close for Freddie's comfort. She backed away from the door. Where could she hide?

She heard a second door shut, farther down the hall. Her knees weakened in relief. She sat on the edge of the settee as she waited for her heart to calm. It hadn't been the duke, after all.

She shook her head. *What am I doing?* She was no spy. She wasn't prepared for this sort of thing. Maybe she should leave, ensconce herself in her room and stay there for the remainder of the party.

You're so close. Are you a coward?

She didn't have to be a coward to be afraid of what the French spies would do to her if they found her. But she'd left them in the library, and she'd taken a shortcut through the passageway to get here. She still had time to search Lord Graylocke's room, if she hurried.

She slipped into the hall. Muffled voices emanated from the room directly across from the duke's. She slipped past. The room next to the one with voices opened to reveal an empty adjoining bedchamber. The locked door in the duke's room must lead to one, as well. She continued down the line. The next door she opened led to Lucy's room, judging by the feminine décor. The one next to hers also contained muttering. It must be Lord Gideon. Freddie slipped across the hall and tried the next door.

It opened to reveal a room that was clearly in use. The hearth was cold, but there was a candle on a table by the door, burned halfway to the holder. Clearly, it had been left so far from the rest of the room in order to prevent anything from catching fire.

Nothing in the room was neat. Didn't Lord Graylocke have a valet? Even if he didn't keep one —the man was absent, after all—one of the other servants should have tidied his room. The room was smaller than the duke's, made to seem even more so from the clutter. The bed was made neatly, though a man's banyan had been carelessly tossed across the foot. On a low table beside the armchair facing the hearth were piles of books. Some had pieces of paper sticking out of them, marking the place where he'd left off. Lord Graylocke's house slippers had been abandoned at the foot of the armchair, though they had been arranged neatly. Spare coin littered the top of the sideboard, along with scraps of paper and other trinkets. Was that a rabbit's foot? How bizarre. Freddie's head reeled as she tried to take in the full breadth of the chaos.

She didn't have time to linger. She had to search. At least, unlike with the duke's room, she didn't have to worry about putting things back in their place. There didn't seem to be any sort of order to the mess whatsoever.

At least this room didn't contain a larger-than-life portrait of Lord Graylocke. If Freddie had had to be subjected to his shrewd gaze while she searched his room, she might have swooned.

She began with the books beside the armchair. The plush, oriental-patterned rug muffled her footsteps. She sank to her knees as she rifled through the books, even flipping through them to ensure that no secret correspondence was hidden between the pages. She found no red book with a gold-embossed seal on the front. She ran her hands over and beneath the armchair. Nothing.

Why was the fire in Lord Graylocke's room out, whereas the hearth in the duke's bedchamber was lit? Curious, Freddie crouched in front of the hearth and explored the neatly-swept fireplace. She found no loose bricks, even when she reached as far up the chimney as she dared. The only thing it earned her was soot-blackened sleeves and gloves. She turned her gloves inside out and stuffed them in her reticule along with her detachable sleeves. The small bag bulged with the contents and she couldn't draw it all the way closed.

Irritable, she moved along the room as quickly as she dared. She found no secret compartments, no books hidden behind paintings, no lumps or hard items in the pillowcases or mattress. When she reached the table next to the bed, she paused. She perched on the edge of the mattress as she picked up one of six miniatures collected on the bedside table. Lord Graylocke's parents and siblings. He kept portraits of them next to where he slept? She traced the frame with reverent fingers. He loved his family.

Then why betray his country and endanger his family? Unless they were in on the conspiracy, as well.

Impossible. Lucy couldn't possibly know, let alone participate, not with the protective way her brothers wouldn't even let her conduct her writing research. Besides, Harker had only mentioned the two oldest Graylocke brothers, no one else. They must be the only French spies.

As she carefully replaced the miniature, she couldn't reconcile the kind of man who loved his family so well and yet turned his back on them and his country. Could his brother be at fault? Freddie would have followed her sister anywhere, even into disrepute, in order to ensure nothing happened to her.

It doesn't matter what his motives are. He's the enemy.

As she crouched at the foot of the bed to check beneath it, the latch on the door jingled. Someone was coming in!

Chapter Eight

Freddie squeezed beneath the bed, whisking her skirts out of sight just as a man stepped into the room. His steps were muffled by the carpet next to the door. He was alone.

Freddie wiggled closer to the foot of the bed. Who was here? The shadows stretched across the room, blanketing the underside of the bed and shrouding her. She peeked beneath the drape of the bed skirt.

The man's back was to her. He wore evening-wear entirely of black, from his polished boots to the jacket covering his wide shoulders. The dark color of his clothing brought out brown tints to his dark hair. When he sighed, running his hand through his hair, he gifted her with his profile.

Lord Tristan Graylocke.

"What a headache."

In that, she couldn't agree more. Her heart hammered in the base of her throat, a painful beat counting down the seconds until he found her in his room. She bit hard into her lower lip to keep from making a sound.

The clench of her teeth stifled her gasp a moment later when he swiftly undid the buttons of his tailcoat and shucked it, throwing it over the back of the armchair. He was undressing!

That, she most certainly did not want to be present to watch. And yet, some wild part of her wouldn't let her look away. His cravat came next, the strip of cloth let fall to the floor mere feet away from her. When Lord Graylocke shifted, bending down to tug off his boots, Freddie held her breath and scurried farther beneath the bed.

She wasn't here to gawk at his male form. She was here to find a book. Even that thought couldn't spur her into movement. Fear paralyzed her.

Leaving his boots by the door, Lord Graylocke padded in his stocking-clad feet into the adjoining room, a dressing room. The moment he was out of the room, Freddie lurched into action. She rolled to the edge of the bed.

Wait. What if the book was hidden beneath here, after all? She gritted her teeth. Her fingernails made sharp crescents of pain in her palms as she warred with herself. Releasing an exasperated breath, she leaned beneath and ran her hand along the frame.

The search yielded nothing but wasted time. Her entire body tingled with the near certainty that Lord Graylocke would leave his dressing room in a moment and find her out. She needed to escape.

She darted across the room so quickly, she forgot about the boots he'd left tangled on the floor. She tripped over them and fell against the table by the door, jostling her hip and the candle. She dove for the candlestick, catching it but burning her hand with hot wax in the process. Hissing, she replaced the sputtering flame on the table.

When she looked up, her gaze locked upon the figure darkening the dressing room door. Lord Graylocke. Her mind blanked. She could think of nothing but escape. She lunged for the door. Her fingers slipped on the latch and she wrestled it open a moment too late. Lord Graylocke splayed his palm over the door and shoved it closed, leaning his full weight against it.

His heat bracketed her back. She turned, but she had nowhere to run. The wooden door was cool against the backs of her bare arms. She lifted her chin to meet Lord Graylocke's fierce stare.

"So you are a spy, after all."

Freddie's lips parted, but she couldn't find the words to speak.

He raised his eyebrows. "Don't bother denying it. Not even you can concoct a persuasive argument as to what business you had in my room and why you were attempting to sneak out."

Her gaze dipped to the bare hollow of his throat. The candlelight illuminated his skin, giving it a golden glow. The laces of his shirt were undone, spreading wide to show his collarbone and a hint of the crisp, black hair on his chest.

Freddie's cheeks flushed. "Can we have this conversation while you're dressed?"

He laughed, leaning a bit closer. "No. I like it better when you're off-balance."

Freddie swallowed. She lived most of her life tripping over her feet, not over her tongue. She didn't like this tongue-tied feeling. She forced herself to focus on his chin, not his sharp gaze. The dark shadow of stubble covered his jaw.

She licked her lips, a nervous habit. "Are you going to kill me, Lord Graylocke?" Her heart rattled in her chest like it was trying to escape. What good would she do her mother and sister if she were dead?

"Tristan."

His dark, intimate tone shocked her. She raised her gaze to his. The look in his eye was just as wicked.

"I...I beg your pardon?"

"If we're going to speak frankly, in my room and while I'm half dressed, no less, you ought to at least call me by my Christian name."

Her gaze dropped to his mouth, the sensual curve of his lips. "That isn't proper."

"None of this is. What do you say...Frederica?"

She made a face. "I prefer Freddie."

When he took a step back, she suddenly found herself able to breathe freely again. She gulped for air. It froze on the way to her lungs when he bowed over her bare hand, lifting it to his lips.

"Lady Freddie."

She was no Lady, and never would be. She clamped her lips together, refusing to play his game and point out the error, thereby admitting that she was lesser than him.

She was not. Rank didn't amount to everything.

The moment his lips brushed her skin, tingles cascaded over her hand. She yanked it out of his grasp. "I'd like to leave."

His face hardened as he straightened. "Not yet."

She swallowed at his curt tone. She glanced toward the miniatures he kept at his bedside. Right now, there was no trace of that softhearted man. His every contour was filled with determination.

"Why are you doing this?"

Given his tone, no answer would be to his liking.

She raised her chin. "You wouldn't understand."

At that, his left eyebrow twitched higher. "Wouldn't I? We're both fighting for something."

Again, her gaze turned to the small oval portraits of his family. "I have no idea what you're fighting for."

He no longer leaned against the door. She fumbled for the latch, hoping to yank the door open and escape before he caught her.

Then what? He already knew she was a spy. Perhaps he didn't know for whom. Could she pretend to be on his side? Probably not convincingly, given the hawkish way he examined her.

"I don't expect someone like you to understand. After all, I can't fathom why you've aligned yourself with Harker."

She notched up her chin an inch higher. "Because it's the right thing to do." Her voice was weak. Grouping herself with the likes of him left a bitter taste in her mouth. But she wasn't only doing this for her sake and for Charlie's. She was doing this for Britain. If their allegiances had been the other way around, she never would have agreed, not for love or money.

Tristan grunted, a noise of disbelief. "Even you don't believe that."

Drat! How could he tell?

"Are you being coerced?"

She pressed her lips together to keep from saying a word. She managed to twist her fingers around the latch and carefully draw it out. Almost there! Triumph swept through her.

Until Tristan laid his weight on the door once more. "Close-lipped are you, Miss Vale?" He leaned so close, his breath batted over her cheek. He smelled sweet and a bit spicy, like after-dinner port. "Maybe this will help."

He canted his head and pressed his lips against hers.

Her breath hitched. Her knees weakened. Her fingers tightened over the door handle, the only solid thing keeping her standing. Her head whirled like she'd spun around too fast. All because of the warm weight of his mouth against hers. When he retreated and cooler air rushed in, her lips throbbed with awareness.

"You don't have to work for Harker. We could use a woman like you."

"Never." The word left her lips, scarcely louder than her breath. Even so, when he leaned his head closer again, she couldn't help but tip her chin up to meet him.

His kiss was different this time. Less cajoling and more demanding. She surrendered, transferring her hand from the door to his broad, firm shoulder. When he nipped at her lips, she gasped at the sensation. He deepened the kiss, pressing her against the door. His body was the only thing holding her upright.

Sensation swept her away. The feel of his muscular body against hers. The harsh sound of their breathing. His taste, sweet port with a slight bitter undertone of cheroot smoke. The hungry way he kissed her, as if he couldn't get enough.

Abruptly, he stepped away. She leaned against the door. Her legs trembled. He stared at her as if seeing her for the first time.

"You should leave."

She didn't understand why he was letting her go after catching her spying, but she didn't question him. Her hand slipped as she fumbled the latch free. She stumbled into the hall, drawing the door shut behind her before she leaned her weight against it. She needed a moment to steady herself.

It was a moment she didn't have. A woman's heels clicked against the floor upon her approach. Lucy, it had to be. Freddie couldn't be seen here. She darted for the other end of the hall, and the heavy tapestry shielding the hidden door. Her legs wobbled, threatening to give way. If Lucy found her outside Tristan's door...

Heaven help Freddie. Lucy wouldn't suggest she and Tristan marry, would she? The notion birthed a torrent of desperation. It lent her strength. With difficulty, she lifted the heavy tapestry and pried open the door behind her.

She shut it just in time. The click of the heels paused for a second, then resumed. A moment later, a door opened and shut. Freddie leaned against the cold stone wall, relieved.

It was only at that moment that she realized she didn't have so much as a candle to light her way. She didn't dare return to that corridor, so close to Tristan. Instead, she opted to fumble the rest of the way in the dark. A fitting end to the escapade, considering she felt the exact same way when it came to spying.

Her future was just as murky.

Chapter Nine

Tristan looked like he'd dragged himself through the grime of London's underbelly. The scrape of the razor eliminated the dark stubble lining his cheeks, but after a night spent tossing and turning while thinking of Freddie—Miss Vale—his hair refused to be tamed. Dark shadows ringed his eyes, evidence of his sleepless night.

No woman had ever gotten under his skin this way. Then again, he'd never been pitted against a woman who seemed so innocent. Every bone in his body rebelled at the idea of her spying for Harker, even though he now had irrefutable proof. He did the dirty, dangerous spy work so that innocents like Freddie wouldn't have to.

She's the enemy. Even knowing that she worked for Harker didn't ease the guilt roiling in his gut. Given the reflection staring back at him from the round handheld mirror, it showed in his appearance. At this rate, he would develop a white streak in his hair like his brother. Unfortunately, there was nothing he could do without the help of his valet. Like with Morgan, Tristan's valet was a spy in the network. With Harker in residence, he didn't have the time to devote to traditional valet duties.

Tristan tried to tell himself that his appearance didn't matter. The debutantes at this hellish party were here to ensnare the duke's interest, not his. The knowledge didn't ease the bitter feeling in his chest. With a sigh, he set aside the mirror, tied his cravat, and shrugged on his coat.

Instead of making his way to the breakfast room, he arrowed for Morgan's door. Before he lifted his hand to knock, his brother emerged. He looked startled.

"You look like you just crawled out of Hell."

Tristan grimaced. "I wasn't able to sleep."

"Women troubles?" Morgan quipped.

Tristan's stomach tightened. *More than you realize.* "In a way." When Morgan moved to step past him, Tristan blocked his path. "I found a spy in my room last night."

The duke's face hardened. "Why didn't you send for me?"

"I let her go."

At the disdain that crossed his brother's face, Tristan curled his fists. He added, "I couldn't very well lock up one of Mother's esteemed guests."

Morgan rubbed the furrow forming between his eyebrows. "Miss Vale, I take it?"

Tristan crossed his arms. "Indeed."

"And she admitted to working for Harker?"

He gritted his teeth. *Not in so many words.* It had been implied, however. He'd seen the knowledge in her eyes. She'd known she'd been caught. She hadn't even pretended to be on his side in the war, which he would have expected of a seasoned spy. Why would Harker choose a woman whose every emotion could be read on her face? As a distraction?

She had certainly been that. The feel of her soft curves against his body had driven him wild. The moment she'd surrendered to his kiss, he'd been lost. He'd been seconds away from drawing her toward the bed before he'd realized who she was.

An innocent. A virgin. For all his carousing, he didn't defile young debutantes.

He scrubbed his hand over his mouth. "I couldn't think straight with her in my room. She has nowhere to go while she's here, so I didn't see the harm in releasing her."

The corner of Morgan's mouth crooked up. "I didn't know you were in danger from the plain ones."

Plain? Was he blind? Tristan bit his tongue. It didn't help. "She may dress as if she's been put on the shelf, but beneath those dresses, she is anything but plain."

The glint in the duke's eye intensified. "If you insist."

Tristan scowled. "What are we to do with her?"

The duke's teasing air dissipated. In its place remained the calm, cool spymaster. Tristan could almost see the cogs in his head align as he thought through the situation. This intellect was why Morgan had always been a better chess player than Tristan. He could see five moves ahead in any calamity.

Thrusting his shoulders back, Morgan muttered, "We'll treat her like any other spy we can't touch. We'll feed her the information we want her to know."

"What about the book?" It hadn't been in his room last night—nor had any other sensitive information. Freddie might have been clever enough to find her way into his rooms, but it had been a wasted effort. He didn't leave things around where a curious servant might stumble across it.

Morgan turned down the corridor, leaving Tristan to match his long-legged stride. Tristan buried his annoyance as he caught up. The moment he stepped abreast, his brother spoke.

"If Miss Vale is so set on finding the book, that is precisely what we'll give her."

***

Freddie froze on the threshold of the breakfast room. Her recently-eaten eggs and bacon tumbled in her stomach. The voices mounted, growing distinct. When she peeked through the doorway, she spotted the two oldest Graylocke brothers arguing three doors down the corridor. Tristan had his back turned to her. The duke, gesturing jerkily in the air, didn't appear to notice her. She shrunk back, but cocked her ear to the commotion. A quick glance behind her showed that the other early risers were still more interested in their breakfast than in her odd behavior. One young man even cracked a yawn. Most, like Charlie and Mama, still lay abed.

"Are you mad?"

That was Tristan's voice, the most distinct sentence in the argument yet. Freddie leaned closer to the open door.

"I'm telling you, now isn't the time. I found her out last night. If she discovers..."

Freddie held her breath. *If she discovers what?* They had to be speaking about her! Were they about to reveal the location of the book?

"We can't afford to tarry." The duke's voice was colder, dispassionate. It sank into her skin like a winter chill.

Tristan, she found difficult to imagine as a French spy, considering his obvious love for his family. But the forbidding Duke of Tenwick... He might put on a good-natured mask in front of the *ton*, but what kind of man was he? When he let shine his true nature, such as that moment through his speech, she could all too easily imagine him a traitor.

The duke added, "We've been tasked to pass along the book, and that is precisely what we will do. Today."

Freddie's heart quickened. They must be speaking about the code book! If she didn't discover to whom they hoped to pass off the book, it would be lost to her. Then what would Harker do?

Nothing good, given his wandering eye of late. A lump formed in her throat. She couldn't let that happen. If she couldn't lay her hands on the book herself, she could at least discover its recipient and remove it from their possession instead.

"If she finds out…"

"She won't." The duke's clipped words cut off Tristan's protest. "You'll keep her busy today. Make sure Mother pairs you with her for whatever games she decides to conduct."

I don't think so. Somehow, Freddie would manage to escape. She and Tristan grated on each other's nerves. He wouldn't be able to remain by her side for long before their dislike for each other was apparent to the entire party.

Besides, he was on the wrong side. Freddie was clever, determined, and motivated. Not even Tristan Graylocke could stand between her and the object of her desire.

"And what will you be doing?"

"I'll attend the meeting in the abandoned chapel in the north of the abbey. We've timed it to coincide with Mother's games at two o'clock this afternoon. I trust you'll be able to keep her attention tied?"

"Of course."

Freddie clenched her hands at his smug tone of voice. His easy dismissal of her rankled. It made her even more determined to prove she could outwit him.

Just you wait, Tristan Graylocke. At two o'clock this afternoon, he would see exactly how formidable she could be.

***

"Miss Vale!"

No! Freddie clenched her fists. She'd almost reached the marble staircase leading to the guest quarters. How had Tristan spotted her? His back had been to the door of the breakfast room when she'd slipped out.

His footsteps quickened over the corridor, barely muffled by the runner underfoot. When she turned, irritability lacing every bone in her body, he had his mouth open to call for her again. With a gleam in his eye, he shut it. He stopped out of arm's reach.

"Lord Graylocke." Freddie emphasized the formal address.

His eyebrows raised by a hair. If she hadn't been staring him in the eye, she might not have noticed.

"You look...hale this morning."

She pressed her lips together to keep from snapping at him. Hale? She didn't know whether to laugh or take the remark on her continued good health as a threat.

"I don't know why you would possibly seek my company."

She showed coarse manners by being so blunt but with him, but she didn't give a fig's end. He could think her the most impolite debutante north of the Channel for all she cared.

His hands, encased in tan leather gloves, curled into fists at his side. A moment later, he relaxed his grip. "Did you consider that I might want to apologize?"

For being a traitor? She bit her tongue.

He took a step closer, lowering his voice. "It was wrong of me to kiss you last night. Forgive me."

Never. She stepped away from him. "Consider it forgotten."

The corner of his mouth twitched before it resettled into that stark, serious line. "I doubt you're able to forget the matter so easily."

She crossed her arms, holding her ground. "And why not?"

"Because I haven't."

His low, intimate tone, coupled with the insistent look in his eye shocked her into silence. Was he trying to tell her that he'd enjoyed their kiss?

What was his game? He was a traitor, a spy. The enemy. She couldn't allow herself to soften toward him for even a moment.

Even if she had relived his kiss last night while she'd lain in bed, awaiting sleep. After her father had cocked up his toes, she hadn't thought much about romance or kisses. She'd been too busy keeping her family in one piece. For a moment with Tristan, she'd forgotten the weight of responsibility on her shoulders.

She bit her inner cheek. She couldn't let him know that. Undoubtedly, he sought to use the kiss against her.

As she studied him, she noticed the telltale signs of a restless night. The shadows around his eyes. The disarray of his hair, as if he'd run his fingers through it a dozen or more times this morning. Could he be telling the truth?

It doesn't matter. It doesn't change what he is.

Traitor, blackguard, spy. He wouldn't deter her from her mission—that, she vowed.

Drawing herself up, she said, "I think it's best if we forget everything that happened last night."

"I don't know if I can do that."

He offered the statement with a neutral tone and expression, but there was a flash of emotion in his eyes that she couldn't decipher. Did he mean it or was he merely trying to install himself by her side as long as possible?

The knowledge of what she'd overheard burned inside her like a hot coal. She needed to tell Harker about this exchange. If she did, maybe he would tell her that her task was complete.

No, she wasn't naïve enough to believe that.

She lifted her chin, staring Tristan in the eye. "I'm going to my room." She dared him to argue with her or try to follow.

A voice from behind washed over her like rainfall. "Oh, dear. I hope not."

Freddie forced a smile as she turned to greet Tristan's mother. She hadn't had the pleasure of spending much time with the petite woman up close. She was shorter than Freddie, with a curved figure and an impish set to her mouth and chin. Her thickly-lashed eyes were surprisingly light compared to her coloring, blue-gray like storm clouds just beginning to build. Her hair was a deep, steely gray where it wasn't threaded through with the brown of her youth. Despite the color, she didn't appear to be that old. Not more than fifty, at Freddie's guess.

Her smile, when she turned it on Freddie and Tristan, was so bright it nearly blinded. "I was just about to round up those out of bed to begin the first game."

Freddie's stomach dropped. She tried not to show it. "So soon? Most of the guests are still abed."

A twinkle entered the dowager duchess's eye as she folded her hands across her stomach. Her wrist-length, white gloves contrasted with the rich green color of the dress. "Why should we have to wait for those lay-abouts? Seize the day!"

"Carpe diem." Tristan gave his mother a fond smile. "A fine idea, Mother. In fact, perhaps Miss Vale would care to partner me in the coming game?"

Freddie narrowed her eyes at him. "You don't even know if the game in question has partners." She spoke in a low mutter. If he or his mother heard, they ignored her protest.

Lady Graylocke beamed. "What a wonderful idea! I don't know if we have quite enough players for a game involving partners, but why don't we start up a game of battledore? We don't need an even number of players for that."

"I haven't played battledore in ages," Tristan said. "It sounds like a delight."

Freddie glared at him. He heaped on the praise too thickly to be genuine. His mother didn't seem to notice. She patted him on the arm as she slipped past on her way to the breakfast room.

"Why don't you fetch the shuttlecock and rackets while I round up a few more participants? I'll meet you on the lawn."

Freddie smirked. *At last*. She had a spare moment to slip away.

When she took a step, Tristan deftly stepped around her and into her path. "Miss Vale, may I beg your assistance with the rackets? There are a fair few and I could use an extra pair of arms."

She chanced a glance down the corridor. Lady Graylocke had slowed her paces and seemed to be waiting to hear the answer. Fiddlesticks! Freddie couldn't refuse without upsetting the host. She didn't want to dream of how that would reflect on Charlie if she did.

She pressed her lips together, letting Tristan know with her glower that she was not amused. "I'd be delighted to help." Her voice was tight.

"Wonderful!" He reached out, tucking her hand onto his sleeve and guiding her down the hall.

She glanced wistfully at the stairs as she passed.

With a sigh, she returned her attention to Tristan. The muscles in his forearm were stiff beneath her palm. Clearly, he took care to keep himself in fighting shape. As a spy, did he face physical danger often?

Would she? Her fingers curled on his sleeve, digging into the flesh beneath. Thus far, he hadn't seemed as though he would grow violent with her. But if he aligned himself with the French, anything was possible.

Perhaps she could distract him—and herself—with conversation. "I know what you're doing," she said, her voice clipped.

He cocked an eyebrow. "Oh?"

"You're trying to rob me of a proper rest."

He laughed. The rich, mellow sound warmed her from the inside out like a warm cup of chocolate. His grin transformed his face, turning his appearance from ragged to rakish.

He leaned his head closer to hers. "It seems only fair, seeing as you've robbed me of mine."

"Sleeping with one eye open, are you?"

The sound that escaped his throat was a mixture of disbelief and mirth. "It wouldn't help. Your wiles followed me into the dream realm last night."

Was he flirting with her? She didn't spend much time in the company of gentlemen, let alone those schooled in the art of flirtation. She nibbled on her lower lip as she considered her response. They turned down another corridor, aiming for a door at the end, before she answered.

"If you continue to keep me awake, you won't have to worry about my wiles much longer. Without my beauty rest I'd have nothing with which to tempt you."

She regretted the words the instant they left her lips. *You aren't Charlie.* She knew she wasn't a diamond of the first waters like her sister, but she was on Tristan's arm and Charlotte was not.

For a moment, Freddie wanted to forget about the gravity of her situation and enjoy the moment.

Tristan seemed more than willing to oblige her, judging by the upturn of his mouth and his mutter of, "I wouldn't be so sure of that." He spoke so low, she almost didn't hear.

The moment dissipated along with the flattered flush of her cheeks as she recalled the person with whom she played this dangerous game. Tristan Graylocke wasn't a man she could trust. She'd do best not to forget that.

Chapter Ten

Fluffy white clouds boiled across the sky like a pot about to froth over. Slivers of blue sky peeked between them. The sun's rays battled with the clouds, occasionally shining through for a second before falling behind cover once more.

Freddie looped the hem of her faded beige skirt over her left arm. The embroidered roses marching crosswise down the skirt bunched—Charlie's handiwork. Taking strength from her sister's love even when she wasn't near, Freddie raised her chin and picked her way across the tidy green lawn after Tristan.

He led her across the broad, sweeping yard toward a shed. In this isolated portion of the grounds, the abbey looked like a looming castle without a moat. Farther east, trees cropped up in groves, but the shed was isolated from them. The only landmark of note, topping a small rise fifty feet beyond the shed, was a tall, gnarled oak. Given the breadth and reach of its branches, it must have stood on the grounds as long as the abbey had, if not longer. Freddie craned her neck back as she examined the branches, so high overhead that the shadow nearly stretched all the way to the shed. This early in spring, tight green buds hadn't yet unfurled into leaves.

Tristan followed her gaze. "That's been there as long as I can remember. I think we have a portrait of one of the old dukes standing beneath it."

Freddie smiled. "It's like a family heirloom." She had precious little of those, seeing as her father had gambled away anything of value.

Tristan barked a laugh. "The only thing of value I've ever gotten from that tree has been a broken bone or two when I fell out."

"Why would you try to climb it? It's gigantic!"

He shrugged. "I was a boy. I liked the lure of danger."

"I'd say you still do." He had become a spy for the enemy, after all. Every day he walked in the shadow of the hangman's noose.

Gravity befell Tristan's features. His gaze dropped to her mouth. "Maybe I do," he muttered under his breath.

He spun on his heel and approached the shed. Freddie stiffened at his abrupt change in demeanor. For the first time since they'd emerged from the abbey, she realized how far they'd ventured. Alone. No one, not even another servant waited nearby.

With trepidation, she approached the shed. She found Tristan collecting a dozen or more rackets. He seemed perfectly capable of completing the task on his own.

She placed her hands on her hips. "I thought you needed my help."

He flashed a grin. Inside the shed, his face was bathed in shadow, but that smile still made her breath hitch. "When did I give you that impression?"

She scowled. "Hand me some of those rackets or I'll return to the house."

Although she expected him to protest and carry them all himself due to some misguided notion of the delicacy of her gender, he willingly divided the pile. If he carried a few more rackets than her, he evened it out by giving her three shuttlecocks to carry.

They left the shed and strode across the lawn. Freddie found it difficult to juggle her skirts and the load at the same time, but she pressed her lips together and made no complaint. When they reached the shadow of the abbey, they found Lady Graylocke waiting along with a half-dozen sleepy, disgruntled guests. Tristan deposited his rackets on the ground, and accepted Freddie's and her burden of shuttlecocks. With relief, she dropped her skirts to cover her ankles once more. Showing her stockings to this mixed group made her uncomfortable.

Curiously, she hadn't felt that way with Tristan. She pressed her lips together, purging the thought from her mind. If only she could rid herself of the awareness of his presence so easily. He stood next to her, his heat like a brand searing her even through her shawl and dress.

The hostess herded the sour-faced guests toward the pile of rackets, which Tristan handed to everyone. Following Lady Graylocke's lead, they formed a ring a few yards away. "Bring only one of the shuttlecocks, Tristan. We'll leave the others for when the rest of the guests awake."

Tristan scooped up one of the shuttlecocks and two rackets. When Freddie reached for one, he held it out of her grasp. "Do I have something you want?"

Was he talking about the racket or the code book? Or, heaven forbid, his kiss. Her gaze dropped to his mouth. She forced herself to look away.

Bending, she snatched a different racket out of the pile left over. "You'd best remember that I don't need your cooperation to get what I want." She turned, striding toward the group without a backward glance.

Tristan followed. As she took up her position in the ring, he claimed the spot next to her. The group shifted, moving farther apart to give them room.

Tristan began, bouncing the cone-shaped shuttlecock toward her. With the cage-like sides, it fluttered delicately. She whacked it out of the air, toward the gentleman on her right. Turning to Tristan, she rolled her eyes. "I'm not going to fall to pieces if you lob the shuttlecock toward me properly. I'm no delicate flower."

His gaze darkened. "Made of more mettle than that, are you?"

"Certainly."

"I should expect nothing less from a woman so eager to engage in…battledore."

Freddie narrowed her eyes. Did he reference her spying abilities? If he did, none of the other guests appeared to attend the conversation.

As the shuttlecock circled back around, she caught it easily and continued it on its journey around the ring before she answered.

"You say that as if you disapprove, but it is the very sport you chose to engage in."

The corners of his mouth turned down, though he battled to keep the scowl off his face. "That's different."

"Why? Because you are a man and I'm a woman?"

Freddie's voice carried. To Tristan's left, a young woman snorted behind her hand. She pretended not to listen, but her eyes twinkled as she followed the path of the shuttlecock. On the other side of the ring, a young man missed the cone and it fell to the ground. He relinquished his racket with what looked like relief. Freddie suspected that he'd lost on purpose, for the excuse to return inside. The game resumed with one less player.

Tristan sidled closer, lowering his voice. "Far from it. I disapprove because you are innocent of the rules."

Freddie tightened her grip on her racket. "I'm a quick study."

"I don't think you realize how hazardous the game can be." As the shuttlecock reached him, he batted it with an elaborate flick of his wrist. The cone whizzed to the ground near Freddie. She lunged forward and barely managed to position her racket beneath it in time. Once the shuttlecock buoyed through the air on its way to the gentleman on her right, she glared at Tristan.

He shrugged.

"You weren't born knowing the rules," she said, her voice stiff.

He met her gaze, his eyes glittering and cold. "No, but I was a sight older than you are when I learned them."

Across the ring, his mother exclaimed, "What lies are you telling? You've been playing battledore since you were a boy."

His expression tightened.

We aren't talking about battledore.

He didn't admit as much, however. With a thin smile, he said, "Maybe so, but I didn't fully comprehend the rules as a child."

"What rules?" His mother laughed. "It's a simple enough game. You must keep the shuttlecock in the air for as long as possible. If you drop it, you've lost and must forfeit your spot. The last person standing wins."

Freddie fixed Tristan beneath a falsely sweet smile. "See? It sounds simple enough to me. If you can do it, so can I."

A few chuckles emanated around the circle.

The game continued. More debutantes, chaperones, and gentlemen exited from the abbey to form rings of their own. Occasionally, those who had lost in Freddie's ring but still cared to play went over to other groups. Their group shrank to only four members—Tristan, his mother, Freddie, and the gentleman to her right. Tristan's hits grew steadily more challenging as he tried to trip Freddie up. When his toss combined with her clumsiness nearly earned her a mouthful of grass, she glared at him.

Tristan didn't seem bothered by her animosity. "I don't know what lured you to play battledore. You can barely keep your feet."

Were they still talking of spying? As the shuttlecock swiftly came around again, Freddie lobbed it toward the gentleman next to her with a bit more force than necessary.

"Circumstance." She bit off the word.

"I don't know of any circumstance that could lure me to join."

On his left, his mother frowned. "If you don't like the game, Tristan, by all means, you don't have to play. You can return to sleeping the day away whenever you'd like."

Tristan rubbed at his temple. "That isn't what I meant."

Of course it wasn't. They were speaking about the war again. At least they seemed to do it in such a way that no one else seemed to catch on.

"Then what do you mean?" Lady Graylocke's voice was clipped.

"Nothing. Please, forget I said anything. I withdraw the comment."

Freddie lifted her eyebrows. "Forfeiting to a woman?"

He made a face. "I have done it when my opponent is worthy."

"I'll be sure to keep that in mind when I emerge the victor."

He made another elaborate pass, which Freddie caught easily, for once. She was growing accustomed to the give and take of the game. She'd staked out a steady little square of even footing and had managed to work out a way to move about without stepping on her hem.

In a blasé tone, Tristan said, "I will never forfeit to *you*."

"Tristan," his mother exclaimed, aghast. "I didn't raise you to insult my guests."

She focused the full brunt of her attention on him and missed the shuttlecock. It fell to the ground by her feet. She made no move to pick it up. Although she was a small woman, her displeasure was like a sharp-edged weight on the air. Freddie was glad the hostess didn't turn that look on her.

Tristan cringed. He bowed stiffly in Freddie's direction. "Please forgive me. I meant no offense."

Lady Graylocke harrumphed. "I should hope not. If you insult one of my guests again, you can hie yourself back to London and your whores." She stormed away from the group. The air rang with her departure.

Freddie's mouth fell open at his mother's crude words. Her cheeks flushed, even though she wasn't the person to whom the words were addressed. Freddie didn't have any comparison, but the kiss he'd delivered her had felt masterful. Did Tristan pay for the privilege of enjoying a woman's...company?

It isn't any of your business if he does. Their kiss aside, she had no intention of surrender to him again. In passion or in any other way.

The conversation's abrupt tone scared away their last competitor. With a muttered excuse, the man dropped his racket and left to join the line of those practicing archery. At some point during the morning, the servants must have set up the targets, two of them facing each other fifty yards apart.

His cheeks ruddy, Tristan bent to scoop up the shuttlecock. "I suppose the game has run its course."

Freddie raised her chin. "Why? Because it's only the two of us?"

His dark eyes glimmered with an unspoken emotion. "My dear, this game has been between the two of us from the beginning."

"Then let's play. I won't forfeit to you."

His chiseled features hardened. "Nor I to you."

"Throw the shuttlecock."

He did. The game rapidly devolved into a heated match between them as they each tried to force the other into submission. They were evenly matched. When Freddie grew hot, she doffed her shawl and removed her sleeves.

Tristan's face was set with determination. He watched the shuttlecock, never faltering a step, but also kept Freddie pinned beneath his examining gaze. What was he thinking? Beneath that shrewd stare, she was much less graceful than she'd hoped, but she held her ground.

"What circumstance leads you to align with the wrong ally?" He still spoke in cryptic terms, in case the ladies and gentlemen strolling past listened in. Their match drew quite a few gazes.

Freddie wiped the sweat off her upper lip. "You're the one who is allying themselves with the wrong side."

He raised his eyebrows. "You can't possibly seek to defend your relative."

From his dark tone of voice, she gathered he meant Harker. She gave a one-shouldered shrug, but her next volley at the shuttlecock was weak. "You can't choose your relatives."

"No. But that doesn't mean you have to follow them blindly."

Freddie bit her lower lip. That was exactly what she suspected he'd done with his brother. He had no right to comment on her decisions, when he'd clearly chosen to do the same. At least she aligned herself with Britain instead of with the enemy.

"You don't know the decisions I've made. I'll thank you not to condemn me because of choices you don't understand."

He lobbed the cone back in her direction. She stumbled as she lunged to catch it in time.

"If you expect me to look the other way and let you win, you're in for a disappointment."

She scowled. "I don't expect you to change your tune." Even if it would make her life easier. "But don't expect me to give up, either."

He met her gaze for a moment as he bounced the shuttlecock lightly on his racket. "Then, Miss Vale, may the best man—or woman—win."

***

The hour must have grown close to two of the afternoon by now. The guests had begun filtering off the lawn and into the house to change their clothes and search for vittles. Freddie's arms ached from holding up the racket for so long. Given the beads of sweat on Tristan's forehead, he was just as uncomfortable beneath the blazing sun, which had departed from its bed of clouds near to an hour ago.

Their tense battle of wits had grown quiet, though neither was willing to surrender. Freddie's heart throbbed with the urgency to leave the match and make her way to the abandoned chapel in the north of the abbey. If she left soon, she still had a hope of reaching the location before the duke and his spy contact.

Unfortunately, Tristan seemed determined to stop her. His jaw was set, his eyes hard. He focused more on her than he did on the game, though he seemed to have more difficulty hitting the shuttlecock after so long. He was sluggish to respond, though her weaker hits didn't give much of a challenge. Between volleys, he tugged at his cravat, as if he dearly wanted to remove it.

His single-minded focus on her convinced her that he wouldn't let her out of his sight long enough to sneeze. She needed a distraction or an excuse even he couldn't refute.

Arm in arm with Lucy, Charlie approached. Freddie watched her sister from the corner of her eye, but couldn't greet her without forfeiting the match. She continued to play.

"I'm going to change and sit down to lunch. Will you two be joining us?"

A burst of relief radiated through Freddie as she grasped on the opportunity. She made a half-hearted attempt to catch the next throw, but purposefully let her racket fall short. The shuttlecock buried itself beneath the trampled grass.

"Oh, dear. It looks like I've lost." Dropping her racket on the ground in defeat, she bit her lower lip to keep from smirking. "Charlie, I might as well accompany you."

Tristan snatched the shuttlecock from the ground and held it aloft. "Wait. I call foul. You missed that on purpose."

Lucy rolled her eyes. "Tristan, give the poor woman a break. You've been at it for hours."

"But—"

Freddie linked arms with her sister. As the three women walked away, she wiggled her fingers over her shoulder at Tristan. He stood on the green, his hands clenched around his racket and the shuttlecock.

She expected to feel relieved to finally leave him behind. Instead, her shoulder blades tingled with the weight of his gaze.

And with the urgency of what she had to do next.

Chapter Eleven

The moment the shadow of the abbey fell across Freddie in a cool wave, her heartbeat sped. She'd escaped Tristan's eye, but now she had to slip away from her sister's grip. Her mind's eye wandered to the north side of the abbey, which hadn't been included in Lucy's previous tour. How much longer did she have to reach the meeting place?

They entered a side door into a smaller antechamber than the main entrance. Between two doors directly ahead was a grandmother clock. It read a quarter past one of the afternoon. Freddie tried to relax.

Twin staircases climbed the edges of the cavernous room, one leading to the east wing and one to the west. Charlie dropped Lucy's arm and started to walk toward the east staircase.

"Freddie, might I have a word alone, please?"

Freddie's grip on her sister's arm went slack as she met Lucy's eager gaze. She exchanged a glance with Charlie, who frowned, but shrugged. "I'll meet you upstairs."

"Of course," Freddie murmured, an instinctive response.

Lucy's gaze trailed after Charlie as she mounted the marble steps. The click of her heels echoed in the room. At the top of the stairs, Charlie dawdled. Clearly, her curiosity won out.

Turning her back on the staircase, Lucy leaned close to Freddie and lowered her voice. A furrow of concern deepened in her forehead.

"I hope you'll forgive my brother. I don't know what came over him." She sounded contrite, almost ashamed at Tristan's competitive behavior.

Freddie couldn't help but grin. "I believe it was my fault for provoking him."

Lucy wrung her hands. "Still, he doesn't have to act like such a boor. He isn't usually so competitive, not unless he's pitted against Morgan."

So the Graylocke brothers had a competitive relationship. Is that why Tristan had joined Morgan and the French, to prove himself a better spy? Freddie chased the notion away. No answer would satisfy her. In her eyes, betraying her country was unforgivable.

"Consider it forgotten."

"He's usually a delight to be around." Her dark brown eyes, so reminiscent of Tristan's, bored into Freddie's, as if willing Freddie to believe her.

Delightful...for a French spy. Freddie managed a thin smile. "I'm sure he is."

Lucy's mouth twisted. "Except when he's being overprotective."

The smile came easier to Freddie's lips. "I can understand that. He loves you."

Her gaze drifted to the second level, to Charlie. Freddie's breath stalled as she realized Charlie wasn't alone. Harker was standing next to her.

When Freddie returned her attention to Lucy, she must have managed to hide her alarm, because Lucy seemed relieved, rather that worried.

"Then you won't hold it against him?"

Hold what? Freddie's head spun as she tried to recollect the conversation. "I promise I won't hold his competitiveness against him."

In regards to his allegiance, Freddie made no promises.

Lucy squeezed Freddie's arm. "Thank you. I'll see you at lunch."

Freddie's ears rang as she returned her attention to the staircase above. Harker still stood with her sister. Even closer, in fact. Charlie's back was pressed against the wall.

As she mounted the steps, Freddie's lungs burned like she'd inhaled fire. She stamped down the sensation, hurrying to her sister's side.

The moment she stepped within earshot, Harker gave an oily smile. "Ah, Frederica. Precisely the woman to whom I'd hoped to speak."

Charlotte stiffened her back. Her fists balled at her sides, as if she hoped to step in.

Freddie relaxed her shoulders from around her ears and tried her best to appear nonplussed. "Why don't you hurry to our room and change, Charlie? I'll be along shortly." For all Freddie's efforts, her voice was stiff.

The whites showed around Charlie's brilliant blue eyes. She cocked up her chin and licked her lips. "Are you sure?"

Harker's gaze dropped to Charlotte's pretty mouth.

Freddie's stomach swished. "Quite sure," she said, her voice clipped.

Reluctantly, Charlie slinked down the hall. Freddie held herself tall, waiting until her sister was out of sight before she turned to Harker.

"What are you doing here?"

He raised his eyebrows. "I didn't know it was a crime to speak with my own ward."

Freddie's fingernails bit through her gloves and into her palms. "I'm doing your bidding. You can have nothing to say to her."

Inspecting his fingers, Harker drawled, "Now that you've mentioned it, let's talk about that."

Freddie gritted her teeth. "What about it? I put my life on the line last night searching the Graylockes' quarters. If I'd found anything, you would have it."

His eyes glinted, like cold, glittering pieces of ice. The temperature in the corridor seemed to cool. Gooseflesh rose on Freddie's bare arms.

"You seem to be getting yourself acquainted with Tristan Graylocke."

Freddie made a face. "He...suspects me. I can't help that."

Something convinced her to hold her tongue on how Tristan's supposed 'suspicions' had been verified.

Harker leaned closer. He must have eaten beans this morning with his breakfast. His breath reeked of them. "You appear to be getting awfully cozy with him. Almost like lovers."

Freddie's hand itched to slap him. She bit the inside of her cheek. Violence wouldn't help her situation.

"I assure you, that isn't the case." Her voice was high and thin. She pressed her lips together, unable to muster another word.

Harker narrowed his eyes. "I wanted to make sure you know what's at stake here. Your future." His gaze traveled down the hall, where Charlie had escaped. "And your sister's."

Freddie stiffened.

Almost as an afterthought, Harker added, "Many more lives hang in the balance, too. This is a matter of national importance."

Freddie gritted her teeth. "I know that. I've been trying to slip away from Lord Graylocke's side all morning. I know where the book will be at two o'clock this afternoon."

She expected Harker to demand details. Instead, he waved his hand in the air dismissively. "Then go and retrieve it."

Retrieve it yourself. Freddie clenched her fists. "Don't you want to do that yourself? Of the two of us, you are the trained operative. You have more experience."

His cheeks puffed out in affront. "I told you, I'm under too much scrutiny while I'm here. It's the reason I recruited you."

I'm under scrutiny now, too. Freddie held her tongue. "Very well. Then I shouldn't dally any longer."

Without waiting for Harker's response, Freddie strode away. She stormed blindly down the hall, soon finding herself in front of the room she shared with Charlie. Mustering some semblance of serenity, she opened the door.

Charotte sat on the plush settee. Lisane must have neatened her appearance, because she wore a fresh placket-front dress in blush pink, patterned with roses no bigger than Freddie's thumb. The moment Freddie stepped into the room, Charlie jumped to her feet.

"Are you all right?"

"Of course I am. Why wouldn't I be?"

Charlie's expression darkened. She looked murderous. "Harker…"

"Only wanted to ensure our comfort and treatment during our stay here. I assured him all was well."

By Charlie's narrowed eyes, she didn't believe Freddie. In the corner, Lisane rifled through the wardrobe, pulling out a new dress for Freddie.

Freddie gulped. "Please, Lisane, put that back."

The thin woman turned her sharp gaze on Freddie. With her high, cutting cheekbones, her expression was all the more potent. "You don't agree with my choice, Miss Freddie?"

"I'm tired." That, Freddie didn't have to feign. A bone-deep weariness swept over her. She kept standing for Charlie's sake alone. She needed to complete this mission, no matter the cost. She offered her sister a smile, but it felt wan. "It's been a long morning."

Charlie wrinkled her nose. "Yes, I imagine so. You were already outside by the time I came down to breakfast. What possessed you to play for so long? You don't normally get so swept away by anything that isn't a book."

Freddie shrugged. "Perhaps I needed to exercise away some excess energy."

Charlie snorted. "All you've done is exhaust yourself." She sighed. "Very well. Come on, Lisane. Let's leave her in peace. I'll give your excuses, but even then you'll have no more than an hour or two before we have to change for dinner."

"I know." Freddie snatched Charlie's hand and squeezed it. *I love you.* She didn't speak the words, trying to infuse her actions with the truth.

Charlie squeezed her back. "Sleep well, Freddie." Lisane shut the curtains and they both left the room.

The moment she was alone, Freddie sank onto the vacant settee. Her knees felt like jelly. She lowered her head into her hands. How long could she keep this up?

As long as you must. Freddie recalled all her reasons for following Harker's demands. With renewed energy, she thrust herself to her feet. She didn't have a lot of time to make the rendezvous. She would have to hurry.

***

The ancient oak door, as old as the one in front of the portrait hall, loomed in front of Freddie. Black iron scroll hinges held the age-worn wood in place. The handle jutted out, taunting her. It was edged with rust.

You can do this. Despite the encouraging words, doubts nagged her. She was no spy. If she was caught... She would have the duke to contend with this time, not Tristan. Although she didn't know what had convinced Tristan to allow her to flee last night, she didn't believe the duke would be as courteous. Even though she was in the middle of English country at a house party, she couldn't allow herself to be fooled. This was war.

Mustering her courage, she opened the door. The hinges creaked, the ghastly sound echoing in the room beyond. From deeper in the abbey, a clock chimed. Two o'clock. Freddie gulped. Was she about to step into the middle of a clandestine meeting?

If someone was in the room beyond, they'd undoubtedly noticed the door opening. She had no choice. She had to step in.

Her footsteps resounded along the stone walls. She stepped into a room lit sporadically with daylight streaming in from fallen sections of the roof. The former chapel seemed to soar as high as the heavens. Long, narrow slits high in the walls formed glassless windows. The wall near the peak of one had crumbled away. The rectangular window opened into a jagged hole near the top of the room.

If there had once been a bell in here or pews or any other form of religious artifact, they were long gone. The elements had worn away this room. The only things littering the flagstones were piles of rubble. One towered over her height. Loose pebbles and chunks of stone littered the ground, along with animal droppings, the remnants of nests, and bones that she didn't care to examine too closely.

Rustles echoing along the walls indicated wildlife, but she couldn't spot the source. In the distance, bird wings flapped. Not a soul lingered in the room. Her stomach dropped. Had she missed the exchange?

Maybe they're late. She squared her shoulders. Her breaths came thickly, threatening to overwhelm her. The only place to sit and watch would be behind one of those piles of rubble. If Morgan and the other French spy were on their way, she didn't have long to hide. She hurried farther into the room with quick, clipped steps. The debris crunched beneath her shoes.

As she took her fifth step into the room, the door to the chapel slammed shut behind her with a resounding *boom!* The thunderous sound deafened her. She spun. The door was shut.

Panicked, she raced to it and pushed. The inside had no handle. It should have swung outward on its hinges. Instead, the door remained shut. Firm. She threw her shoulder into it. It felt as though a bar had dropped across from the other side.

A flood of emotion swept through her as she turned her back against the door, searching for another way out. The nearest opening in the stone was at least two stories over her head.

She was trapped in the chapel with no hope of rescue. No one knew she was there.

Chapter Twelve

When Freddie launched away from the door—barred from the outside by Morgan—panic infused her expression. Her brown eyes were wide. They seemed darker in the dim light. Her ivory skin blanched to such a degree that the smattering of freckles across her nose and cheeks stood out like flecks of paint. Her mouth thinned.

She bolted away from the ancient, solid door and stumbled into the old chapel. Her slipper caught on a chunk of rock and she nearly careened onto her face. From his position in the shadow of the tallest mound of rubble, Tristan fought the urge to help her. He clenched his fists.

Frederica Vale worked for Elias Harker, a man worse than scum. Tristan could afford to give her no mercy. She'd made her choice when she'd decided to come here and infiltrate a clandestine meeting.

Not that any such meeting would have occurred in a place like this. Frustration built in

Tristan's chest over the fact that he still hadn't heard word from their contact at the party—whoever it was. No one had made an overture indicating that they were a friendly party. Not to Tristan, at the very least. Perhaps his and Morgan's valets were having better luck ferreting out to whom they should pass along the book.

That person was certainly not Freddie, however beguiling an enemy she made.

As she stepped past him, her footsteps ringing in the vaulting chamber, Tristan silently detached from the shadows of the rock. He trailed her as she searched the length of the chamber for another exit—a futile effort. He and Morgan had settled on this place because there was no other way out. Everything from her posture to her movements was frantic, desperate, frightened. He could almost pity her.

He hardened himself to the emotion. She was the enemy. He couldn't forget that.

He continued to approach even when she stopped short, staring at the rear of the chapel, encased in stone. When she whirled, he met her gaze unflinchingly.

Tears gathered along her lower lashes. Her eyes had reddened, granting her gaze a green tint. She stared at him, lips parted. Her chin trembled.

"You did this."

Her words were so faint, he almost didn't hear them. He crossed his arms, drawing himself up. "You aren't supposed to be here."

She stared at him for a moment, her expression unreadable. Myriad thoughts crossed her face, all of them indecipherable. Tristan matched her impassive demeanor, staring her down.

Tears swamped her eyes. They leaked from the corners, flowing like a river down her cheeks. Impatiently, she brushed them away. "Not now." Her chin wobbled.

The look on her face cut him. He hated to see a woman cry. At that moment, she appeared more innocent than ever. What had he done? He stepped closer.

"Don't!" Her voice was venomous as she recoiled. The tears continued to fall from her eyes, thicker now.

What kind of spy broke into tears at the first sign of opposition? He resisted the urge to rub his temple. He felt like a blackguard for forcing her into this.

Was she innocent or was it a ploy? His gut churned. Her cheeks were growing splotchy with color from crying. No actress was good enough to feign that. If she was so innocent, he didn't understand how she'd found herself in Harker's employ. Even if Harker had approached her with the notion of spying, a woman as inexperienced as she was should never have accepted. Freddie was many things, but bird-witted wasn't one of them. She was smart enough to know better.

So why had she accepted?

As she wiped her eyes, she muttered under her breath. "I didn't ask for this."

His breathing hitched at the sad, broken quality to her voice. It barely met his ears. He doubted she meant for him to hear. The sudden desire—no, *need*—to encircle her with his arms, to protect her from the harsh realities of the world, surged within him. Undeniable.

He approached her like he might a skittish lamb. More tears bubbled up as he slipped within arm's reach. He reached out, gently wiping the moisture from her cheek. When she didn't shy away, he wrapped his arms around her shoulders, drawing her close. She was a tall woman. He rested his cheek on the top of her head. She smelled like lavender.

"Shhh," he whispered. "It's all right. No one will see you here."

She sobbed into his collar. Her shoulders shook. She rested her hand on his tailcoat, over his swiftly-beating heart. Her touch was light, delicate.

"When did my life get so complicated?" Her voice was thin and high. "All I want is to keep that blackguard away from Charlie."

Tristan stiffened with jealousy. Who was this Charlie?

"Has Harker threatened you?" Tristan's voice was soft. He mediated his tone, pretending as if he didn't care for the answer.

Inwardly, he seethed. Slime like Harker shouldn't be permitted to walk the street. But, despite knowing that he was the enemy, Tristan and his brother had been expressly forbidden to lay a finger on Harker. Considering that he knew about the code book and yet hadn't made a move against Tristan directly, Harker must have similar orders from his superiors. If Harker got his hands on that book, hundreds of spies in England and abroad could be in jeopardy. Tristan couldn't let that happen. Their cover was the difference between living and dying for many of the spies. In more than one case, Tristan had been put in a similar corner where exposure would have endangered his life.

But he couldn't let Harker twist young maidens into unfavorable situations, either.

As Freddie thrust herself away, he became acutely aware of the absence of her curves against his body. An ache blossomed in his gut, one he tried to ignore.

She turned her back on him. "Harker has never issued a threat. He doesn't have to. You wouldn't understand."

Desperate to touch her again, he grazed his palm over her shoulder. She jerked away and rounded on him.

"Maybe I might, if you gave me the opportunity to listen." Tristan's heartbeat quickened. The muscles in his throat worked, but he couldn't think of another word to say. This was supposed to be an interrogation of sorts, to discover if he could deter her without harming her.

The alternative... Tristan didn't want to contemplate it. Unlike Harker, he and Morgan had been given no instructions not to detain or even torture her if necessary. Details about Harker's reach could help his superiors immensely.

If Freddie had any details to provide. She seemed too innocent, too inexperienced at the spy game for Harker to have used her before. He was playing her. Who knew the lies he had spread as motivation?

But Freddie didn't strike Tristan as a woman easily tricked. He didn't know what to think, but his gut told him she had no business being involved in Harker's game.

Her gaze hardened, glittering like ice. Her tears had dried, but her eyes were still red, her cheeks still colored up. "You are the enemy," she spat. "I will never tell anything to you."

Her tone was lethal, her gaze direct. She believed with all her heart that she was his enemy. As she stormed past him—where she thought to go, he didn't know—he turned and followed on her heels.

"I don't have to be your enemy, Freddie."

Her eyes flashed with anger. "I will never be anything else to someone like you."

She spoke the words with such vehemence that he was struck dumb. What had Harker told her about him to make her hate him so viciously? He fisted his hand at his side, wishing he could plant it in Harker's hideous face.

Freddie pounded on the ancient door with the flat of her palm. "Open this door immediately. If *he's* in here with me, I know someone must be out there."

Her words echoed throughout the lofty chamber, growing dimmer each time they were thrown back. They faded into silence.

From the other side of the door, wood scraped. A moment later, the door was yanked open from the other side. Morgan stood on the threshold, his expression forbidding.

Shock radiated through Freddie's body. It was evident in the hitch of her shoulders, the way she turned reflexively to face Tristan, her eyes wide and frightened.

She feared his brother more than she feared him? For some reason, the notion mollified him somewhat.

He tried not to let it show. In a grim voice, he warned, "You won't win. You're playing for the wrong side."

She firmed her chin and brushed past Morgan, out the door.

Chapter Thirteen

"We should never have let her go."

Tristan clenched his jaw to keep from snapping at his brother. They'd been having some variation of the same argument ever since the encounter in the abandoned chapel earlier this afternoon. Throughout the evening, the guests had kept Morgan from harping on him, but even then, Morgan had shot Tristan pointed looks.

To save himself the need of answering, Tristan took a sip of brandy. He savored the burn as it slid down his throat.

Morgan paced the length of his study. Although the long, narrow room seemed large when he was ensconced behind the massive desk taking up one corner, as he strode down the middle, his face set in disgust and frustration, the air in the room seemed to shrivel and compress. Tristan set his tumbler down on the sideboard. Maybe he should stop drinking. He stepped to the side, out of his brother's path.

"She'll tell Harker."

Tristan gulped a deep breath before he answered. "What will she tell him? The entire debacle was arranged to trap her. She knows nothing."

Morgan glared. His grey eyes pierced like a blade. "She knows we're spies."

"She knew that before this afternoon."

"If she exposes us..."

Tristan released an exasperated breath. "She would be exposing herself. She has no proof and she won't find any."

Morgan crossed the length of the room again, his long-legged stride devouring the space. When he turned, his gaze settled on Tristan. It was assessing, maybe even accusing. "I suggested the trap today so we could interrogate her, discover what Harker knows about us and our efforts."

He knows about the code book. At least, so Tristan thought. It seemed to be what Freddie was after.

Blindly, Tristan reached for his tumbler. He swallowed the last sip. "I think...I think Harker is coercing her into spying for him. He must be."

Morgan's posture stiffened, as though he turned to stone in front of Tristan's eyes. Even his expression was as immovable as one of the busts in the portrait hall. "You have no proof."

I have her crying into my shirt. Tristan gritted his teeth.

Ever since their father had died ten years ago, Morgan had taken over as the head of the household. He'd been heaped with responsibility and looked toward for answers. Growing up, Morgan had been the golden boy to Tristan's black sheep, but they had been close. By the time Morgan had become the Duke of Tenwick, that closeness was nothing more than a memory. Tristan had had to live in Morgan's shadow, never being noticed except as the duke's younger brother. It had put him in an ideal position to become a spy—but Morgan had entrenched himself in that, as well.

Tristan clenched his fists. The empty tumbler in his hand squeaked against his glove. He set it down on the sideboard.

Anger unfurled in his chest, but he tried to keep a tight rein on it. Being at odds with his brother wouldn't help their mission, even if it would give him some measure of satisfaction.

Keeping his voice low and controlled, Tristan said, "You don't venture into the field, brother. I have years of experience. I think by now, I'm able to tell when someone is making an enemy of us of their own free will."

For a moment, the study was so silent, their breaths trumpeted in contrast. Tristan locked gazes with Morgan. He refused to look away.

The duke grimaced. "Does it make a difference whether or not she was coerced? She is still spying on us."

"Ineptly. I'm sure she hasn't been trained. And now that we know about her we can monitor her."

Morgan shook his head. A lock of his black hair curled onto his forehead. "Our resources are focused on Harker, as they should be. While she's engaged in party activities we can keep an eye on her, but there is still a chance she could break away, and in a stroke of luck uncover our secrets."

"The book is well hidden," Tristan snapped. "And I change the location regularly. She won't find it."

"You've earned her attention. If she follows you..."

"I'll send my valet."

Morgan's lips thinned, but he said nothing.

"Miss Vale isn't a threat," Tristan insisted. "I didn't get into this game to harm innocents."

The duke turned away. "Bloody hell if I did, either, but we may not have a choice. She isn't doing this with her eyes closed. She knows the dangers."

Does she? Tristan had tried to warn her, but in her obstinacy, he doubted she'd taken his warning to heart. He envisioned her oval-shaped face, pale and awash with freckles, the parted bow of her lips as he confronted her. Something primitive surged at the image. He didn't want to hurt her, directly or indirectly.

"Maybe I can change her mind."

Morgan's gaze sharpened as he pinned Tristan beneath his stare.

Tristan fought the urge to swallow. Why did he say that?

Because there's no other way.

"How?" Morgan's voice was thick with disbelief, disdain even.

Tristan's hackles rose. His brother didn't think he could do it. That, more than anything, made Tristan determined to succeed. He straightened, thrusting his shoulders back.

Freddie's curvaceous figure and pretty face flashed across his mind again. The memory of her pressed against him mounted.

"Seduction." The word left his mouth before he thought twice. He swallowed, but didn't take it back. He didn't want to.

He met his brother's gaze. "No woman betrays a man she's fallen in love with."

Morgan's mouth twisted in a wry smirk. "I suppose we'll shortly find out."

***

Freddie wove through the throng of people meandering up the wide, grassy lawn toward Tenwick Abbey. To her right, the small shed was dwarfed in the shadow of the giant oak tree. Ahead, up a small incline, loomed the abbey, a magnificent sight cutting up from the manicured lawn, carefully cultivated garden, and smaller trees beyond. The stone edifice seemed to rise in tiers, the windows fitted with glass that sparkled in the intermittent sunshine. It was a lofty, regal building perched on the edge of the Tenwick estate, like a benevolent overlord keeping an eye on his subjects.

The guests meandered toward the edifice like pilgrims, taking slow and plodding steps. Freddie elbowed her way between Mrs. Biddleford and Miss Maize, muttering her apologies. They glared at her as they closed ranks, blocking the path of the man who dogged her steps.

Tristan narrowed his eyes. As the sun hid behind the clouds, his dark gaze turned stormy. He pressed his lips together. Freddie turned her back, quickly slipping in and out of the other guests as she made her way toward the manor as quick as she dared. The entire way, she felt his hot gaze on the back of her neck.

He hadn't given her a moment's peace all day. From the moment she'd descended to the breakfast table, early as usual, he'd been waiting. Thankfully, they hadn't been alone. He hadn't spoken a word to her, but his gaze had bored into her while he methodically buttered a piece of bread from corner to corner, filled a cup with a strong, bitter coffee judging from the smell, and consumed it, alternating in sips and bites until he finished both at once.

He'd escorted his sister on his arm down the lawn to the church. The party had opted to walk rather than drive, given the mild spring weather. Even with Charlie and Lucy to serve as a buffer between Freddie and Tristan, she'd still felt his presence like the heat of a furnace.

He'd sat in the pew behind hers during Church, and although Freddie hadn't dared turn her head during the sermon, she'd sensed that his gaze was fixed to the back of her bonnet.

His message was clear: *I'm watching you.*

Freddie couldn't help but shiver at the thought. It was bad enough that, in a moment of weakness, she might have shared too much information with the enemy. Now he wouldn't let her alone. How was she to accomplish her task and lift her family from Harker's eye when Tristan stuck himself to her every move like a burr?

So don't do it.

That wasn't an option. Although Harker had been conspicuously absent from the festivities last night, along with Mama, and hadn't approached her yet today, his beady eyes were upon her as well. The moment she managed to separate herself from Tristan's side, she would have to answer to Harker.

A shudder crawled up her spine at the thought. If she'd only managed to get the book yesterday, this would have all been over. But no, she'd managed to become a watering pot, too bacon-brained to even probe Tristan for the book's location while he confronted her.

She stiffened her spine. She had to do better. *I promise, Mama. Harker won't touch you again, not if I can help it.*

As she reached the front of the group, Charlotte's voice called her name from behind. Freddie ducked her head, pretending not to hear as she stepped beneath the shadows of the manor. The doors loomed, a beacon. She quickened her step and crossed the threshold.

The butler waited to one side, his stiff posture encased in azure livery with silver trim. He accepted her bonnet and shawl. Freddie's shoes clicked, echoing along the long antechamber as she stepped away from the door. Behind her, the guests deluged the butler with garments. Bodies clogged the entryway as they impatiently waited their turns. With a smirk, Freddie hurried farther into the manor.

Her gaze rose to the balcony overlooking the antechamber. She'd first laid eyes on Tristan on that very spot. Had it only been two days ago? Her weariness reached down to her toes. She felt as though she'd fought a battle.

But she hadn't won yet. She hadn't found the book. If her sense of direction was correct, that balcony bordered the west wing. Were the family's quarters connected to it?

You already checked there. You found nothing. She bit the inside of her cheek, even as she acknowledged the truth of the words. If she was going to find the book, it would be in someplace she hadn't looked.

Like the library.

A gentleman and a young lady murmured softly as they left the butler behind. The guests thickened as more poured into the manor. If Freddie wanted to avoid Tristan, she had to hurry. Her heart in her throat, she looped her hem over one arm and bolted from the room. The echo of footsteps and the chatter of voices followed her, growing dimmer.

As she turned a corner, she came face to face with Tristan. Her mouth dropped open. He must have entered by another door. But how had he known she would come this way? The glint in his eye left no doubt that he'd expected to find her.

She shut her mouth with a snap. Glancing over her shoulder, she spotted a few ladies lazily crossing the corridor she'd traversed. Halfway down, they turned up a staircase toward the guest chambers.

Before anyone spotted her, Freddie stepped around the corner and out of sight. Tristan remained rooted in spot, a wall of solid muscle. Even in his conservative, gray Church clothing, with his hair neatly combed and his cravat tied simply, he looked dangerous. Her heart thumped faster. She wiped her clammy palms on the skirt of her flower-patterned yellow dress as she dropped the hem from her arm.

"Are you following me?" She kept her voice low, afraid of it carrying.

Tristan had no such qualms. He laughed, a deep, rich chuckle. They stood so close together, she could feel the air ripple from the vibrations.

"Why do you sound disapproving? It's what you've been tasked to do, isn't it? Keep an eye on me—follow me."

The fabric of her skirt scraped against her palms as she fisted them. *Not even close.* In fact, she expressly tried to avoid his interest. By now, it was impossible.

He leaned closer. His cologne filled the air around her, a sultry whiff of sandalwood.

"In a way, I'm making your task easier. You don't need to search for me when I'm right in front of you."

He leaned his palm against the wall in a casual pose. His biceps strained against the tight sleeve of his jacket. Her gaze darted to that display of muscle. She swallowed, but couldn't find words.

With a charming smile, he added, "Go on. Report on my movements to your master."

She pressed her lips together, but even that couldn't stem the tide of outrage that rose in her. "Harker is *not* my master."

"No? He seems to be able to get you to do his bidding."

If she were prone to violence, she would have kicked him. "What I do with my time is none of your concern."

"No?" He cocked one eyebrow. "It is when I find you places where you don't belong."

She gritted her teeth. "I'm in the middle of a public corridor. I'm on my way to the library. You can't possibly be so arrogant as to tell me that I'm not permitted to read."

He chuckled, a deep sound that matched his eyes. His gaze seemed to envelop her, dark with promise. "You know what I mean."

She took a step back. Without her hem draped over her arm, she tripped on her train. A sickly tear rent the air. Her heel slipped across the fabric of her hem. She lost her footing. She yelped before clamping her lips shut.

In the next instant, strong arms wrapped around her as Tristan kept her from falling. He pressed flush against her from belly to knee, his hands splayed across her back. His gaze dropped to her mouth.

Freddie's ears rang with a steady *click, click, click*.

A moment later, twin gasps punctured the air behind her. While clutching Tristan's biceps for support, she peered over her shoulder.

Mrs. Biddleford, her gaze sharp despite the lack of spectacles perched on her long nose, beheld Freddie with unrestrained glee. Miss Maize, only as tall as her companion's shoulder, fought a smirk. With her cheeks heating, Freddie faced forward, only to be confronted by Tristan's panicked gaze.

He released her with alacrity. Freddie leaned against the wall for balance. Turning his gaze away from her, he said stiffly, "Yes, Miss Vale, the library is this way. Just down this hall. If you'll excuse me, ladies?"

Without waiting for a response, he shouldered his way between the two older women and continued down the hall. His posture was stiff, his movements jerky. Had she noticed some heightened color in his face?

Her cheeks felt like a furnace as she met the two gossips' examining gazes. As their attention roved over her, taking in every aspect of her from her staid coiffure to her modest walking dress, she felt as though they could see through to her very soul. She shifted in place, hoping her secrets weren't shining on her face.

She cleared her throat. "I hope you'll excuse me as well. I seem to be especially clumsy this afternoon. I believe I'll go to my room and lay down."

Mrs. Biddleford cackled as Freddie stepped forward. "Yes, I imagine you are...clumsy."

Miss Maize beamed, her gaze sly. "I imagine I would be too, if I had Lord Graylocke's strong arms to catch me."

When the taller busybody nodded in answer, it looked a bit like the bob of a chicken's head. "Yes, a sight better than the menfolk you're usually accustomed to, isn't it, Miss Vale?"

Freddie's heart pounded faster. Were they talking about Harker? Surely they didn't believe that she...entertained him the way her mother did. Freddie's stomach swished at the thought. She would rather be cast out onto the street.

Ah, but would you rather Charlie was cast out? Freddie swallowed hard. That was a future she dared not contemplate. It wouldn't come to that. She would find the code book for Harker, and that would be that. However clever Tristan thought he was, he would not outsmart her.

She wiped her hands on her skirts. Throwing back her shoulders, she said in a prim tone, "I'm sure I don't know what you mean."

Her eyes gleaming, Miss Maize pounced on the topic like a cat offered catnip. "If you'll forgive us for saying so, that Lord Harker is hardly a pleasant one to look at."

Freddie offered a tight smile. It was the closest to a pleasantry as she could come. "I hardly employ my time staring at him."

When she tried to step past the pair, they shifted to block her.

Mrs. Biddleford added, "He does seem rather odious. One might wonder why you find yourself in his company at all."

Freddie's head spun. She bit the inside of her cheek to grant clarity. "I hardly have a choice. Lord Harker was kind enough to take my family in when we had nowhere else to go. Now, if you'll excuse me..."

She stepped past the pair, her heart beating faster as she heard the rustle of muslin that indicated movement. Would they try to stop her?

Mrs. Biddleford called after her, "Is that why you're so adamant in pursuing Lord Graylocke? To provide another choice."

Breathing became difficult, like she tried to inhale sludge. She swallowed hard, but even then, couldn't come up with something to say. Instead, she beat a hasty retreat. Her legs shook by the time she reached her chamber.

I'm not pursuing him. He's pursuing me—and not for the reason you think.

Chapter Fourteen

Lace tickled Freddie's nose. She batted it away, fighting a sneeze. When she opened her eyes, it took her a moment to puzzle out why the room was sideways. She must have fallen asleep. Guilt nagged at her stomach over a wasted afternoon—the light slanting in through the window indicated that sunset approached. She sat up, rubbing her eyes.

Charlie stood in front of her, beaming. A mint-green underdress was draped over her arm. The bottom six inches were tiered in lace with small white flowers embroidered above where it had been hastily added to the hem.

"I promised I would finish it, and I did."

Freddie's mouth fell open. "When did you find the time?"

Her sister grinned. "I made the time. You'll wear it tonight, won't you? I want to give you every advantage."

Freddie reached out. When her fingers touched the smooth waterfall of fabric, she had to blink away tears. *I want the same for you, Charlotte.* She waited until she had her emotions under control before she craned her neck back to look her sister in the eye. Freddie's throat was thick with tears. Her sister radiated satisfaction and pride.

"Is there no one who catches your eye here, Charlie?"

Her sister made a face. "No. Freddie, I've told you, I'm not interested in marriage yet. I have time yet before I have to decide."

Not if I don't procure the code book for Harker. Freddie's chest filled with a hot burn. She gritted her teeth. The look in Charlie's eye, if anything, made Freddie even more determined to do his bidding. She would earn that promised cabin and dowry for her sister if it was the last thing she did.

She smiled. "Thank you. I appreciate it. Will you take the rest of the party to enjoy yourself?"

Charlie draped the dress over the royal blue settee and straightened. Her smile was blinding in its brilliance. "I will, as long as you promise to do the same."

Freddie choked back a laugh. Now that Tristan knew of her spying arrangement with Harker, she didn't know how that would be possible.

***

Freddie sat squarely in the middle of the long table. The white tablecloth tickled her legs. To her right, at the very end of the table, was the Graylocke family, seated in a square next to the guests of honor, who Freddie gathered were also related to the Tenwick title in some peripheral way. The youngest, Lucy sat opposite her mother with the duke in between them. Diagonal from her, on the dowager duchess's right, was Tristan. Several yards and myriad people separated them, but even so, every time Freddie cast her gaze toward the head of the table, she found Tristan staring at her. At that distance, in the shimmering light cast by the chandelier overhead, she couldn't make out his expression.

Pressing her lips together, she focused on the food on her plate, spiced beef and creamed parsnips. With Tristan's gaze on her, her stomach jumped and buzzed like it was filled with grasshoppers. She moved her food around her plate, but didn't eat.

On Freddie's left, her sister leaned closer. "I think Lord Graylocke is staring at you."

Freddie didn't look up. "You must be mistaken."

"Am I?"

The wondering note in Charlie's voice made Freddie rear her head in alarm. Her sister wasn't paying the least bit of attention to her anymore. Instead, she was busy staring at the head of the table. Her eyes were narrowed, her thick brown eyelashes jutting out like the accusing point of fingers.

"I thought I caught him paying attention to you during Church this morning."

Freddie didn't like the look on her sister's face. She gulped a hasty sip of wine. "How would you know? He wasn't sitting with us." Her voice emerged high and thin, not at all natural.

Charlie didn't seem to notice. Her attention remained, unwaveringly, on Tristan. "He sat in the row behind us with his brothers. I saw him when I stretched my neck."

Charlie always had a more difficult time concentrating during Church than Freddie.

She hazarded a gaze at Tristan. He appeared to notice her sister's regard. A frown pulled at the corners of his mouth. He said something in reply to his mother and picked at his food, but a moment later, his gaze returned.

"Aha!"

The exclamation was no louder than a whisper, but Freddie cringed all the same. A quick glance down the table proved that no one appeared to have noticed. For that reason alone, Freddie was glad that Charlie had tenaciously claimed the seat next to her instead of adhering to the seating schedule that paired women with male partners on either side to encourage conversation. Freddie doubted that a man seated between them would have stopped her sister from engaging in this conversation. At least this way, they weren't overheard.

Charlie leaned so close that the artfully arranged curl by her temple tickled Freddie's cheek. "He did it again. He is definitely looking at you."

"Are you certain he isn't looking at you?"

Charlie wrinkled her nose. "Why would he be staring at me? We've scarcely exchanged two words."

"And you think he and I have held a debate?"

"You spent the morning with him yesterday in battledore."

Freddie winced. She was right.

And, judging by the shrewd gaze Charlie turned on her, her sister knew it, too. "You know him infinitely better than I do."

That is closer to the truth than you know.

Freddie had difficulty finding her voice. She spluttered. "I would-ldn't say that I know him well. He... He and I..." She stared around the room, hoping for an excuse. Weakly, she ended, "He is c-competitive, is all. We didn't speak. At least, not much. We—"

Stop talking!

Freddie shut her mouth. She didn't like the gleam in Charlie's eye.

"If you're certain," Charlotte said, drawing out her words.

"I am." Freddie answered a touch too quick, judging by the smug look in her sister's eye. She remedied, "You're bosom friends with his sister. He must be looking at you."

As the servants emerged in a parade to clear away the guests' plates and serve the dessert course, Charlie held her tongue. Freddie was thankful for the respite. She didn't dare look at the head of the table now, whether or not Tristan was staring at her.

Somehow, she had to find a way to escape his company this evening, before her sister came to the wrong conclusion.

***

As the ladies engaged in needlework, the chatter in the drawing room was low, like the soft buzz of insects on a calm summer's day. Leaning forward in her seat, clad in a pink dress with seed pearls sewn into the bodice, Lucy matched the strength of the whispers. She laid her hand on Freddie's knee.

"I hope you aren't still angry with Tristan."

"Angry with him? For what?" Freddie abhorred his association with the French, but Lucy couldn't possibly know that.

She drew back, making a face. "For his crude behavior during battledore yesterday."

Freddie shook her head. It seemed a lifetime ago. "I assure you, it is forgotten."

Lucy perked up a bit. A black curl tumbled into her forehead, lending her a girlish look. Her brown eyes gleamed. "Then you like him."

Not in the least. Freddie caught herself from gritting her teeth and tried to smile instead. "I like him as well as may be."

Lucy exchanged a sour look with Charlie, on Freddie's other side. They had boxed her into their usual corner, not allowing Freddie to move so much as an inch without gaining a sharp glare. Both women now looked as though they'd bitten into a lemon.

Good. They can suck on that response for a while. With luck, it would convince her sister that she and Tristan harbored no feelings for each other whatsoever. None, at the very least, that didn't sprout from acting as spies on opposite sides of the war.

In the corner of the room, the pendulum clock swung back and forth with a steady tick, tick, tick. Each swing settled between Freddie's shoulders, growing tighter and reminding her that she had a mission to complete. She'd already wasted two days.

She had to find that code book at all costs.

"I'm dreadfully tired. I believe I'll turn in early for the night." Freddie's voice was strained and her cheeks were hot. She didn't think her claim was that far from the truth.

The moment she stood up, Lucy—on her left—latched onto her arm. "You can't!" Something close to desperation lit Lucy's voice. "Not yet. The festivities are about to begin."

Between her dark gaze and Charlie's light one, Freddie felt as though she treaded a thin line. She bit her lower lip, uneasy. She hesitated just long enough for Charlie to grip her other arm. Her sister's blue eyes turned pleading.

"Please, Freddie? Stay a moment more. I didn't spend all that time on adjusting the dress for you to sit in your room."

Guilt sank its claws into Freddie's stomach. Charlie had worked hard on the dress. Beneath one of Freddie's thin, net muslin overdresses, it looked divine. The neckline plunged a bit too low for Freddie's comfort, but she'd solved that problem handily by wearing a fichu. The gloves she'd chosen, with the sunny yellow flowers on the back, sported leaves that closely matched the color of the underdress. Even her slippers were embroidered with threads that complemented the shade.

Slowly, she slipped back into the chair. "Thank you again for your effort, Charlie. I don't mean to be ungrateful."

Charlotte beamed. "Not at all. I'm happy you like it." With a smirk, she retracted her hand and returned to her embroidery.

Freddie hoped she wasn't altering another of her dresses, but she was too afraid to ask. She leaned back in the chair, surveying the room as she searched for her mother's comforting face. She couldn't find her. Where was Mama? She'd seated herself alongside Lady Graylocke earlier this evening.

Swallowing the sudden lump in her throat, Freddie dropped her gaze to her hands. She couldn't have returned to her room to await Lord Harker, could she have? No, not two days in a row. It would have been suspicious in the eyes of the guests.

Not to mention in Freddie's eyes.

To her left, Lucy held her lower lip between her teeth as she furiously scribbled her thoughts into her notebook. As Freddie watched, Lucy filled a page with indecipherable script and turned it to cram more words on the other side. Whatever her idea, it must have a tenacious grip.

On Freddie's right, Charlie shivered with a jolt. A moment later, she did it again.

"Are you cold?"

Charlie made a face. "Only a touch. It's my neck. I should have worn a fichu tonight."

Without thinking, Freddie's hand rose to her neck. "Take mine." In an instant, she pulled it free and offered it to her sister. A thin, sheer bit of cloth, it wasn't much protection, but it was better than nothing.

With a sweet smile, Charlie said, "Thank you, Freddie. How thoughtful of you." She tied the triangle of cloth around her neck as if she hadn't a care how fashionable it looked.

Freddie's fingers twitched. She itched to adjust the set of the fichu, but she feared offending her sister. Finally, she could take it no longer. "Let me fix that." She leaned forward, straightening the neckline filler until it hung better.

Although Charlie usually fussed when Freddie straightened her clothes, tonight she remained quiet. Freddie narrowed her eyes, but didn't comment on that fact.

A moment later, the gentlemen poured into the room. Lucy bounded to her feet, waving her hand through the air. "Tristan, over here!"

Freddie's stomach dropped. Lucy had positioned herself facing the door, but Freddie had only to look to her right to spot Tristan's tall, muscular form. The other women in the room appeared to be staring in his direction as well. At least, those whose attention was not squarely focused on Freddie's group. She battled a blush as she leaned back in the chair, thanking her luck that her back was to the rest of the room.

Two men separated from the flood at the door, Tristan and the duke. The duke's expression was stoic, almost forbidding as he crossed a pace behind Tristan to reach them.

When he reached the three women, the duke raised a sardonic brow. "A wave would have sufficed, Lucy."

For a moment, a dark expression crossed Tristan's face. He shot his brother a look of annoyance, likely since the duke had taken it upon himself to comment on Tristan's behalf. Freddie wouldn't have liked being ignored like that.

Once again, she had to wonder if Morgan had betrayed his country first, and Tristan had followed him out of loyalty to his family. She pressed her lips together, doing her best to play invisible.

The moment Tristan stepped abreast of the chairs, his gaze settled on Freddie. Her breath hitched as she locked eye contact with him. Without words, she tried to tell him to stop. Stop looking at her, stop speaking to her. Their siblings were forming ideas, coming to unfortunate conclusions that Freddie couldn't convincingly combat without spilling the truth.

That was out of the question.

Fortunately, Tristan looked away to address his sister. "You seem unusually enthusiastic this evening."

With absent strokes of her hands, she smoothed her dress. "I am. I managed to fill three pages of my notebook!"

He smiled, though the expression had a wary edge. "It must be a riveting idea."

"It is. Oh, silly me, why don't you sit?" She motioned to the armchair she'd just vacated.

The duke's second eyebrow rose to join the first. "There aren't enough seats, Lucy."

Again, that annoyance crossed Tristan's face, quickly buried.

With a light, tinkling laugh, like wind chimes, Lucy slipped between the two brothers and laid her hand on the duke's arm. "Tristan, you can take my seat. Morgan, Mama told me earlier that she'd like a word with you. Why don't we get that out of the way?"

Lucy should have been the spy, not Tristan. She handled her brothers with such a suave grace that they barely noticed they were being manipulated. Morgan straightened his cravat and pulled on the cuffs of his tailcoat as he muttered under his breath.

"What could Mama want this time?"

Freddie would have wagered her family's annuity that Lady Graylocke hadn't requested his presence at all. She bit her tongue as the pair walked away.

Tristan remained behind. His gaze gleamed, the clear, deep brown of his irises reflecting the candlelight, as he took the chair next to Freddie. She stiffened, and pointedly turned her face away.

Charlie set aside her embroidery. At least Freddie would have one ally against him, even if Charlotte didn't know the true depth of his character.

However, the moment she tucked the embroidery into its basket, she stood, hoisting the basket onto her arm. "I should return this to our room. I won't be but a moment, Freddie."

As was polite, Tristan stood as well. Charlie offered him a neat curtsey, and turned away.

"Wait—"

Freddie cut off her words when she glimpsed the smirk playing around Charlie's lips a moment before her back fully turned. Freddie clenched her fists in her skirts. Charlie knew, just as well as she did, that their maid Lisane would collect the embroidery when the room was vacant. The only reason her sister had left had been to thrust Freddie into Tristan's company—alone.

With a flick, Tristan arranged the tail of his coat and dropped into the seat next to her once more. He stretched out his legs in front of him, barring her path. His gaze twinkled.

"We meet again, Miss Vale."

I'd rather meet a pit of vipers. She bit the inside of her cheek. Although no one joined them in their corner, the guests now mingled throughout the room, the chatter rising considerably. Some plucky young debutante had seated herself at the pianoforte again. No one seemed to be paying her much mind. The noise obscured the sound of their conversation somewhat, but not enough to disguise their words to those who stood near enough.

Freddie took a deep, steadying breath. She prepared for a war of wits. "Please don't feel like you have to keep me company, Lord Graylocke. I'm perfectly content to sit here alone."

"Nonsense!"

Freddie cringed as he raised his voice a touch too loud for comfort, drawing more attention.

"It's my pleasure to sit with a beautiful woman."

Blooms of heat lit her cheeks like fireworks. She narrowed her eyes. What was his game? After darting a glance to the gathering—more and more eyes turned in their direction, and she was certain the whispers behind gloved hands were centered on them as well—she leaned closer to Tristan.

She kept her voice low, so hopefully no one but him would hear. "What are you doing?"

His smile grew. "Speaking to you. In turn, you respond to me. I believe it's called conversation."

She glared. "Stop. People are starting to get the wrong idea."

He crossed his ankles, leaning back in a relaxed pose and threaded his fingers over his stomach. "And what would that be, my dear?"

She balled her fists. "Don't call me that. They'll think you intend to marry me."

He laughed. The sound was soft at first, but one corner of his mouth turned up. He lost the battle and threw his head back.

Freddie kicked at his ankle to draw his attention. "It isn't funny. Your sister is embracing the idea. As is mine."

That convinced him to shut his mouth, but a twinkle of mirth remained at his side. "Is it farfetched for a man to pay court to a woman?"

"You know very well that it is out of the question when we are the man and woman in that scenario."

A predatory look crossed his face. Sitting upright, he leaned his elbow on the arm of the chair and rested his chin on his hand. "And why is that?"

She lowered her voice even further, the barest hiss. "Because we are enemies!"

His eyelids lowered, a languid expression. "We don't have to be. In fact, if you gave me a chance, I'm sure you'd find that there are many advantages to having me as an ally."

Never. Never, never, never.

Freddie counted to ten as she forced herself to take a deep breath. When she released it, she felt no better.

"I will not be your ally. You are wasting your time."

Moreover, he wasted hers! With Charlie and Lucy preoccupied, this would have been the perfect time to dash out the door without anyone being the wiser.

"Do you find me so odious?"

"Yes." She narrowed her eyes. "You know why."

"Do I?" He reached out and captured one of her hands. As he drew it between them, he gently loosened her fist. When he'd curled each of her fingers away from her palm, he pressed his lips to the spot he'd exposed.

Freddie stifled a gasp. The touch of his hot breath and lips on her palm burned her like a brand. The thin silk of her gloves proved no barrier. She colored up, but didn't dare peek behind her to see if anyone had noticed the gesture. She didn't want to know whose wagging tongues were at play.

Tristan's eyes darkened with an emotion she dared not name. "I'd like to propose a truce."

She stiffened. She didn't have time for compromises or truces. Even now, with their words veiled, Freddie knew that his main aim was to keep her from finding the code book. She would not give up.

"I will not enter a truce with you." Her voice was strangely breathless.

Did he look disappointed? When he retracted his hand, his fingertips grazed the back of her hand from her wrist to the tips of her fingers. She shivered involuntarily.

He raised his eyebrows. "Not even to ensure that I turn my attentions elsewhere?"

Freddie gritted her teeth. Didn't he know that by pretending to court her, he ultimately did her reputation harm? When they inevitably parted, if the rumors didn't place her in a compromising position, it would seem as if he, the son of a duke, had shunned her. She'd never marry.

She hardened herself. It didn't matter. After all, she didn't intend to marry. She refused to be dependent on a man, left destitute when he cocked up his toes because he couldn't control his gambling habit. Most men of the *ton* gambled. Freddie knew that she couldn't forbid the habit, but she didn't have to indulge a man deep in debt, either.

No. She would find the code book. She would attain the promised cottage for herself and her mother. Charlie would marry well.

Freddie refused to allow Tristan to taint her reputation, and thereby Charlie's.

Balling her fist, she stood. "I am done conversing with you."

He rose with her. The chairs, squeezed into the tight corner, were so close together that when she stood, she found herself inches away from his body. Her gaze roved over his eveningwear of its own accord. This evening, he wore a bit of color with an emerald green tailcoat and tan waistcoat and breeches to offset his milk-white cravat and black Hessian boots. She couldn't help but admire the way his broad shoulders filled out his coat. Did he pad them? No, she'd seen him without his jacket and he'd been every bit as broad. Swallowing to moisten her dry mouth, she dropped her gaze to her shoes.

As another young woman poised on the seat of the pianoforte, someone gave a call. The exclamation was muffled, but Freddie caught the word 'dancing.'

The cry was soon taken up by others and the gentlemen worked together to clear the furniture from the center of the room. In the bustle and cacophony, Freddie tried to slip away.

Tristan blocked her path. "Would you do me the honor of standing up as my dance partner?"

Freddie's breath caught. He wore his usual, fashionably bored expression, the air of someone unflappable. A burn of embarrassment spread throughout her chest as she ducked her head. "I... can't."

He leaned closer. The sandalwood smell of his cologne swirled around her, making her light-headed.

"Don't think for a second that I'll let you slip away to search my chambers again." His voice was low, intimate, and disapproving.

She firmed her chin, but didn't look up. "I can't dance."

"You must be jesting." His voice was thick with disbelief.

With a glare, she reared her head to look him in the eye. "I taught my sister, but didn't have time to practice, myself."

One eyebrow twitched, as though he battled a sardonic expression. "You just admitted you can't dance. How can you teach another?"

"I only know how to lead." It hadn't been an issue before tonight. Compared to Charlie, Freddie faded into the background. She was happy there, a wallflower, unnoticed.

But Tristan seemed determined to expose her. He held out his hand, palm up. "I'm certain the steps aren't that dissimilar. Try it. I promise, I won't make this a competition."

A smile tugged at the corners of Freddie's mouth. "Good, because I don't know if I'd care for a repetition of battledore."

He gave a wry, one-shouldered shrug, looking at once chagrined and unapologetic. Reaching out, he caught her hand and brought it up between them.

"What do you say? Will you dance with me?"

This is a bad idea. Even so, she found herself wishing that she had practiced, that she would be able to show to advantage. When she hazarded a glance around the room, men and women were pairing off, but some people looked toward her and Tristan with unveiled curiosity. Mrs. Biddleford and her companion were two such people.

Freddie couldn't, in good grace, refuse a man so closely tied to the hostess of this party. Even if he was her enemy.

She nodded, stiffly.

The woman behind the pianoforte played a lively tune. Her skills were imperfect, but the cheerful beat hid many of the slips of her fingers. Tristan drew Freddie away from the wall and took up a ready stance for La Boulangere. He took both her hands in his. The heat of his long, broad hand seeped into her palm as he tightened his hold.

"Are you ready?"

Other couples had already begun to dance. Freddie nodded, a short, curt movement. She and Tristan stepped forward at the same time. Their abdomens brushed as they nearly collided before Freddie took a hasty step back. She hung her head, wishing that her hair was loose to hide her hot complexion.

When she glanced up again, she found Tristan admiring her form. She realized that, without her fichu, her cleavage was on full display. He didn't seem to dislike what he saw.

Freddie opened her mouth, then shut it again. She'd never been ogled by a man, at least no man other than Harker. When she attended soirees or excursions, it was always with Charlie by her side to draw the male gaze. Being the object of a man's attentions—and a handsome man, at that—made her giddy. She fought the feeling.

Tristan caught her gaze and held it. "Relax. Trust me." His voice was gentle, his expression earnest. The rest of the world melted away. For a moment, she could almost forget that they were enemies on opposite sides of a war. And that scared her most of all.

A tide of panic caught her chest, rising quickly. She stepped back, shaking her head. "I can't." Yanking back, she gathered her skirt and ran from the room, her heart beating quickly.

As she crossed the few steps to the door, her gaze unwillingly fell on Harker. Her breath caught. Mama wasn't here, so why was he? His piercing gaze warned her that she treaded a dangerous path. She crossed the threshold, her heart in her throat.

She knew what was at stake. She couldn't let herself forget what would befall her family if she failed Harker's task.

Above all, she couldn't trust Tristan. She couldn't fall for him. He was a French spy, and they would always be enemies.

Even if she wished their relationship could be different.

Chapter Fifteen

The cooler air of the corridor granted Freddie clarity. Without Tristan nearby to muddle her senses, she was able to focus on his real aim in lavishing attention upon her. To distract her from her mission, to thwart her from finding the code book.

She clenched her hands. "Not today."

Instead of making her way toward the wide marble steps leading to the guest wing, she turned toward the library. With Tristan occupied, this might be the only chance she would find to search it without being subjected to his scrutiny.

By now, the path was imprinted on her mind like rote. She kept to the center of the runner, her footsteps muffled as she avoided the fragile items on pedestals along the hall. She held her breath, for fear of drawing someone's attention if she exhaled too hard. Although she passed several servants as she walked, they each stepped to the side to let her pass without comment.

At last, she reached the library door. She ran her fingers over the wood for a moment before grasping the handle. If this journey had been different, she might have been able to lose herself in one of the many magnificent books beyond this door.

She gritted her teeth and chided herself. *Stop it. You can't afford to be fanciful.* If she was wishing her life to be different, she might as well wish Harker out of it. And she knew exactly how to do that.

Inside the library, a fire burned in the wide hearth. The air was stale with cheroot smoke, a bit bitter of a smell. The armchairs, facing the fire, were vacant. All around the room, shelf after shelf of books soared as far as her eye could see.

"How am I supposed to find the book in here?"

That would be the point, a clever way of concealing the sensitive code book in plain sight. She squared her shoulders and decided to start to the left of the door. The two stories of wall-to-wall bookcases taunted her, but she refused to shy away from a bit of hard work.

Harker had told her that the book she sought was encased in red-dyed leather, the size of a pocket book with a gold seal on the front. She hadn't thought to ask what the seal would depict. Hopefully, she didn't find two books that met that description.

Looking around the room, filled with books primarily brown, she laughed. It was a low, bitter sound. She would be lucky if she found one book meeting that description, let alone two.

You'll never find it if you don't search. She crouched to start on the lowest shelf, running her fingers over the spines as she searched for a slim red volume. As she found no such volume, she moved her way up the shelves to the top, beneath the shadow of the balcony ringing the room. Although she was tall, the topmost books eluded her. She needed the ladder. She dropped the ladder on her foot and nearly toppled one of the shelves, but eventually wrestled it into place beside the door. Her stomach dropping somewhere in the vicinity of her shoes, she climbed.

When she stepped high enough to read the glimmering gold lettering on the spines of the books, reflecting the cozy light of the fire, she ran her hand along the shelf as far as she could reach, searching for the book. Not there. She hurried to the ground, all the while afraid that she would trip. Her luck held.

So she continued around the room. She wasn't always as lucky coming down off the ladder. In fact, she managed to rip the lovely lace of her hem and nearly land on her face at one point. She pulled out books and slid them back into place, but found no red book with a gold seal. By the time she searched the bottom story and mounted the steep, narrow steps to the balcony, the late hour caught up to her. Her jaw cracked with the force of her yawns, coming thicker and thicker. Stubbornly, she continued in her task, even though it meant looking at books two or three times to make sure she hadn't missed the one she sought.

She didn't find the book. Dejected, she sat on the top step of the spiral staircase leading down from the balcony. If it wasn't in the library and Tristan didn't keep it in his rooms, where had he put it? Her head swam as she contemplated the dilemma. She was too tired to piece together another likely hiding place. She would have to think harder.

Tomorrow. Tonight, all she wanted was to take one of these lovely books into her room and lose herself in its pages. She'd even set aside her choice, a tale by Mrs. Radcliffe that she hadn't read yet. Clasping the book in her hand, she rose and gathered her hem over one arm to keep from tripping over it. She descended the stairs carefully. When she reached the bottom, she sighed.

She turned toward the door, and for a moment, her heart skipped a beat as she saw Tristan standing there.

No, not Tristan. Lord Gideon. Her eyes were deceiving her. In the firelight, his short, disarrayed hairstyle and the regal cut of his features made them nearly interchangeable. But Lord Gideon was nearly a head taller, without shoulders nearly so wide in proportion to his frame.

She clutched her book to her chest, but didn't relax knowing that it wasn't one of the traitorous brothers who had happened upon her.

Was Lord Gideon a French spy, as well? She hated suspecting every member of Lucy's family, but her interactions with Tristan made her wary. She didn't expect a traitor to be devoted to his family. Was it possible that a recluse who spent more time with plants than with people had also defected to France?

Unlikely. Harker had only mentioned the eldest brothers.

Even so, she couldn't rid herself of the strange notion that she'd been found out. Lord Gideon's gaze was piercing. As he beheld her, his expression turned impassive. He stepped into the room and shut the door.

Belatedly, she recalled his status of a lord due to his parentage. She dipped in a shallow curtsey, still clutching the book. "My lord."

"I didn't expect to find you here." His voice was soft, but sharp at the same time.

She gulped. "I came for a book." A beat later, she hefted her prize, proof.

Lord Gideon narrowed his eyes. For a man with so absent an air on the other occasions she'd encountered him, he now seemed alarmingly present. Not to mention astute. Did he know, could he know the extent to which she and his brother were at odds?

For a long, drawn-out moment, he said nothing at all. Then, in that same stiff, quiet tone of voice, he warned, "Don't play with my brother's heart. He's fragile."

Tristan, fragile? The corners of Freddie's lips twitched. Her mirth died a quick death at the forbidding expression on Lord Gideon's face. He meant his words.

If so, he obviously didn't know his brother very well. A strong, rakish man like Tristan couldn't possibly be fragile. If there had been a crack in his armor, Freddie would have found it by now.

She straightened her spine. "I assure you, I have no intention of doing anything at all with your brother, least of all with his heart." *His black heart.* "Good night."

Her pulse galloping, she brushed past him into the hall. He made no move to stop her, but long after she'd passed out of sight, the hairs on her neck stood at attention, as if she was being watched.

This house party might be the most lauded one of the Season, but Freddie, for one, couldn't wait for it to be over.

Chapter Sixteen

Rain splattered against the glass window in Tristan's bedchamber. Usually an ill omen for the day ahead, today, he was glad for the morose weather. It would keep Freddie confined indoors, where she would be easier to watch. Even if it would keep all the rest of the guests indoors as well, and he wouldn't get a moment alone with her.

As he straightened his cravat, he squelched the eagerness he felt at the thought of seeing her again. She was quick-witted, and a worthy sparring partner. Not to mention a pleasure to look upon. When Freddie took it upon herself to wear fashionable clothing, like the low-cut green gown from last night, she shone brighter than any other young woman in attendance, even her sister. Miss Charlotte had a youthful sort of beauty about her, but it wasn't accompanied by Freddie's presence, her determination and iron will. Although Freddie was an innocent, and his instincts continually told him that she shouldn't be in the spying game, he couldn't deny that she was made of sterner stuff than most debutantes. She was a woman to be admired.

No, she was a woman to be watched, lest she foil his efforts. He clenched his jaw as he fiddled with his cuffs, ensuring that they hung straight. He ran his palm across his chin in case he'd missed a spot shaving.

"She is the enemy," he muttered under his breath. Above all, he couldn't forget that.

Even if she did look fetching in green.

Battling a yawn—he usually didn't wake until noon—he stepped out into the corridor and shut the door to his chambers behind him.

"There you are! I thought you intended to sleep the day away."

Tristan jumped at his sister's voice. When he turned, he found her bright-eyed and perky. Her hair was neatly swept up off her neck in a simple style, though a few ebony locks escaped her coif to frame her face. Her dark eyes gleamed. Her mouth curved up in a sly smile.

Before he could so much as greet her with a polite, 'good morning,' she latched onto his arm and towed him along the corridor with her en route to the breakfast room.

She leaned closer. Unlike Freddie, his sister didn't stand taller than his shoulder. She clung to him with her fingers as sharp as claws. "I notice you've been spending a prodigious amount of time with Freddie—Miss Vale."

He opened his mouth, but couldn't at first find the proper words to speak. Lucy was bound to take whatever he said and twist his words. He didn't like the mischievous look on her face. He cleared his throat. "Do you mean to imply that I should avoid her?"

It would certainly be easier for his sanity if he did. Unfortunately, he couldn't let a spy run amok in Tenwick Abbey, even an amateur one. If he didn't keep an eye on Freddie, his brother surely would.

For some reason, the thought of her spending any amount of time with Morgan made him bristle.

When he glanced to the side, he found Lucy glaring at him with unveiled irritation. "She is a lovely woman, as you well know."

With his free hand, he loosened his cravat. Clearly, he'd fiddled too much with it while dressing, because now he had trouble swallowing properly.

He didn't respond to his sister's statement.

She dug her fingers into his arm. "What are your intentions toward her?" Her voice was high, thin, and disapproving.

I intend to keep her from making a bloody fool of herself trying to best Morgan and I. I in-

tend to keep her from putting herself in harm's way. I intend...

Tristan could say none of the sentences that blossomed to his lips, so he lied. "I have no intentions toward her at all."

Lucy dropped his arm. "Tristan Graylocke! I am ashamed of you."

They'd reached the end of the west wing. If he darted down the corridor, he could ensconce himself in the breakfast room, where a surplus of witnesses would make it impossible for her to continue to carry this conversation.

Then again, knowing Lucy, she might continue to pester him regardless of who heard.

Stifling a sigh, he turned to face her.

Lucy crossed her arms over the bodice of her cream-colored walking dress. She hiked her chin higher, meeting his gaze without flinching. He looked away first.

"How could you trifle with a young lady's affections like that?"

Tristan snorted. "Believe me, she is under no misconception about my designs on her...affections."

"How can you say that?" Lucy threw her hands in the air. "A blind man could see the way she looks at you."

Had his sister fallen and hit her head? The only way Freddie looked at him was with unbridled animosity. She loathed him.

Why, he couldn't believe to fathom, because he hadn't done any harm to her. And he had had plenty of opportunities to do so, as well as just cause.

He rubbed his forehead, where his pulse throbbed violently.

"You're mistaken, Lucy. She feels no affinity for me, nor I for her. She's an intelligent woman, perhaps the only one at this blasted party, and that's the only reason I've been keeping her company."

Lucy took a cautious step forward. "So you do like her."

"I do," he admitted. It was what she wanted to hear. He tried not to examine how close to the truth that statement veered. "But not in the way you imply. She and I are..." Enemies? Friends? Acquaintances? No words he conjured seemed quite right. He shrugged. "...temporary companions."

Lucy stared at him for a long moment. He met her gaze squarely, afraid that if he looked away, she would take it as a sign of something he didn't wish her to deduce. After a moment, she let out an audible breath.

"Very well."

His mouth dropped open. He couldn't recall the last time he'd won an argument against her. Certainly not since she'd learned to talk.

Stepping forward, she slid her hand onto his arm once more, less tenacious this time. "Let's go to breakfast."

He didn't argue. They strode the rest of the way in silence.

When they reached the cozy rectangular room, Lucy dropped her hand from his arm and moved to the sideboard to direct the waiting footman to prepare her breakfast from the rows of covered trays. Aromas swirled through the air—eggs, bacon, sausage, coffee, tea, and the sweet scent of marmalade. Only a half-dozen people sat at the narrow table. Among them was a woman with brown hair who had her back to him.

His breath caught. Was it her? Freddie had always risen early on the other days during her stay at Tenwick Abbey. He battled his reaction to the thought of her.

Then she reached out to refill her tea cup. Her profile faced him and he confirmed her identity. His stomach flipped at the sight of her. The curve of her nose, the sweep of her mouth, the way one brown curl seemed determined to escape her pins and caress her cheek. She wore a high-necked dress again today, in a vibrant sky blue that seemed to light up the room.

Or, at the very least, it lit up her eyes. Suddenly, the day seemed much brighter.

Tristan bypassed the sideboard and claimed the seat directly across from her. He poured himself a cup of coffee. He emptied the pot, getting the strongest dredges from the bottom. The bitter aroma curled into the air along with the steam from his mug. He handed the carafe to the footman. Once he took a cautious sip of the brew—strong enough to wake the dead, just as he liked—he helped himself to a slice of bread and reached for the butter.

Across from him, Freddie was just finishing her meal. The last thing she ate was a slice of toast smothered with marmalade. He took a bite of his bread—freshly made and still soft and warm—as he watched her consume the last of her meal. A fleck of marmalade clung to the side of her mouth. She darted her tongue out to catch it. The sight stirred his desire.

He gulped his coffee, hot enough to singe his tongue. Anything to get his mind off of Freddie's allure. She was an innocent, an enemy, and he'd best treat her as both.

He leaned back in his chair, taking his time with his bread. He didn't like to eat a lot in the morning, when he was usually still queasy from stale cigars and strong whiskey consumed while carousing and gathering information. This party was a rare respite from the wild nights he kept in London.

As Freddie finished the last of her meal and wiped her mouth on her napkin, Lucy claimed the chair next to hers. Lucy's breakfast was piled high on her plate. How could she possibly eat so much? It boggled the mind.

"Good morning," Lucy chirped as she snagged a piece of bacon from her plate.

A genuine smile crossed Freddie's face, one that lit her eyes as she returned the greeting. So she liked his sister. That was another point in her favor. If only she wasn't so bent on aligning herself with Harker.

The mere thought of the man drew Tristan's gaze to the door, but the breakfast room remained blessedly untainted by the man's presence. Bad enough Harker festered somewhere beneath the same roof, like a fungus waiting to take over and weaken the structure.

Unaware of the dark turn his thoughts had taken, Lucy conducted a cheerful conversation with Freddie. Freddie answered with more reserve, though not with disapproval or malice. Like in most social situations, she held herself back, trying not to draw attention to herself. Whether that was her aim or she did it unconsciously, Tristan didn't know.

He knew what it was like to live in the shadow of a sibling, but she didn't seem as affected by Miss Charlotte's beauty as he was by Morgan's popularity. In fact, Freddie seemed perfectly content to wait in the eaves until her sister had taken the *ton* by swarm.

What, then? Did Freddie hold designs toward matrimony once her sister was taken off the market? The polite thing for a man to do would be to offer for Freddie first, but as she hadn't tried to engage the affections of any man at this party—at least, not that he'd noticed—he had no doubt that Miss Charlotte would be the first to marry. If Tristan had been a woman, that knowledge would have stuck in his gob, made all the more potent by the fact that Freddie wasn't a homely woman. She had a quiet sort of beauty that filled the edges of a room, rather than shining like a bright beacon in the center.

Lucy asked, "Would you like to take a walk with me to the portrait hall? Your sister is still abed and I have an idea I need to percolate. I'd love to have your company so I can talk it through aloud."

Freddie opened her mouth, but Lucy wouldn't let her get a word in edgewise.

She continued. "I'm sure you'd be able to give more insight into my idea, since you love books so much. Charlie, I'm afraid, doesn't offer much advice on my plots, but she's great fun and helps in other ways. In fact, I'm basing a character off of her."

At this, a look of concern crossed Freddie's face. It bunched her freckles together and created a little crease between her eyebrows. "Oh?" Her voice was weak, matching her expression.

Lucy didn't seem to notice that her enthusiasm had waned. "It's true! I've set her character—or rather, the character I created that most resembles her—to be the heroine in my next novel."

"I...I'm sure she's pleased."

Tristan drained his coffee mug to keep his smile hidden. Freddie didn't look as pleased. In fact, if anything, she seemed more worried.

A look which deepened when Lucy added, "I think she will be. I made her a swashbuckling princess."

Tristan couldn't hold back his amusement any longer. He chuckled and came to Freddie's defense. "Don't you base your books on personal experience, Lucy?"

She frowned at him. "I do..."

"You aren't a princess."

She raised her chin. "I'm the daughter of a duke. It's almost the same thing."

Drat, she might be right about that. "I didn't know you learned to swordfight." He let his tone and his gaze convey his disapproval, in case she had snuck behind his back to learn the dangerous sport.

She narrowed her eyes. "There are books about swordplay in the library."

"Ah, but reading about it is not the same as doing it."

She batted her eyelashes at him. "Does that mean you're willing to bring Morgan around to granting me some fencing lessons?"

Lud, had she already broached the topic with him? "Indeed not."

She sighed, overly dramatic. "And here I thought you might hold some sway over him. Oh, well."

Tristan gritted his teeth. He knew she only aimed the barb because of his competitiveness with his brother, but it still cut him to the quick. Unfortunately for her, he and Morgan saw eye to eye on the subject of fencing lessons.

Before he mustered the ability to politely answer, Freddie jumped into the conversation. "Didn't you say you wanted to visit the portrait hall?"

Lucy jumped to her feet, leaving half her plate of food uneaten. "Oh, yes, of course. Tristan, won't you join us?"

From the look of pain that Freddie tried badly to hide, she clearly wanted him to decline. He took a perverse pleasure in disappointing her. With a grin, he stood. "I would love to."

With a resigned expression, Freddie followed Lucy to the doorway. When he offered his sister his arm to be her escort, she gave him a sweet smile. "No need. I need both hands free to jot down my ideas. Why don't you accompany Freddie instead?"

His stomach dropped. Blast! She had finagled for just such an eventuality.

He couldn't very well decline. Keeping his smile pinned in place—although it had begun to feel forced—he offered his arm to Freddie instead. She didn't have a notebook to hide behind, and had no choice except to lay her hand on his sleeve. The light, delicate touch seared through his jacket.

Lucy conducted a lively conversation as they made their way to the ancestors' hall. Tristan barely heard a word. He couldn't get his mind off the feel of the woman striding beside him. She kept enough space between them to please even the strictest of gossips. As he walked, he was acutely aware of that space. He burned with the need for her to lean closer. Even an inch...

By the time they reached the ancient door leading to the portrait hall, he was losing his mind. He nearly made his excuses and left them alone, but the thought of Morgan's disapproval weighed on him. If nothing else, he would prove to his brother that he could do this. He could sway Freddie into aborting her quest to steal their code book.

If he was lucky, maybe she'd even be willing to give them something they could use to expose Harker and take him out of the spy game once and for all. The notion was appealing, but didn't satisfy his desire. With Freddie's touch muddling his head, he would gladly surrender to Harker if only he got to press his body against hers once more.

He'd never seen the appeal of having a wife, but if most men were as enamored with the thought of finding themselves alone with their wives as Tristan was with Freddie, then maybe the concept had merit.

Lud, had he just considered marrying Freddie? He couldn't have.

It would be one way to ensure she was no longer subjected to Harker's coercion.

No, the very idea was mad! He was definitely losing his sanity.

Lost in thought, he stepped through the old door, which Lucy held wide. The doorway was wide enough for him and Freddie to walk abreast, but in order to do so, she had to press closer to him. A whiff of her lavender perfume met his nose. The soft, gentle scent made his head spin.

They stepped into the wide, cavernous room. Before Tristan took more than three steps, the door slammed shut with a resounding crash that echoed throughout the room. As Freddie's hand slipped from his arm, they both whirled toward the door. Lucy was gone.

Tristan bolted to the door. The light in the room, filtering through the rain-splattered glass high above, was thin and wan. He could see the outline of objects in shades of gray, but no more. As he reached the door, he grappled for the latch.

It was stuck. Something was securing it from the other side.

He pounded on the door with the flat of his palm. "Lucy! Let us out this instant!"

"No!" Her voice was muffled. The tinkling of rain on glass, amplified by the echoes in the vaulting room, almost drowned her out. Tristan strained to hear. "You like her, she likes you. Talk about it! I'll let you out when you agree to marry."

Tristan fisted his hands. His leather gloves saved him from the pain of his fingernails, but barely. "We are *not* going to marry, Lucy. Give up the notion."

She didn't answer. Had she left? Tristan tried the latch again, but it still wouldn't budge. He slammed the palm of his hand against the door.

Behind him, the crash of metal signaled that the suit of armor had fallen to the ground. From the rustle of fabric, Freddie must be caught under it.

"Bloody wretched thing," she muttered under her breath.

He couldn't agree more, though his sentiments leaned more toward their situation.

Balling his fists, he turned away from the door. Freddie flailed, half-trapped beneath the suit of armor. He crossed to her in ground-eating strides and bent to help. Within moments, she disentangled herself, but when he tried to lift the suit, the components fell apart and scattered on the ground. He left it there.

"Thank you," Freddie muttered as she dusted off her dress. Judging from the way she was angled away from him, she didn't care to meet his gaze.

"Think nothing of it," he answered, his voice stiff.

"What are we to do now?"

He ran his hands through his hair. "We find Lucy and lock her in her room for the rest of the day. If only the abbey had a dungeon."

Freddie laughed, a light and happy sound that pinched him in the gut. "I warned you this would happen."

"You warned me that my sister intended to lock us in a dusty old hall where no one would come looking for us?" He crossed his arms. "Do tell when we had that conversation."

"Don't be a chucklehead. I warned you only last night that she was forming erroneous assumptions."

"So I recall. If I'd thought she would resort to childish antics like this, I would have taken your warning to heart."

Freddie sighed. "There's no point in assigning blame now."

Tristan shook his head. "Not unless we're laying it squarely at her feet." He ran his fingers through his hair, trying to get it to lie flat again, to no avail. "We may as well get out of here."

"Oh. Right. The secret passage. She didn't choose the most opportune location if she wanted to keep us locked away."

To the contrary, his younger sister was more devious than he'd dreamed. In order to get out, he and Freddie would be forced into even more intimate quarters. If they were seen together in his family wing on the other side of the passage, he might, indeed, have to marry her.

He gritted his teeth and kept the foreboding to himself.

Given her penchant for clumsiness, he decided it better if he kept close by her. He ignored the strange, warm feeling in his chest at the thought. Reaching out, he groped for her hand and threaded his fingers through hers. Like him, she wore gloves.

"Tristan, what—"

"The door to the passage is this way."

Her words cut off as he coaxed her forward. Her fingers tightened on his, but she didn't try to break free.

Although he tried not to dwell on the fact that she'd called him by his Christian name, his ears rang with the memory of the word on her lips. He swallowed hard and ran his hand down the door to the ring serving as the handle.

When he opened it, he insisted Freddie enter first.

"Why?" she asked, her voice suspicious. "You aren't going to lock me in here, are you?"

He snorted. "What good would that do me? I'd have no way to get out."

"Maybe you crave the solitude."

The mirth in her voice was infectious. His dark mood lightened somewhat. "With a sister like mine, would you blame me?"

"At the moment? I'm surprised you don't swear off the world and live as a hermit."

"Now, what fun would that be?"

He guided her into the passage and entered after her. He had to release her hand in order to do it. He flexed his fingers at the loss and pulled the door shut behind him.

Without the dim light cast by the windows, he couldn't see anything. Not even Freddie's form in front of him.

"I can't see a thing. Can you?"

"No," he answered. "Feel your way ahead but don't go too far."

"Why not?"

Her voice was edged with defiance, as if she lived to oppose his wishes.

He rolled his eyes. "We can't come out in my family's personal wing. At this time of day, someone might see us. We'll have to take one of the other exits."

"There are other exits?"

He frowned. "Yes, of course. Why have a secret passage that runs the length of the abbey if there is only one destination?"

"I didn't see any when I was last in here."

Ah, yes. In vivid detail, he conjured the night he'd found her in his room. She had smelled a little musty and he'd suspected she'd used the passage Lucy had shown her. Now, his suspicions were confirmed. Apparently, she hadn't taken the time to investigate the passage.

"There are four other exits to the passage, that I've found, but they use hidden doors. You need to press a trigger to get them to open." Even then, the passage had been there for centuries. Some doors had languished for too long and were in dire need of oiling.

When he stepped forward, he bumped the back of her. The brief press of her body against his ignited his desire. He took a healthy step back. "Forgive me."

"It's fine. What do I have to feel for to find this trigger?"

"I'll find the door. Walk slowly and I'll be right behind you."

The soft click of her heels indicated her compliance. Tristan had to angle himself to the side in order to navigate the passage comfortably. He pulled off his gloves and kept his hand on the wall to his left, feeling for any shift in the rough stone.

He'd never done this in the dark before. Would he miss the doorway?

He found one before too long. The crack in the wall was barely perceptible. "Stop," he called, his voice soft.

The rustle of movement halted. "You found an exit?"

"I believe so. Give me a moment and I'll push the trigger."

The mechanisms were usually at the level of his shoulders. He felt along the wall until he found the familiar crevice. He delved his fingers inside, praying that he'd found one of the doors that opened easily. The longer he spent in the passageway with Freddie, the more the stale air started to smell like her. He couldn't get her perfume out of his head.

He exerted pressure and the wall clicked as it started to move inward.

"Thank Heavens," Freddie exclaimed.

He raised his fingers to his lips. A line of light entered from the other room, which could indicate that the room was occupied. Slowly, he pushed out the wall enough to peer past it.

He'd found a sitting room, and a lesser-used one if the hodgepodge of furniture was any indication. He released a breath. "We're safe." He pushed out the wall enough to exit and held it open for Freddie.

She dusted off the skirt of her dress, chasing dirt into the air. He battled a sneeze. She needn't have bothered with the action; her attire was hopelessly sullied.

"I suggest you return to your room," Tristan said.

When she straightened, she almost looked hurt.

He added, "I don't know about you, but I could do with some tidying up."

She raised her hand, patting her hair. Her questing fingers found the piece of cobweb near her temple. As she pulled it away, she made a face. "I think you're right. Shall we meet back here in an hour?"

Tristan frowned. "Whatever do you mean?" She'd been trying her best to avoid him. Suddenly, she sought out his company?

The corners of her mouth twitched as she raised her eyebrows. "Surely you didn't think I'd let you retaliate against your sister without me."

He grinned. "What, exactly, did you have in mind?"

Her eyes twinkled, a brown that looked like expensive brandy in the light filtering through the window. "Let's show Lucy how it feels when someone else plays matchmaker."

Not precisely locking her in a dungeon, but judging by the mischief in Freddie's eyes, the gratification was bound to be infinitely sweeter. Still holding the wall open, he captured her hand with his free one and lifted it to his lips.

"You, my dear, are brilliant."

As he parted ways with her, he thought he noticed heightened color in her cheeks. The notion brought a bloom of satisfaction to his chest. She might pretend at indifference, but he had some effect on her, after all.

Chapter Seventeen

In the end, Tristan had only one rule for their revenge—Lucy had to be chaperoned at all times. He wanted to get even with his sister, but he didn't want to send her into ruin or a forced marriage.

Seated side by side in the parlor that had been divested of its furniture in order to accommodate a ring of chairs large enough to seat every guest, Tristan and Freddie surveyed the prospects. Who would they throw into Lucy's path to keep her occupied?

Freddie leaned closer to him. The second walking dress she'd donned this morning—yellow, this time—had a lower neckline than the first. A small, flowery line of embroidery followed the swoop of her bodice over her breasts, just low enough for him to see a hint of cleavage. If she was going to wear gowns with lower necklines each time, perhaps he ought to lead her through the secret passage a time or two more. How many would it take before she wore the alluring green dress from last night?

Oblivious to the turn his thoughts had taken, Freddie whispered, "What of the young man scratching his chin?"

Tristan's next deep breath brought the soothing scent of her perfume. He forced himself to attend to the conversation and searched the group for the man in question.

"Davenport? He'd be too frightened to talk to my sister."

She let out a huff of impatience. "Perhaps you should suggest one, then. You seem to know them much better than I do."

He bit his tongue to stifle a laugh. They scribbled on their papers, folded them over, and passed them down the line as they contributed to the game of Consequences that his mother had arranged. Whispers eddied around the circle as various couples spoke in low tones—including Lucy and Miss Charlotte.

Tristan's stomach jumped, as if trying to escape out his throat. He tore his gaze away. He didn't like their pointed examination of him and Freddie, no more than he liked their sly expressions as they spoke in heated whispers. They were concocting a scheme. He doubted he would care for it.

He folded his page, cutting off the line he'd written and waited for his mother to make the rounds to collect the completed papers. He leaned his head so close to Freddie's the teasing curl at her temple brushed his cheek. It was soft, like silk.

"We may have to find someone to occupy your sister. She seems to be scheming with mine."

Freddie grinned. She raised her gloved hand to cover it, keeping the expression for his eyes alone. His chest warmed at the twinkle in her eye.

"Such scheming things our sisters are. Mine certainly didn't inherit the habit from me."

Laughter bubbled to his throat and slipped out. The sound drew the eye of several people nearby, including his mother. Freddie didn't appear to notice. Her smile widened, and his chest warmed. He no longer cared whether someone noticed their conversation.

"Do you doubt me?" she asked, her voice low and teasing.

"I think you are a master at scheming. You taught her everything you know."

She worried her lower lip between her teeth. The dimple her teeth made in the plump flesh drove him mad. He would give anything to be able to lean over at that moment and taste her lips.

"Not everything," she whispered, her voice so low it barely carried to his ears.

He smiled. "Good. We'll need all your expertise if we're to emerge victorious."

Her eyes glinted as she met his gaze. "I don't care to lose, if you recall?"

She had forfeited during their battledore match in the end, if only to escape his company. Today, she didn't seem as adamant to part from him as before. Could his design to woo her be working?

For some reason, the thought left his chest flat. After he convinced her to give up her alliance with Harker, then what? He couldn't marry her. Their keeping company was for show, nothing more.

He swallowed, trying not to think of it. He had become a spy to make a difference. That didn't change because of one alluring woman. Even one who underestimated her charm.

He offered the slip of paper to his mother as she passed. She continued around the circle until she returned to her place, a bundle of folded pages in her hands. She sat and chose one to begin reading out.

The following half hour was filled with laughter over bizarre gifts, ludicrous declarations, and unlikely pairings. The duke was featured in more than one tale; Tristan's name emerged twice, from Lucy and Miss Charlotte, he was willing to bet. He had put his sister into one tale, as had several others, likely gentlemen. Miss Charlotte was even mentioned once or twice, but not her sister. Freddie didn't seem to mind.

He pressed his lips together, pretending to hold back a laugh when he covered another emotion instead. How could they overlook her?

His mother's voice penetrated the warm haze of anger as she read the last line from the sheet in her hand. "...and the consequence was that he fell under her spell!"

The group laughed, but Tristan's chest tightened. Had he written that? He needed to pay more attention when he committed words to the page. Or else, his head was still muddled from the drink he'd nurtured last night after Freddie had fled.

That sheet marked the last to read aloud and the circle of guests disbanded to seek other amusements. Footmen filed into the room to collect the chairs and return the furniture to its natural order. Tristan stood and offered Freddie his hand. She slid her delicate palm into his and he helped her to her feet.

"Are you ready?" Tristan murmured as he guided Freddie's hand onto his sleeve. His sister and hers had risen and made their way to him with impish looks on their faces.

Freddie cast him a sly sidelong glance. "Let's make them regret this mad plot of theirs."

He couldn't help but match her smile.

In a deft movement, he drew Freddie to the left, hiding them both behind a cluster of gentlemen. He tapped the nearest one on the shoulder.

Freddie's hand slipped from his arm as she rounded to the fellow's other side.

The man who turned to him, a weak-chinned young man with a broad nose and beady eyes, looked suspicious as Tristan smiled. He slung his arm over Digby's shoulders, pulling him close.

"I think my sister's been eyeing you."

Digby perked up immediately. "She has? Are—are you certain?" He spoke rapidly, stumbling over his words with mixed excitement and disbelief.

Tristan infused his stance with confidence. Digby often joined in the late-night card games at the gaming hells. He was the easiest to read, a bit frightened of the women who joined the table, and he always treated them with respect. A harmless sort of fellow to throw in his sister's path.

"Didn't you notice, man? She kept casting glances your way during the game."

"She...she did? I thought she looked at you."

Tristan rolled his eyes. "I'm her brother. Why on Earth would she care to look at me when there are other gentlemen present?"

At this, Digby straightened. He fiddled with his cravat. "Do you think I should t-talk to her?"

"Absolutely. If you have honorable intentions, it's best to capitalize on her interest now before someone else catches her eye."

"Oh. Oh, of course." Digby held up his hands. "My intentions are pure, I assure you. I would never disrespect her, not *your* sister."

Tristan frowned at the odd way he emphasized the relation. He decided not to examine the slip of the tone too closely. Digby often had an odd manner of speaking. Slapping the man on the back, Tristan said, "Then I wish you luck."

When he stepped back, Digby took off like a racehorse.

Tristan bit back a grin. He turned his attentions to how Freddie was doing with her mark. She smiled up at a tall man, batting her eyelashes.

The urge to smile evaporated. Something disapproving and primal took hold of him. He clenched his fists, battling it down.

Freddie didn't seem to notice his unease. She tapped the man on the arm, a light brush of her fingertips. "Why, Lord Harington, my sister adores horses! She can't hear enough of them."

The man had a long face, rather reminiscent of a horse himself. His eyes brightened and he turned, craning his neck to see above the crowd.

"Have you been introduced?" Freddie asked, her voice light and encouraging.

Like a punch to the gut, Tristan realized that this was likely the way she would behave as a mother. Bright, gentle, encouraging. Everything a son or daughter could ask for.

Tristan shoved the thought away. He'd never thought much about children, and he didn't care to start now. No one cared whether he sired an heir and a spare.

Lord Harington nodded, but the movement was hesitant. "I have, while she was in the company of Lady Lucy."

"Well, it appears as though Lucy is otherwise engaged. This might be your chance to engage my sister in conversation."

"Yes." He straightened his cuffs and threw back his shoulders. "Good day, Miss Vale." He didn't look at her as he prepared to stride away.

A slim smile stretched her lips. "Good luck, my lord."

The moment Freddie stepped away from the other members of the group, Tristan installed himself at her side. She didn't look triumphant. In fact, if anything, she looked worried.

"What ails you?" he asked, his voice a whisper.

When she turned her head, her mouth skimmed so close to his chin that she nearly brushed his skin. He pulled away marginally.

She raised her gaze to his. In the strong light of the sitting room, her eyes glowed like embers. "I feel bad for lying to him."

Tristan raised an eyebrow. "You wanted him to engage her in conversation, did you not?"

"Yes, but I gave him the wrong impression. What if they might have made a good match, had

I not given him to believe that she was horse-mad?"

She looked so genuinely distraught over the idea that he nearly pulled her into his embrace to offer comfort. He fisted his hands at his sides instead.

Before they'd launched this plan of revenge, he hadn't considered that she might be interested in matchmaking. Tristan didn't tend to think of such things. But, then, he wasn't a woman.

"If you hadn't told him such a thing, he would never have sought out her company. Any match that comes to fruit between them will be because of you."

"I suppose so…" She still sounded concerned.

If Freddie considered marriage for her sister, did she also seek a match for herself? It was a maddening question, and one he didn't care to dwell on for long. Whatever her intentions for marriage, she'd clearly set them aside during the interim of this house party.

She had, after all, set herself squarely in his path. As his enemy.

He tried for a charming smile. He practiced it often enough in the gaming hells and other suspect locations in London. But, in this case, he felt as though Freddie could see through the pretense.

Impossible. No one sees you. Not even when he was in plain sight, drawing attention to himself. Other people only saw Morgan's younger brother and temporary heir.

Freddie let out a yelp as she suddenly pitched forward. Tristan caught her, his arms wrapping around her as her soft body pressed against his. The feel of her was like a conflagration. He battled his reaction as he set her on her feet and took a healthy step back. What had prompted that?

With a pugnacious glare, Freddie turned. Several feet behind her stood Lucy, wearing a smug smile. She must have shaken Digby off her tail. She cocked one brow in challenge.

Tristan exchanged a glance with Freddie. Her gaze simmered with mischievous intent. He grinned. "Are you ready to go to war?"

She matched his smile. "Let's do this."

***

The afternoon's battle wore thin quickly. Lucy, realizing what Tristan and Freddie were about, soon sought to thwart his efforts by being inseparable from Miss Charlotte. He and Freddie had to concoct elaborate schemes to convince young men to approach the formidable young women in pairs. Lucy must have gotten to Mother as well, for the indoor games took a decidedly romantic bent. How else would he have pulled the word 'kiss' from the hat during Pantomime? Through every game, he was paired with Freddie, which would have been more pleasurable if not for the knowing stares of his sister and his mother.

Even the respite of the dinner table was thwarted by his mother announcing that the family would mingle with the guests tonight. Somehow, Tristan found himself seated beside Freddie. Not that she wasn't an adequate dinner partner—they kept up a lively conversation, mostly about their sisters—but he was starting to feel the stares of the others in his family.

Particularly Morgan. Even though Tristan tried to reassure his brother with a look that he knew what he was doing, Morgan looked disapproving. That, if nothing else, made Tristan determined to continue. For the remainder of dinner, he applied himself to making Freddie smile and laugh. Each one was a reward in itself.

As the gentlemen and ladies rose to depart the room and go their separate ways, Tristan laced his fingers through Freddie's and tugged her toward the door. She stumbled, but soon caught her balance and the delicate pink skirt of her evening dress. This dress, like her walking dress, had a lower cut neckline than most of her other dresses. A pearl necklace drew attention to her creamy skin.

"What are you doing?" she whispered.

"We've been under their scrutiny all day. Don't you want a moment away from your sister to breathe?"

Hesitation crossed her face and burdened her footsteps.

His hand slipped on hers. He hadn't worn gloves this evening, hoping to better feel the heat of her skin. She wore gloves, dainty little things that felt like sliding into a cool pond on a hot summer's day. Her hand tightened on his, keeping him from moving away.

Was his plan successful? Had he seduced her onto his side? The only way to be sure would be to take her back to his room.

No. He couldn't do that. She was an innocent. He'd done many things he'd later regretted in the name of spying, but he'd never defiled a virgin. As much as Freddie tempted him, his conscience wouldn't let him start now. There were other ways to test whether or not she had fallen for his charm.

He cocked an eyebrow. "Unless you'd rather subject yourself to Lucy and your sister."

She made a face. "You have a point."

Triumph surged through him, at least until he glanced past her and spotted his sister bounding toward them. From her determined expression, she fully intended to take him to task—or worse. Adjusting his grip on Freddie's hand, he intercepted the path of Mr. Catterson.

"Catt!" Tristan greeted him with a grin.

The young man narrowed his eyes as he peeked past Tristan toward Freddie.

"Just the man I was talking about earlier with Lucy."

If anything, that made him even more suspicious. His eyebrows, so pale they were difficult to discern in the light cast by the chandelier, knit together.

"You and Lucy were talking about me."

"Yes, and Rocky, too. In fact, Lucy was telling me how much she admires Rocky."

Catt's expression darkened. "Indeed?"

Tristan pretended not to notice the change in his demeanor. "Oh, yes. She told me how Rocky is able to cultivate so much more with so little to work with, unlike you and Gideon."

The young man scowled. His reddish-blond hair flopped into his eyes as he twisted to scan the throng. "She'd best not be repeating that to anyone else." Darkly, he stormed off toward Lucy.

Tristan bit his tongue to hide a laugh. He towed Freddie through the door and into the cooler corridor. The servants had set out candles during dinner and the corridor twinkled as if imbued with starlight.

"Who is Rocky?" she asked.

"Our gardener," he said over his shoulder. "She and Catt are always arguing about botany."

The glance over his shoulder was just enough to espy the glimmer of a smile chasing across her lips. "You employ a female gardener?"

"We do. She's the best. Perhaps even better than Gideon—but don't tell him I said that."

The low tinkle of her laughter swirled around him. A happy, innocent sound. "I wouldn't dare."

Something dark and mischievous lit her voice. He didn't dwell on it, but quickly guided her down another corridor. "With Catt and Gideon occupied, the orangery should be free." Within moments, they stepped through the door leading to the wide corridor. The sun hid below the horizon, casting a purple-orange glow along the horizon line, with the deeper canopy of stars opening overhead. The corridor was unlit, though a light from the orangery drew him onward.

The moment he opened the door, the steam curled around him like a warm, wet blanket. He pulled Freddie inside and shut the door. The floral aroma made him a bit lightheaded. It reminded him of Freddie's scent, though hers was a muted version.

A half-shuttered lantern on the work table illuminated the space. The light blotted out the stars through the glass overhead and cast long shadows over the various leafy plants gathered. Most had furled their petals for the night, but a few lifted their heads to the sliver of moon overhead, their petals washed golden in the orange light.

Tristan sighed, happy to be alone at last. Freddie's hand shifted in his and he recalled that he wasn't alone. He was with the enemy.

At that moment, with shadows swathing them and sheltering them from the censorship of others, she didn't feel like an enemy. In fact, he felt as comfortable with her as he did when he was alone.

The lamplight glinted off her irises. It cast a golden glow on her cheeks, hiding her freckles. He found himself wishing to see them. Although Society disparaged freckles as a sign of homeliness, on Freddie he found them charming.

Her lips parted. "Tristan, what are we doing?"

He couldn't look away from her mouth. "Do you ever get the feeling that you're about to do something horribly wrong, but you can't bring yourself to stop?"

She stiffened. She tried to tug her hand away, but he tightened his hold.

He swallowed hard. His voice went hoarse. "Because that's the way I feel right now."

Unable to resist any longer, he dipped his head to capture her lips. They slackened beneath his for a moment with shock. Panic overwhelmed him. Did she not feel the same about him? He started to pull away.

Freddie twined her arms around his neck, threading her fingers through his hair as she kissed him back. He took full advantage, sliding his hand down to the small of her back and pressing her luscious curves against him. His head spun, that enticing feeling of falling while he still had both feet firmly planted on the ground. He clutched her tightly as he surrendered himself to the moment. Her hands drifted down his torso in a slow slide toward his waist. He burned in the wake of her touch.

A man cleared his throat. Tristan broke the kiss to swivel his face toward the door. Gideon stood there, his eyebrows raised in disapproval.

Tristan met Freddie's gaze—except she wouldn't look at him. She removed her hands from his jacket, her gaze averted. The expression fell over him like a dip in icy water.

She'd removed her hands from over his jacket pockets. Where she'd been searching his clothing for the code book. He thought she'd been falling under his spell as much as he had under hers. He'd been wrong. The only person enthralled was him.

He stared at Freddie, at his brother, and then stormed from the room. He was a damn, bloody fool to ever think she saw him as anything other than an enemy.

Chapter Eighteen

The condemnation in Tristan's eyes chased Freddie all the way to the east wing of the house. She couldn't bring herself to step into the sitting room and face her sister and Lucy's interrogation. Perhaps, once she gathered herself, she would be able to go down. If Tristan was there…

I did what I had to. Even if she'd lost herself to Tristan's wit and charm this afternoon, finding herself beneath Harker's livid stare at dinner reminded Freddie why she was here at this party. They would never have garnered the invitation without Harker. She had to find that book. If it wasn't in Tristan's room or in the library, the next logical conclusion had been that he carried it on his person.

She'd felt no lumps in his pockets of the telltale shape of a book. Worse, now that he'd caught her searching for it, she'd caused a rift between them.

That isn't worse. It's what must be. He was a very good spy, because he had her doubting whether or not she should continue with this mission. She had to, even if Tristan was the enemy against whom Harker had pitted her. Her family's future was at stake. As someone who loved his family so well, Tristan would understand that.

Even if she could never tell him. He was the enemy. He was working for the French. She still hadn't reconciled why a man like him would resort to such treachery. She didn't dare ask. For all that she had enjoyed herself in his company this afternoon, their time together would soon end. They weren't companions, they weren't friends. They were enemies.

Her steps slowed as she turned the corner into the guest wing. The bedchamber she shared with Charlie resided near the end. Candles rested on pedestals along the long corridor, reflecting off round mirrors. It looked nothing like home.

Home didn't conjure thoughts of Harker's townhouse in London, but rather of the tidy little home in which Freddie had grown up. Less lofty than that of the peerage, the little two-story townhouse had been squished next to their neighbors. From the outside, it had looked a little lopsided, as though leaning for support against the house next to it. Memories surged, of her and Charlie running through the house in a game, shrieking and laughing. Of Mama's gentle gaze as she did needlework in the evenings. Of Papa's ready grin as he concocted mad, fantastical stories and acted them out during the telling.

Tears clung to Freddie's eyelashes. She'd hardened herself for so long to Papa, clinging to his misdeeds as a means of holding the pain at bay. Anger was easier to weather. These days, she often forgot that she loved him. When she remembered, like now, the wound in her chest ripped open, once again raw.

"Freddie, darling?"

Freddie thrust her shoulders back and wiped at her eyes. She forced a smile as she turned. "Hello, Mama."

Her mother looked worried. The glow from the candles cast shadows across Mama's face, making her look older. She stepped closer, as serene and poised as Freddie often tried to be. She reached out to clasp Freddie's hand.

"Why aren't you down at the party?"

"I don't feel well," Freddie lied. "I thought I might lie down for a spell."

"Oh?" Mama squeezed her hand. "You seemed to be enjoying yourself earlier. You've caught the attention of one of the Graylocke brothers. That's something worth encouraging."

Freddie glanced sidelong at her mother. Mama's voice was gentle, but filled with earnestness. She truly believed that Freddie catching Tristan's interest was a good thing. Maybe, if Harker hadn't pitted them against one another, it might have been. But Tristan was a French spy. If Mama had known, she wouldn't have been so encouraging.

"I'm afraid that's his sister's doing. She and Charlie have been playing the matchmaker this afternoon."

Did Mama look disappointed? If she did, the expression soon smoothed from her face. "I see. Are you sure there isn't something more between you?"

"I'm sure." Freddie was proud of the strength in her voice. Even now, far away from the orangery, she could feel the pressure of Tristan's lips against hers, of his body nestled against her. Had his reaction been feigned? She hadn't been able to hide hers, not even when she'd recalled herself enough to search his pockets.

Mama tugged at her hand, drawing her down the hall. "Come. Why don't we sit for a moment and have a chat?"

Freddie hadn't found more than a few minutes to speak with her mother since arriving at Tenwick Abbey. She tightened her hold on Mama's hand and followed, grateful to be spared the need to be alone. If she was alone, her thoughts would return to Tristan, and she couldn't have that.

Mama led her into her chamber. Like the one Freddie and Charlie shared, it was richly decorated, in emerald green to their royal blue. She tugged Freddie toward a narrow settee at the foot of the large bed. They sat side by side, their hips touching.

Freddie stared at the vanity on the wall directly across from her. Even that piece of furniture, nestled against the white and green toile wallpaper, screamed of luxury. When they'd been a family, Mama had kept a worn writing desk in the corner of her room that she had also used as a vanity.

"Do you ever miss Papa?" Freddie's voice was so weak, she barely heard herself speak.

Mama tightened her hand. "Every day." Her voice was soft, but vehement.

Freddie's lips parted. "Even after he—"

Ruined us.

Left us.

Died.

Canting her face away, Mama brushed at her eyes. "Your father wasn't perfect, Freddie. Nobody is. I love and miss him more every day." Her voice lowered to the barest whisper. "Maybe someday soon we'll be together again."

Her voice was filled with such longing that for a moment, Freddie wasn't able to speak. Was Mama talking about dying? She clutched her mother's hand, a reflexive reaction. "You're young yet, Mama. You'll be with us a long time."

Mama didn't say a word. She didn't look at Freddie, either. The silence drew on between them, strained and painful. Freddie swallowed around the lump building in her throat.

"If you love Papa so well, why do you let Harker—" She couldn't finish that sentence. She couldn't even think it.

"I do what I must for those I love."

She'd never heard Mama speak so fiercely. When she glanced at Mama, her pale hair hid her face. Freddie tightened her hand.

"You don't have to. At least, not for much longer. Charlie will marry and..."

Freddie didn't dare speak another word. If she did, she might confess about her arrangement with Harker. Mama would only try to complete the task for her. Freddie had already exposed herself to the Graylocke brothers as Harker's agent. She didn't want her mother to be put in the same danger.

So she didn't speak a word. Instead, she laid her head on Mama's shoulder. "Everything will be better soon," she murmured.

It had to be. Somehow, even though she hadn't found the book in the last four days of residence, she had to find it soon. What would she—and Harker—do if she failed?

She couldn't afford to find out.

***

Tristan paced the library. He'd rejoined the guests for an hour after leaving Freddie, but his surly mood had soon soured the evening to the point that Mother had made a thinly veiled suggestion that he should retire for the evening.

He couldn't sleep. Not with the feel and taste of Freddie's body still fresh in his mind—or the memory of her betrayal. He'd thought...

He should have known better than to think she saw him as anything other than an obstacle. He clenched his fists.

A fire roared in the grate, lighting up the vacuous room. His muffled footsteps on the rug were the only sounds aside from the chuckling fire. Tension coiled in his shoulders, his instincts clamoring that he couldn't wait for Morgan any longer. Freddie was the enemy and he had to do something about her. Anything.

Even if she was an innocent, even if she didn't deserve to get caught up in this. She had made her choice.

The memory of her sobbing into his shirt in the abandoned chapel as she confessed to Harker's coercion rose unbidden to his mind. His knuckles cracked as he flexed his fists. The person he truly wanted to punish wasn't Freddie. It was Harker.

Not for the first time, Tristan cursed the command he'd received not to touch the known enemy spy. Tristan wanted blood, and tonight he was destined to be denied.

When the door to the library opened, he whirled to face the intruder. Morgan stepped through the door, his expression tight and a bit weary. He shut the door behind him.

"Good, you're still here."

Tristan opened his mouth, but he didn't know what to report. He had spent the day with Freddie, he'd done his best to woo her and he hadn't made a dent in her resolve to oppose them. The knowledge brought bile to the back of his throat. He couldn't confess to Morgan that he'd failed, that Morgan had been right all along.

Fortunately, Morgan didn't seem to be waiting for a report. He ran his hand through his hair as he stepped forward, a habit that he indulged in only when he was at his wit's end. It wasn't something that Tristan saw from him very often.

Tristan stiffened. "What is it? What's the matter?"

Morgan stopped abreast of his brother. His eyes were as piercing as cold steel. He confessed, "The moment the Vales arrived at Tenwick Abbey with Harker, I franked an inquiry to our contacts in London about their father."

Their father? Tristan should have thought of that. He should have asked Freddie about him. Why were the Vales in Harker's company? Tristan would have preferred to keep company with a snake.

But...what good would it have done to learn about a dead man?

"Did you hear back?"

"I did. Today."

Tristan braced himself. For what, he didn't know, but Morgan's expression and his tone of voice didn't bode well.

"He's dead, isn't he?"

Morgan raised his shoulder in a half-hearted shrug. "I thought it might be worthwhile to know what sort of man their father was. What traits he might have passed on."

Reluctantly, Tristan nodded. "And? What did our contacts have to say?"

Gravity befell Morgan's features. He stood straighter. A muscle in his jaw twitched, a sign of frustration. "I've been ordered to stop looking into the matter."

Tristan frowned. "What do you mean?"

Morgan's mouth thinned. "I can't know for sure because no one will say so outright, but...I think he was a spy. Tristan, I think he was on our side."

Tristan's mouth dropped open. He tried to speak, but couldn't find the words. Could it be true?

No. Impossible. Freddie was working for the enemy now. The apple couldn't possibly have fallen so far from the tree.

Chapter Nineteen

The day dawned gray and drizzly, but unlike the previous day, Tristan didn't have anything to look forward to when he rose from bed. He dressed sluggishly, wishing that his valet hadn't been occupied with Harker, so at least he would have had a bit of company. He tried to avoid thinking of the company he would have liked to have had.

It was bad enough that he would have to see her this morning. And keep a close eye on her, at that. He scrubbed a hand over his chin, feeling stubble but mustering no desire to shave it clean again. With a sigh, he left his room and trudged down to the breakfast room. At least Lucy wasn't waiting to pepper him with questions about Freddie, this time.

As he reached the threshold of the breakfast room, he gathered himself, threw back his shoulders, and strode in.

Freddie was waiting for him. She perched on the edge of her seat, an empty teacup resting in its saucer, the last remnants of her breakfast. The moment he stepped into the room, she raised her gaze and met his. She smiled.

She might as well have gutted him. It felt the same.

Launching to her feet, she lifted a mug and napkin. She held it out to him.

He eyed the offering warily. "What's this?"

"Think of it as self-preservation. You're always a beast in the morning, and I know you plan on dogging my heels all day. I might as well do what I can to put you in a sweeter mood."

Cautiously, he accepted the bundle. He took a seat across from her at the end of the table. When he unfolded the napkin, he found a single piece of warm bread smothered with butter from corner to corner, just the way he liked it. His coffee was strong and bitter—not as hot as he might have liked, but he had obviously made her wait.

When he met her gaze again, she gave him an eager smile. "Does it meet your approval?" Her voice was chipper, cheerful.

He nodded. His murky head started to fade as he gulped the coffee, alternating with bites of bread. She'd remembered his chosen breakfast, even though they hadn't known each other for more than four days.

Could it be that she noticed him, after all? Not Tristan the spy or Tristan the duke's brother, but Tristan Graylocke. The man he was when no one was watching.

Something warm unfolded in his chest, but he tried not to look at it too deeply. Freddie was still his enemy...wasn't she? He didn't know what to believe—or what he wanted to believe.

He busied himself finishing his breakfast as she tapped out a cheerful beat on the tabletop. Suddenly, the day's events seemed much sunnier.

***

Tristan barely spoke two words to Freddie while he ate. She tried not to take his churlishness to heart. After all, as she'd said, he always acted a beast in the morning. If he treated her no differently than he had the day before, did that mean that he'd forgiven her for her transgression last night?

She gritted her teeth. The beat she drummed onto the table faltered. *It is not a transgression.* After all, he'd known when he'd started to romance her that they were on opposite sides.

She battled the urge to lower her head into her hands. Whatever Tristan was interested in, it couldn't be romance. Not with her. No, if anything, he was trying to trick her to give up the mission Harker had set her. She resumed the beat of her fingers against the wood table, slower this time. If Tristan thought he could trick her, she should be proud to have proven him wrong.

Instead, she felt guilty for fighting the pull of his kiss, even for a moment. His gaze lingered on her face. She averted her eyes.

The moment he finished his breakfast, she jumped to her feet. "Are you ready to seize the day?"

The noise of derision he made drew her attention. He raised his eyebrows as he slowly straightened. "It's raining out. The day is shaping up to be miserable."

A sly smile curved her lips. "The day is whatever you make of it."

He stepped around the table, falling in line with her. "Given the look on your face, I gather you have an idea of what you'd like to make of today?"

Her smile widened. "I hear you're a formidable chess player. I thought I'd trounce you a time or three and teach you some manners."

A wicked glint entered his gaze as he grinned. Her heart skipped a beat under the full force of that smile. It was a formidable weapon. She swallowed, trying not to show how effective it was.

He is the enemy, she told herself. Unfortunately, that argument was getting weaker and weaker with each repetition.

He leaned closer, so close her senses hummed with the spicy scent of his cologne. "You can try, but don't think I'm going to let you win."

"I like a challenge." Her voice was a bit breathy. She glanced away before his nearness conjured memories of his kiss.

Too late. Her body tightened with an ache she hadn't been able to appease since last night. All she wanted was to turn back time and lose herself in that kiss once more.

Tristan offered his arm to her. "In that case, shall we adjourn to the library?"

"Of course." She tried to act confident but that mien vanished the moment she laid her hand on his sleeve. The muscular flesh of his forearm only served to remind her of a time not too long ago when he'd encircled her with that arm.

He didn't appear to be afflicted by the same wayward thoughts. Had it been a calculated seduction? If so, he was certainly an asset to the French. Even knowing that they were on opposite sides didn't stop her from wanting to kiss him again.

The moment he led her into the hall, Freddie stiffened. Harker stood in the doorway to a sitting room diagonally from the breakfast room. His beady eyes narrowed as he beheld Freddie on Tristan's arm. Had he been waiting for her?

When he smiled, the expression did not meet his eyes. "Frederica, may I have a moment?"

No. Every bone in her body rebelled at the idea, even as she knew she had to accept. She clenched her teeth and started to withdraw her hand from Tristan's sleeve.

He pinned it beneath his. The glare he leveled at Harker could be considered nothing less than lethal. "I'm afraid we have an engagement elsewhere." He half-turned, shielding her with his body as he urged her in the opposite direction. He didn't once look at her, but the fierceness in his tone and stance left no doubt that he was protecting her.

From Harker, the man everyone accepted as her relation, and therefore a man she could trust.

At that moment, she wanted nothing more than to melt into Tristan's embrace, to let him hold her up for just a moment while she caught her breath. She was always the shield, the barrier keeping Harker from her family. Mama played her part—Freddie couldn't prevent that—but she did what she could to mitigate it. No one stood up to place themselves between her and Harker, not the way Tristan did.

It felt good to be protected, even if she couldn't let herself get used to it.

"I won't take more than a moment of her time."

Harker's voice was cutting. When Freddie shut her eyes for a moment, gathering herself, she saw her sister's bright, smiling face. Freddie laid her free hand on Tristan's arm. The bunch of his muscles beneath her palm was an ominous sign.

"This won't take long, I promise." Her voice was faint. She didn't look him in the eye. Instead, she fixed her gaze on the tight muscle in his jaw. It twitched.

His hand loosened over hers as he nodded curtly. She retracted her arm and he took a step back, but he didn't move far. She hoped her voice wouldn't carry.

She pinned Harker beneath her stare. At that moment, she'd never disliked him more.

No, dislike was too tame a word. She loathed him. She didn't understand why the British government would employ such a snake. Could it be they didn't know his character?

Perhaps they didn't care, so long as he served their purposes. Right now, Freddie was the one putting herself in harm's way while Harker looked on disapprovingly.

"What do you want?" she asked, her voice blunt. She didn't care if she displayed coarse manners. Harker had...

What? His only crime this morning was in approaching her and Tristan when she'd rather not be gifted with the ugly sight of his face. She and Tristan were supposed to be enemies. In fact, they were, they must be, despite the protective way he'd tried to keep her from Harker. Perhaps it was yet another ploy to draw her onto his side.

It won't work. Her family's future was at stake—and her future, too.

Harker's lip curled as he leaned closer. His breath reeked, stale from sleep. "You haven't found me the book, yet. You said you knew where it was."

"I was mistaken." The words cost her dearly, but she could offer no others. Her last lead on the code book's whereabouts had led her into a trap.

"At this rate, the party will end and you will be left empty-handed!"

She swallowed hard. A painful lump formed in her throat. She could barely speak around it. "I'll find the book." Was she lying? The words tasted sour.

What if she couldn't do it?

She grappled for any excuse. Peeking over her shoulder, she found Tristan staring in their direction, his expression dark.

She swung back to face Harker. "I'm making progress. In case you haven't noticed, I'm beguiling the man who has possession of the book."

Was she? Or was he beguiling her?

She swallowed again, thickly. "Once I've gained his trust, he'll lead me to where the book is hidden."

Harker's expression grew even colder, glacial even. He drew himself up, even though he wasn't much taller than Freddie. Staring down his nose at her, he said, "You'd do well to find it sooner, rather than later. Your poor sister is looking dreadfully out of sorts to be left all by her lonesome while you tarry."

Horror washed over her, quickening her pulse. It throbbed painfully in the base of her throat. Was that a threat? Surely he wouldn't touch Charlie, not while under the Graylockes' roof.

He won't touch her after, either. That, Freddie vowed. No matter the cost, she would keep her sister safe.

When she turned, she met Tristan's gaze. His dark brown eyes were sharp, disapproving. He was the key to keeping her sister out of Harker's clutches. Her personal feelings for him didn't matter. She had to find that book at all costs.

With a faked smile to hide the unease seething inside her, she approached him. "I'm terribly sorry about that. Shall we continue to the library?"

He nodded, stiffly. His steely gaze drifted past her, to Harker, as he offered his arm. She slid her hand into place and composed herself as they walked away.

The library granted her some comfort. The soaring shelves of books loomed over her like benevolent guardians. She relaxed as Tristan led her to one of the seats by the fireplace. A fire had been stoked in the grate, but it must have been a while since the servants had attended to it because it had started to burn low. Upon helping her into the padded arm chair, Tristan positioned a high, square table next to her and retreated to fetch the chess board.

He seemed perfectly content to ignore the fact that they were enemies, each fighting on opposite sides of a war. Freddie's country relied on her to filch the book from him—but that would not have mattered a whit to her if the mission had threatened the well-being of her family. How did Tristan feel about his duty? Had Britain ever offered him employment or had they turned him away? Freddie found it hard to believe that the government would choose to employ Harker over Tristan. At least Tristan didn't send others out to do his work; he faced it head on. That, or else he didn't find Freddie to be a formidable opponent.

She clenched her fists. *I'll show him.* When she found the book and delivered it to Harker, she would show everyone. Most of all, herself.

As he seated himself across from her and set up the board, she mused, "There are enough books in here to educate an army. I can only imagine how many of them are scattered in other places throughout the abbey."

He didn't rise to the bait. Instead, he presented her with the white side of the board, graciously allowing her to take the first turn. She did, moving her knight out from behind her row of pawns. His eyebrows twitched as he beheld the move. Most people led with a pawn.

Freddie preferred to remind him that she was not most people.

As he made his move—moving his pawn one square away from the queen—he said, "I am quite proud of our collection. We have some tomes in London, of course, but not to this extent. Have you explored our selection?"

"I have." She moved one of her pawns, freeing a path for her bishop.

His eyes narrowed as he surveyed the placement of her pieces, measuring her strategy. She waited, unconcerned, for him to make a move.

Almost absently, he asked, "And did you find something to your liking?"

"I didn't find what I was looking for."

He raised his gaze, his eyes sharp as his fingers hovered over the head of his pawn. "Not every book is available in our library, extensive though it may be."

For some reason, the disapproval in his eyes and voice as he caught on to the fact that she referred to the code book shredded her gut into ribbons. She waited for him to finish his move, then quickly made one of her own.

Heaven help her, but she craved his good opinion. She liked the amiable truce they'd formed. She didn't want to bloody well do this spying business anymore.

She had no choice. But it was obvious from his tone that he wasn't about to tell her the location of the code book. She would have to find out on her own, when she could rid herself of his company.

Not now.

She cleared her throat. "I did borrow a novel by Mrs. Radcliffe that I hadn't read yet."

Some of the tension in the air eased with this neutral topic. "Oh? And how did you find it?"

She countered his move and took one of his pawns. He frowned. She grinned. She wasn't going to let him win, either.

"Actually, I was a bit disappointed in it. I like her later novels better."

He leaned his elbow on the arm of his chair and propped up his chin as he mulled over his next move. Freddie counted only three viable options to put him in a favorable position, and she'd already lined up her pieces to counter the one she thought him most likely to choose.

He surprised her, proving himself a worthier opponent than she'd earlier assessed. She might have to take more time to think over her moves going forward.

He said, "And what sort of book impresses you?"

"I prefer not to see women painted as weak and malleable. Men can be just as weak."

His eyebrow twitched as she made her move. At her play or at her words? She kept her finger on the top of her bishop, holding it in place as she reconsidered the move. No, she liked it. She let it stand.

"Are you referring to *The Monk*?"

She smirked. "You've read it too, have you?"

"I have, though I have to say, I don't know how well I'd like to be cast in Ambrosio's role."

She grinned. "Exactly."

He gave a rueful shake of the head as he met her gaze. "You're something of a feminist, aren't you?"

She bristled. "Is that a bad thing?"

"No." He offered the word with a shrug of his shoulders. It was a casual statement, a fact.

She'd half-expected him to belittle her.

He added, "There are weak and malleable women in this world—men, too, I'm sure. But you, Freddie Vale, are not in danger of becoming one of them."

His adamant tone teased a smile from her lips. "You aren't one, either."

That seemed to please him. The grin that curved his mouth was nothing less than radiant. Her heart lurched as he asked after other books she liked, leaning closer to her as if the answer was vital to him. As if he cherished her opinions.

Was there any way that Harker could be wrong about Tristan being a French spy? Maybe he was a double agent. Anything would be better than him being her enemy.

Because, deep down, a small part of her feared that it would be very easy to fall in love with him. And that was the one thing she couldn't afford to do.

Chapter Twenty

Tristan put out his cheroot and drained his tumbler as the other gentlemen got to their feet. Some groaned at the thought of rejoining the ladies—those who were unlucky in love or, worse, had a matchmaking mama on their heels. Frankly, Tristan was surprised that his brother, Morgan, wasn't among their number. Every lady in attendance had set their cap for him, barring perhaps the Vale sisters.

The thought of Freddie flirting with his brother set jealousy simmering in his stomach. She might only be spending time with him because they were swept up in a battle of wits, but if she set her cap for Morgan, it might ruin him.

Did Freddie think of marriage? She must. All young ladies considered it, even those who fancied themselves feminists. Until the day they could hold fortunes of their own, they were dependent on the men in their lives to care for them.

The man in Freddie's life was Harker. That man never adjourned with them to the library, and with good reason. He would receive hostile treatment even from those who had no notion of his spying allegiances. It was no secret that he was rotten to the core.

With a sigh, Tristan got to his feet. The other men slapped each other on the back and ribbed each other as they filed through the library door. As Tristan moved to follow, his brother called his name.

He held back, gritting his teeth as he sought to find composure. If this was about Freddie... He turned to face Morgan.

For once, Morgan didn't look disapproving. He looked weary and worried. A furrow formed between his eyebrows. If he wasn't careful, the white streak near his temple would engulf the rest of his black hair.

Morgan eyed the doorway, waiting for the last man to vacate the library before he spoke. Tristan braced himself for a reprimand.

Instead, Morgan spoke through clenched teeth. "I haven't been approached by our contact. Have you?"

Tristan shook his head. "I've installed myself at Miss Vale's side, to keep her from ferreting out the book. No one has approached us."

Morgan hung his head. He covered the small, defeated motion by running his hand through his hair. It didn't fool Tristan. His brother was distraught.

"I've had my aide investigate the luggage of every servant and guest, to no avail. The party won't last for much longer. If we don't pass along the book here..."

"Then we'll do it in London. Damn what anyone thinks. They shouldn't have changed our contact at the last minute."

Morgan rubbed his forehead. "Our contact might not be from London."

"Didn't Mother choose all the guests from those who came down for the Season?"

"Not all."

Tristan pressed his lips together. "Then perhaps focus on the ones we won't be able to reach in London."

"And if our contact is a temporary servant?"

Tristan wasn't used to seeing his brother so out of his element. Usually Morgan was calm, composed, the voice of reason. He gave the assurances, he didn't need them. Tristan often chafed beneath his brother's direction, but now that the tables were turned, he felt queasy. Gingerly, he reached out to clasp his brother's arm and offer comfort.

"It sounds to me like you're doing all you can. We don't know who the replacement is. We have to await the signal. If they don't give it, then the fault is theirs, not ours."

Morgan didn't leave things undone. For that matter, Tristan didn't, either. He caught his brother's gaze. "We have a few days, yet. We'll see this through."

Morgan accepted Tristan's platitude without argument. That, more than anything else, worried Tristan. Why was this mission so important to him? The code book was important—it would give their operatives a new method of communication unknown to the enemy—but in the grand scheme of things, it wouldn't end the war. Their lives would continue as usual.

Wrapped in thought, Tristan traversed Tenwick Abbey at his brother's side. When they reached the parlor where the ladies were gathered, Tristan paused in the threshold, searching for the one woman he hadn't been able to get out of his thoughts.

He found Freddie, dressed in a muted blue evening dress tonight that scooped just beneath her collarbone, next to the notorious gossips, Mrs. Biddleford and Miss Maize. Freddie's stance was hostile, her expression was livid. Color flushed her cheeks. A few strands of her hair escaped their pins, forming an angry halo around her face. She looked ready to do violence.

Lud, what was she about to do? He had to stop her before this went too far.

***

If the disparaging comment had been about Freddie, she might have been able to walk past with her head held high. She'd faced censure before, after all, when Papa had died, leaving such a weight of debt on their shoulders. She'd survived that, shielding her mother and sister from the worst of it.

But Mrs. Biddleford and Miss Maize weren't talking about Freddie, or her no doubt suspicious attachment to Tristan of late. They spoke about her sister.

"Look at the way she bats her eyelashes. That Miss Charlotte doesn't seem to care how many fall under her spell."

Freddie stiffened. Outrage beat at her breast. She struggled to subdue it, but she could not walk away. She turned to the two busybodies. Tonight they were dressed in eye-searing colors—fuchsia for Mrs. Biddleford, with her sheer fichu tucked into her bodice, and leaf-green for Miss Maize. Miss Maize wore a necklace of fat peridots following the lower cut of her dress. Both ladies shut their mouths as Freddie turned.

She glared down her nose at them. Harder to do with Mrs. Biddleford, considering she was of a similar height, but Freddie managed all the same. She clasped her hands in front of her stomach, fighting the urge to do violence.

No one said a word against Charlie. *No one.*

"Perhaps I should caution you not to repeat untruths about people whose characters you don't know."

Her voice was clipped, but even. *Well done.* She held herself stiffly. As the gossips' gazes turned predatory, she realized this battle was far from over.

Mrs. Biddleford narrowed her eyes. "To the contrary, Miss Vale. I believe the young lady in question has made her character quite clear."

Freddie's jaw slackened. Her ears rang as if she'd been slapped. Pain radiated from the fingers of her right hand, clenched so tightly in the left.

"Forgive me, but I don't believe I heard correctly."

Freddie thought the words so vehemently, they spouted in the air—from a different mouth. She turned as Tristan stepped smoothly to her right, installing himself at her elbow. His expression was tight, his gaze unforgiving. He rested his hand on Freddie's back and turned his gaze down to her. His eyes softened.

The tension in her posture eased, as though some leached into his body. Was this what it was like to have a partner, someone to face the evils of the world alongside? Freddie had always shunned the notion of marriage, but she'd never felt supported like this. If this was what marriage felt like, maybe it wouldn't be so bad.

She hardened herself to the thought. She had no fortune, no prospects, and no beauty. Charlie would do well for herself, that Freddie vowed, but she knew better than to hope for the same luck.

To Tristan, she said in a cool voice, "I believe they were insinuating that my sister's reputation is less than pure."

"Oh?"

Freddie didn't know how the raise of an eyebrow could appear dangerous, but Tristan made it so.

He turned to the two busybodies. "Then my sister must be in danger as well, for the two have been inseparable from the moment the party began." His tone deepened, lethal. "You would never dream of speaking out against my dear sister, would you?"

Mrs. Biddleford's eyes widened until she resembled more owl than chicken. Miss Maize's mouth dropped open. They clamored atop one another to reassure Tristan that they would never do any such thing.

He smiled, a mirthless expression that bared his teeth. "Then it is settled. Whatever you heard about Miss Charlotte must be false as well, wouldn't you say?"

"Oh, yes."

"Of course."

The pair made a hasty excuse and left. Tristan stared them down until they reached the other side of the room. When they were a safe distance away, he dropped his hand from Freddie's back. She felt the loss of the touch deeply.

He turned to her, a smug glint in his eye. "That ought to silence them, wouldn't you say?"

Yes. She opened her mouth to say something—maybe to thank him—but the words that tumbled out were not the ones she intended.

"Why did you do that?"

His face fell. His eyebrows knit together in a frown. "I beg your pardon?"

She wiped her clammy hands on her dress. "Why did you defend my sister? Please don't misunderstand me—I am grateful—" *Grateful* didn't begin to describe the snarl of emotions knotted in her chest. "—but you can't possibly know for sure that she's been with Lucy the entire time. The pair have a tendency to escape their chaperones, as you well know."

Tristan's tongue teased his lower lip. He didn't appear to notice, deep in thought as he searched for an appropriate response. Freddie noticed. Her eyes dropped to his mouth. Her lips started to throb with the memory of his kiss.

She forced herself to meet his gaze once more. Not a trace of his usual humor lingered in his eyes.

"You looked as though you were about to exacerbate the situation. With vultures like these, you must retain a cool head."

He sounded as though he had experience. What kind of condemnation did a man like Tristan ever have to face?

She crossed her arms. "Being the son of a duke doesn't hurt."

A teasing grin swept across his face. Her heart flipped at the sight of it. He had no right to be so devilishly handsome. Or to come to her rescue like some knight in shining armor. She could take care of herself—and her family—on her own. She always had before.

His gaze twinkled with good humor. "Exactly. It was my duty and my birthright to help you."

She tightened her arms across her chest, half-hugging herself. "You still didn't have to defend me. What do you care about my family's reputation?"

That serious look re-entered his gaze. "It's important to you."

She threw her hands in the air. "You don't even like me!"

Gravity befell him. "To the contrary. I like you a great deal." His voice was soft. It carried no farther than her ears.

Her arms dropped limp to her sides. She opened her mouth, but couldn't speak.

She liked him too, a great deal. More than she had any other man. And certainly much more than she ought to.

When had she stopped hating him?

Chapter Twenty-One

I like you a great deal.
Tristan didn't realize how much until the words left his lips. His chest tightened with a warm, expansive feeling. He wanted nothing more than to reach out and touch her. Her arm, her cheek, it didn't much matter where.

'Like' wasn't a strong enough word for the depth of his feelings. He admired her resilience, her loyalty and love for her family, her cleverness. He cherished her smiles and the way she nibbled on her thumbnail when she contemplated a chess move. Heaven help him, but somehow in the last few days, he'd fallen in love.

The realization was like a blow to the head. It left his ears ringing with the knowledge. The truth. He wanted to spend every last minute of his day with her. He never wanted to be parted from her, not tonight and certainly not at the conclusion of this house party.

He'd never been in love before.

He opened his mouth, then shut it again. What if she didn't feel the same? They'd started out as enemies. His opinion of her had gentled, but hers might remain the same. After all, they'd only known each other for a few days.

The way she treated him wasn't just Tristan the spy, or Tristan the duke's younger brother. She made him feel like she saw him, like she knew him. He hadn't realized how much he'd needed that until she'd given it to him.

"I...I like you, too." Her voice was husky, her gaze vulnerable.

For a moment, he couldn't speak. Was she telling the truth? Lud, but he hoped so.

He couldn't think about the future. Right here, right now, they were two people who...liked each other. The word didn't feel right, but he couldn't confess the depth of his emotions when they had chosen opposite sides of a vital war. Tonight, he wanted to forget about that. At least for a while.

He leaned close. "Maybe you'd care to join me in my room so I can show you exactly how much I like you. I trust you recall where it is."

His pulse beat painfully in the base of his throat as he pulled away, gauging her reaction. He'd propositioned women before, and been propositioned. None of those encounters mattered as much as this one. His body hummed with the desire to touch her and show her that in an ideal world, they weren't enemies.

Tonight, they could forget about the war.

Her cheeks flamed as she caught his meaning. Swallowing, he stepped back. If she was going to reject him, it would be safer if he wasn't exposed in front of so many people.

What if she came to his room just to further her mission from Harker? If anything, that would be worse than if she stayed away. He clenched his fists. Without looking her in the eye, he murmured, "I don't keep the book in my quarters, as you well know. If you come with an aim to find it, you'll be disappointed."

With a stiff incline of his head, he turned on his heel and left the room. His heart thundered through the corridor. His reflection—paler than usual, a byproduct of his nerves—was thrown back at him from the myriad mirrors along the route back to the family wing. By the time he reached his door, his palms were clammy. He wiped them on his breeches before he gripped the handle and strode inside.

The fire in the grate was out, a testament that his valet was still occupied with spying business. For once, he was grateful. Stoking the fire gave him something to occupy himself. Once the flames caught, he started to pace. His body was alive with nervous energy, far too much to sit.

She might not come. In fact, if she had any sense, she wouldn't. Now that he'd finally admitted to himself how much she meant to him, he burned with the need to touch her, to join with her. She was a gently-bred young lady, likely a virgin. If she joined him tonight, he should respect her virtue.

But if she came and participated willingly, he would be lost. At that moment, he needed her more than he needed his next breath.

She might not come. If she still viewed him as the enemy, she certainly wouldn't.

That thought should have consoled him, but it only increased his torment. He wanted so much more from her, even if they would be on opposite sides of the war come morning. With a sigh, he dropped into the armchair and rested his head in his hands.

How long had he waited? Half an hour or more?

She might not come.

The latch on the door jingled as it was opened from the corridor. He lurched to his feet as a woman slipped into the room. Freddie. She shut the door behind her, but didn't move away from the wall. Her hand rested on the latch.

His chest ached and he realized he'd forgotten to breathe. He took a deep breath, hoping to organize his thoughts enough to put her at ease. She looked uncertain, just as nervous as he was. At least he wasn't alone in that.

"You came." His hoarse voice sounded overly loud in the silence, its only companion the thunderous beat of his heart.

"I did."

I love you. Tristan pressed his lips together before the words spilled out of his mouth. Now wasn't the time to speak them.

He crossed the room in ground-eating strides to enfold her in his arms and kiss her senseless. She met him halfway.

***

The moment Tristan's lips met hers, Freddie forgot her own name. She forgot to breathe. The jangle of her nerves faded. The only thing that mattered was the feel of his body pressed against hers. His arms encircled her, holding reality at bay. She sank into his hold, twining her arms around his neck to keep him near.

He kissed her with a ferocity that stole her breath. As if he didn't think he would ever get another chance.

Maybe he won't. They were on opposite sides of the war, after all.

She didn't care to think about that just now.

When he broke away from her mouth to trail his lips over her jaw and neck, tingles erupted in his wake. Her breasts ached, as did the secret spot between her legs. She canted her head to give him better access. Her body tightened and she clutched his shoulders.

Was she mad for surrendering to him like this? She had her future to think about. She gasped for breath.

"Tristan, wait."

His hands tightened on her back. With a low groan, he raised his head from her neck. He rested his forehead against hers instead.

Butterflies took wing in her stomach. When he held her like that, as if he cherished her, she could all too easily fool herself into believing he loved her. Because she loved him, and that notion terrified her. There was no future for the two of them. There was only right now.

"Yes, Freddie?" His voice was hoarse. His breath played across her lips, close though he made no move to kiss her again.

She swallowed. "Is there a way to...do this without losing my virginity?" She couldn't risk pregnancy, after all.

He nodded, his forehead still pressed against hers. After a moment, he separated and stepped back. He held out his hand to her. "There is. Do you trust me?"

"Yes." The word left her lips without forethought. The color of his gaze deepened. She slipped her hand into his.

They both wore gloves, muting the sensation. The clasp of his hand was a comfort as he led her farther into the room. Toward that big bed of his.

The ache between her legs intensified. She wanted...she didn't know what. Him, certainly. Her legs began to tremble as she neared the bed. When she met his gaze, her nervousness melted away.

Tristan would never hurt her.

Gingerly, she sat on the edge of the bed. Tristan knelt in front of her, still holding her hand. He laid his lips to her silk-covered knuckles, then without taking his eyes off her, he slid his hand up to the top of the glove, just above her wrist. The movement pushed up her sleeves, bunching them around her elbows to display a swathe of skin between them and the gloves. With his thumb, Tristan stroked that skin. Her lips parted at the surprisingly potent sensation.

"May I?"

She nodded. She could no longer find her voice.

With a slow movement, he slid the glove down over her wrist. His glove was warm from the heat of his hand beneath. He pressed his lips to the inside of her wrist, over her pulse.

She gasped. Her heartbeat sped. When he flicked out his tongue, she couldn't hold back the moan that escaped her throat. His gaze turned wicked as he stripped her glove the rest of the way off, pressing open-mouthed kisses to her skin as he went. She pressed her thighs together, squirming in place.

After doffing his gloves and tossing them aside, he set to work on her other hand. The sensation, skin on skin, was magnified tenfold. As he dropped her glove and reticule to the floor, she cupped his cheek. The shadow of stubble scraped over her skin. He turned his face to press a kiss to her palm.

Unable to resist, she leaned forward to meld her mouth to his. Their breath mingled an instant before their lips touched. The kiss was light, leisurely, exploring. When she broke away to catch her breath, he leaned forward, following the arc of her mouth as she straightened.

"You taste like Heaven," he murmured.

She smirked. "Have you tasted Heaven before?"

"Never. But I don't need to in order to know that nothing on this Earth could taste as good."

She bit her lip as she ducked her head. Heat in her cheeks indicated she was flying her colors again. She didn't mind. No one had ever professed anything so sweet to her.

With deft fingers, Tristan removed her shoes. He wrapped his big hands around her ankles and slowly slid his palms up her calves. Her breath hitched as his hands disappeared beneath her skirts. She met his gaze once more. His eyes held a salacious promise. She pressed her thighs together, quivering, as he traced the outside of her legs.

He found the ties to her stocking. Slowly, with great care, he pulled the bow free. He hooked his fingers beneath the silk and teased the fabric down her leg. She lifted her legs, eager to help him along. When the fabric pooled around her ankles and he shifted his grip to attend to one foot at a time, she ran her finger around the rim of his collar. A shiver coalesced on his broad back and he raised his gaze to hers once more. His eyes darkened. He licked his lips.

All thought of proceeding with care disappeared beneath the weight of their hunger for each other. She fumbled with his cravat as he divested her of the stockings. Once the fabric around his neck was free, he stood.

With his knees, he urged her legs open and insinuated himself between them. He planted one hand on the mattress, the other cupping her jaw as he kissed her deeply. He trailed his hand down her neck and over her shoulder, to the buttons on her dress. One by one they slipped free as she tackled the stubborn buttons on his waistcoat. Within seconds, he unlaced the short stays on her back and her dress gaped over her breasts. When he broke the kiss, his face turned downward, his gaze locked on the shadow of her cleavage. Desire etched across his face, unmistakable.

Undeniable, too. She reached up, lacing her fingers in his hair as she pulled him down for a kiss. He shifted, toeing off his boots and shucking his jacket and waistcoat. When his arms returned around her, he urged her dress up her hips and over her head. They broke the kiss in a tangle of fabric that soon fluttered to the floor.

She was bare before him, but he didn't give her time to be embarrassed. He resumed the kiss, turning it urgent and demanding as he laid her back against the bed. He followed her. The press of his body against hers drove her wild. She clutched his shoulders.

When she leaned her head back, gasping for breath, he kissed his way along her throat. He spread her legs wider, urging them around his hips. The thick bulge of his manhood pressed against her core. The rough tease of his breeches against her feverish flesh made her shudder. When she raised her hand to loosen the laces of his shirt, he caught her hands, pinning them to the mattress above her head.

"Don't I get to see you naked as well?"

His Adam's apple bobbed behind his collar. When he shook his head, a lock of his hair curled over his forehead. "Not tonight," he rasped. "I don't think I'd be able to stop myself if we were both bare. It would be too easy to coax you to beg to take this farther than you want."

As if to prove his point, he dipped his head to kiss along the swell of her breast. Her nipples pebbled into hard points. By the time he reached the peak, she was trembling. He ran his tongue around her areola, making her gasp, before he took her nipple into his mouth.

The pleasure mounted between her legs, as if an invisible string joined the two places. When he lightened his touch, moving away, she arched into his embrace.

His mouth curved into a smile as he teased her with tantalizing flicks of his tongue. "Beautiful and passionate. You're what every man dreams of waking up to."

If she'd had the breath to speak, she would have returned the compliment. As it was, the closest she could come was a moan.

He kissed his way down her torso and abdomen. He lingered near her navel, inducing tingles over her skin before he continued down between her legs. Her cheeks heated as his big shoulders spread her legs wide. He studied her most private part, his gaze rapt. When her legs tightened, trying to close, he twisted to kiss the inside of her knee.

"I want to see you," he whispered. She barely heard him over the merry chuckle of the fire. "All of you."

He pressed another kiss to the inside of her leg, moving upward. By the time he reached the inside of her thighs, his tongue teased her skin with each kiss. And then he pressed his lips to her sex. Heat flooded her chest, but passion won out and she soon found herself lifting her hips to better meet him.

His kisses turned frantic. Her breath came fast and quick. He worshipped her with hands and mouth until she unraveled in his arms.

But he wasn't finished. He nuzzled his way up her body until he took her mouth in a deep, conquering kiss. He tasted tangy with her arousal. As he fitted himself between her legs once more, the bulge in his breeches was bigger than ever. Kneading her breast with one hand and using the other to hold her heady steady for his kiss, he gyrated against her with increasing urgency. Soon, she matched his fervor. The pleasure built, higher and higher until she shattered. This time he followed, shuddering against her as he held her close.

When he rolled to the side, he slipped his arms beneath her and pulled her with him to cradle her against his chest. His heart thundered beneath her cheek. His shirt was damp with sweat.

"That was..."

"Yes." Her voice was breathy. She didn't know what else to say.

Instead, she burrowed her face farther into his chest as she fought to catch her breath. *I love you.*

Don't let go. She bit her lip, keeping the words walled away inside her.

As much as she'd like to fool herself into believing he cared for her just as deeply, she couldn't. When morning dawned, they would be enemies again.

Chapter Twenty-Two

Tristan seemed so much more innocent in sleep. His eyelashes formed a crescent on his cheeks. The stubble was just starting to darken his chin. Freddie was nestled beside him, his arm slung around her waist as he fitted her against him. She didn't want to leave.

She had to.

With a light touch, she traced the curve of his cheek. Making a sleepy noise, he leaned into her touch, as if he craved more of her. An ache ripped open in her chest like a chasm. Gently, she eased his arm from around her waist. As she left the bed, he rolled over onto his stomach.

The fire had dimmed as it ran out of fuel. It cast a soft glow, barely enough for her to see the silhouette of objects. It took her some moments before she untangled her clothes and donned them. Although she bent her elbows at an uncomfortable angle, she couldn't properly reach behind her to lace up her stays. At some point in the night, her hair had fallen free of its pins. She couldn't begin to rectify her appearance. The river of her hair flowing down her back should cover the hastily-secured buttons.

Before long, she tiptoed across the room to the door. She stumbled, catching herself before she introduced her face to the wall. Behind her, Tristan stirred. He softly started to snore. She laid her hand on the latch.

She couldn't leave without saying goodbye, but she didn't want to wake him. Instead, she fished a handkerchief with her initials out of her reticule. More careful this time, she traversed the room to lay it on the pillow next to him.

There. At least this way, she didn't feel like a thief trying to steal out of the room.

Although she wanted nothing more than to slip back into bed and lose herself in his embrace, she turned and marched out the door. The abbey was quiet. With luck, all the guests had gone to bed and she wouldn't have to explain her ravished appearance.

She turned away from the door and came face to face with the duke. Although the candles had burned down, shedding only enough light to make out his profile and the glint of his eyes, it could be no other. Her heart jumped into her throat, throbbing painfully. She opened her mouth, but no words emerged. What could she say?

My virtue is intact. I won't make him marry me.

Even if Tristan asked, she couldn't possibly say yes, could she? They were on opposite sides. Unless one of them bent, they had no future. For her family's sake, if nothing else, she couldn't back down. And for some unknown reason, Tristan had allied himself with the French. He had likely done that for family, too.

She didn't have any guarantee that he would want a future with her, regardless.

The duke's piercing stare paralyzed her. Her mouth dried and her palms grew sweaty. She couldn't look away. Would he take her to task for seducing his brother?

Or worse, tell someone else? If word got out that Freddie had been seen coming out of Tristan's room, her reputation would be ruined. And so would Charlie's, for her relation to someone with a less than pristine standing in the *ton*. Freddie's chest burned as she stopped breathing.

Abruptly, the duke stepped past her. He strode to his room without a word. Without looking behind, he opened the door and slipped inside.

The vise around Freddie's chest loosened. What was that? Her mind awhirl, she crept back to the guest wing across the abbey. She knocked over two candlesticks in the process, but managed to slip into her room without setting anything on fire. Or, better yet, waking Charlie.

But she still couldn't get her mind off the forbidding look on the duke's face.

***

Freddie tossed and turned to such a degree that at one point, even though she slept in a bed across the room, Charlie grumpily complained of Freddie's movements and left to sleep with their mother in the room next door. Even then, Freddie spent so much time studying the ceiling that she could probably paint it in blacks and grays.

With bags under her eyes and exhaustion weakening her limbs, she finally gave up on sleep and dressed for the day. Lisane hadn't yet entered to help, so Freddie left off her stays and dressed herself in a modest lavender day dress. The abbey bustled with servants, but no other guests stirred as she made her way down the corridor.

Only one man was awake and down to breakfast when she entered, and it was one she didn't think to see, given his late night.

As he noticed her falter in the doorway, the Duke of Tenwick fisted the letter he was reading. He was dressed for a morning ride in a high-necked burgundy riding coat and kid gloves. A plate of steaming eggs, kippers, and bacon was heaped on his plate and he nursed a mug. He thrust it onto the table so forcibly that the creamy brown liquid sloshed over the side, wetting the short graphite pencil beside his dish.

"G-good morning, your grace." Her voice was thin and fragile.

The duke's gaze sharpened like steel. He stuffed the paper into his pocket, thrust himself to his feet, and stormed toward her without a word. Freddie jumped to the side, vacating the doorway. The air stirred with the force of his passing.

The livery-clad footman by the sideboard followed after him. Even the servants disdained her.

Her knees weakened. Her stomach shriveled and her appetite fled. She approached the sideboard with shaky legs and poured a cup of tea.

As she carried it past the duke's half-eaten breakfast, a wadded piece of paper caught her eye. It must have fallen from his pocket! Gingerly, she set down her tea before she spilled it and bent to retrieve the paper.

A quick glance toward the door confirmed that she was still alone in the room. Kneeling on the ground to obscure her actions if someone walked in, she smoothed out the page.

It looked to be written in code. It might as well have been written in Egyptian hieroglyphics, for all she understood the inked message. Someone— likely the duke—had added marks in pencil to certain words. Beneath, he had decoded the message.

Freddie's breath caught as she read and reread the translation. This was a spy message! It detailed the time and location—tonight, while the guests were at supper, at the towering oak tree—

for a rendezvous to pass along the coded book. It also detailed the signal the spy was to give the duke to ensure his authenticity.

Her head spun with this information. This was exactly what she needed to retrieve the book. If she reached the point early and gave the signal to the duke herself...

She would be betraying Tristan. An ache rooted painfully in her chest. She blinked away the sting of tears.

"He's on the wrong side," she whispered. She would be helping Britain by completing this task.

More than that, she would be helping her family. She couldn't let her feelings for Tristan get in the way of that. Even if she was sure she was about to make the worst mistake of her life.

She didn't see any other way.

***

Miss Vale, Tristan had been told, had gone out for a walk by the time he reached the breakfast room. By luncheon, he concluded that she was either avoiding him or avoiding the guests, because she didn't soon return. Spending time around the guests—and especially his sister, with her pointed looks and questions—irked Tristan as well. He couldn't smile, contribute to conversation, or act the carefree rake while he combatted the strange burn in his chest.

He'd known that he and Freddie could indulge in only one night, but that hadn't meant he'd wanted to wake without her at his side. Instead, the only sign of her presence was a monogrammed handkerchief on his pillow. FV. Even that felt wrong. 'FG' would look better. He'd thrust the thought aside as he'd stuffed the handkerchief into his pocket. It smelled soft and delicate, like her lavender perfume. Every time he tucked his hand into his pocket, he found himself fingering those embroidered initials and the thought arose anew.

He couldn't ask her to marry him. Every time he told that to himself, a small part of him asked, *Why not?* He hadn't come up with a satisfactory answer, he just knew it was so. If nothing else, his brother wouldn't approve.

And when have you ever given a fig's end for Morgan's approval?

He hadn't, especially not in recent years, but Morgan was the head of the duchy. His word held weight even with Tristan. Especially with their mother. Tristan couldn't go against his family's wishes to pursue love, could he?

It was a moot point. Even if he asked, he doubted Freddie would accept. If she'd wanted to spend time with him, she would have this morning. They could have escaped the guests together.

In a foul mood, he shut himself away in Morgan's study, the one place of solitude in the abbey overrun by guests and family members. The room was dark and cool, devoid of a fire or signs of occupancy. As he shut the door, he rested his forehead against the wood.

Being alone only left him with his troubled heart.

"I've handled our problem with Harker's spy."

Tristan jumped at his brother's voice. He rounded, searching the room for the telltale shape. The daylight drifting from beneath the shut drapes lingered on a figure Tristan had inwardly dismissed as part of the furniture. Not so, considering that it moved.

"What are you doing in here alone without so much as a candle?"

Morgan gave a low chuckle. The leather armchair squeaked as he stood. The carpet muffled his footsteps as he crossed to pull open the drapes. The cloudy day didn't allow for much sun, but a gray light fell into the room, illuminating it and the stacks of papers on Morgan's desk. Nestled between them was a tumbler of brandy, still full.

When Morgan turned around, his eyebrows raised, he said in that calm, even tone, "I imagine I'm here for the same reason you are. I'm damn and bloody sick of Mother's matchmaking attempts."

A thorn pierced Tristan's side, just beneath his ribcage. Mother hadn't tried to throw any young debutantes his way. Did she not think he was good enough for them?

Was he not good enough for Freddie?

Wait—his brother's initial statement registered. "What do you mean you've handled Harker's spy?"

What had Morgan done to Freddie? Was he the reason she hadn't been in the abbey all morning? Something hot and sinister unfurled in Tristan's chest. He didn't move for fear of what he might do to his brother.

Oblivious to the line he treaded, Morgan dropped into his desk chair again. He fingered the rim of his glass, but made no move to drink its contents.

"I left false information for Miss Vale." He shrugged. "I'm sending my assistant out on a fake rendezvous. When she speaks the code word, impersonating an agent of the Crown, we'll arrest her. That's a hanging offense, you know."

Tristan trembled. He felt as though a shadow was eating away at his gut. He opened and closed his mouth several times, trying to compose himself before he spoke. It didn't help.

"You can't do that!"

Morgan never responded well to direct confrontation. His ebony eyebrows hooked together in outrage as he pushed to his feet. His face was livid.

"Can't I? You've gotten too close, Tristan. I had to do something. She was deceiving you."

No, she wasn't. They'd known exactly what temporary insanity it was to indulge in passion last night. Heaven help him, but Tristan wanted more.

Lud, but his chest ached. It felt as though it would rip open at any second. He rubbed at it, trying to quell the pain.

"You're wrong." He tempered the anger in his voice this time.

Morgan clenched his fists. The muscle in his jaw twitched. "Are you going to tell me that she loves you, then?"

How can I when I don't know the answer to that question? Tristan ground his teeth. "No. She never deceived me in that fashion."

"Then it was just coincidence that I found her sneaking out of your room late last night?"

Tristan burned with a protective instinct he couldn't name. He stepped closer. One step at first, then another and another until only the desk separated him from Morgan. He didn't break eye contact.

In a low, lethal voice, he said, "Tell me you have repeated that to no one."

Morgan made a face. "And risk hurling you into the parson's noose? I would never."

Tristan swallowed twice before he was able to speak again. Somehow, his hand found its way back into his pocket. The linen handkerchief, soft from many washes, soothed him. He took strength from it. Freddie wouldn't have left it if she didn't care for him to some degree. He meant something to her, even if he didn't know what that something was.

"I'm a grown man. I don't need you to look out for me."

Morgan's nostril's flared. "If I don't, then who will?" His voice was loud, belligerent.

It shocked Tristan into silence. Morgan's temper wasn't usually this volatile.

In a more moderate tone, Morgan added, "I'm your brother. I care for your well-being."

"I'm perfectly capable of making my own decisions out from under your bloody shadow."

Silence rang as Morgan's face grew slack.

"You don't truly feel that way." There was a note of incredulity in Morgan's voice, a question.

Tristan made a face. "Of course I do. You've been the golden boy ever since we were small, the heir. When you became Duke…"

A shadow fell over Morgan's face like a veil. It cut off any trace of emotion in his eyes. Softly, he admitted, "I never asked for that. I never wanted it."

Tristan recalled that grief-stricken time, when the fun-seeking, carefree brother he'd grown up with had turned into the austere man standing in front of him now. "I know." Tristan's voice was every bit as soft. The words tasted bitter as he spoke them. "But that doesn't change the fact that everyone started to look at you differently. I became an afterthought, more than I already was."

Morgan's eyebrows twitched, a hint of fierceness soon subdued. "You aren't an afterthought. You're important."

"To the spy initiative, yes." Tristan clenched his hand around the handkerchief. "It was the only goddamn thing I had in my life that mattered, that made me feel like I was contributing, but you had to have that, too."

Morgan's gray eyes grew cloudy. "You think it's fun being Duke? I can't go off to war like Anthony. I can barely leave the blasted estate without something requiring my urgent attention! I wanted something that made me feel a little less like a prat who spent his entire life behind a desk."

He still spent his time behind a desk, albeit some of that was for the spy movement.

Fiercely, Morgan added, "I wanted to contribute, too, to keep my family safe."

"I know." Tristan's voice was so soft, he barely even heard it. He knew exactly how Morgan felt, because he felt the same way.

They so often butted heads that he didn't stop to consider that Morgan might chafe at his role in life, too. And, come to think of it, Tristan wouldn't trade him for the world. He wished his brother a long life and an army of sons. Tristan enjoyed his freedom too well to relinquish it for the responsibilities and notoriety of a dukedom.

What about for a wife? He'd always considered marriage to be a trap, a constriction on his life. With Freddie, he didn't feel trapped. In fact, he considered her a ray of light in a bleak and sometimes black existence. He had done many things he wasn't proud of, more than one of them in the name of spying. Freddie didn't know the specifics, but she certainly suspected that he wasn't a saint. When he was with her, she was a balm to his wounds. She made him feel important.

He had to protect her before she unwittingly found herself thrown in prison for Harker's crimes.

Tristan shook his head. "This time you've crossed the line, brother. Even in the name of keeping the family safe. You know I would never do anything to jeopardize our family."

"I know that you are blinded by her."

"I love her!"

Lud, had he just said that aloud? Judging by the hard look on Morgan's face, he had.

"That is exactly why I have to do this. If she wasn't in Harker's pocket, I would give you my blessing, but..."

"So take Harker instead," Tristan spat. "He's the bigger threat to the war."

Shutting his eyes as if in pain, Morgan rubbed at his temple. "You know I can't do that. We've been forbidden to interfere with him."

"Why?"

"Supposedly he's being monitored. Does it matter why?"

Tristan clenched his fists. He still held the handkerchief in his right hand. "It does when you're trying to make me choose between my family and duty or—" *the woman I love.* Tristan shut his mouth. He couldn't bear to speak the words again. With each repetition his conviction grew stronger. What if he couldn't save Freddie? It might kill him.

Morgan's voice turned cold. "The choice should be easy. If you warn her, you'll be tearing apart everything you care about. I know it isn't like you to allow your heart to interfere with your judgment, but...trust me on this, brother. I'm only looking out for what's best."

"No," Tristan spat. "You're doing what you're told. I would have thought a duke would be able to make his own decisions."

As a painful lump built in his throat, Tristan turned on his heel. He couldn't argue with Morgan any longer. He had to act.

But what could he do? His superiors had ordered him not to touch Harker. *They can't know the depth of his depravity.* Then again, neither did he. How had Harker convinced a sweet, innocent, perceptive, caring woman like Freddie to spy for him? She'd hinted, but never told him the specifics.

He needed to know. Now, more than ever.

He couldn't warn her about Morgan's duplicity. His brother was right, he would be turning his back on his country and family, not to mention Morgan's trust. He hadn't realized until that moment that for all their squabbles, he valued his brother's trust. At the end of the day, they were family.

But if he kept his silence, the woman he loved could die. His head throbbed with the force of his predicament. He didn't have much time to decide. There had to be another option.

Chapter Twenty-Three

Freddie waited for her sister to look the other way before she stumbled on the way to the door to their room. She purposefully snagged her hem on her toe and leaned her weight into it. The resulting *rrrrip!* sliced through the air. For once, her clumsiness came in handy, even though she landed on the carpet.

Charlie bounded to her side, hiking her skirt to her knees. "Freddie, are you all right?" She kneeled to help Freddie to her feet.

I'm in pain. Freddie bit her tongue to keep from admitting as much. Her plan had been to rip her skirt, not fall face first onto the floor. At least she'd accomplished her goal. She twisted to examine the tear in her skirt. She fit three fingers through it.

Charlie batted her hand away. "Who cares about your skirt! Are you hurt?"

"I'm fine," Freddie said. She accepted her sister's help to stand. A twinge stabbed her ankle, but she leaned her weight onto the other foot and hoped it would go away soon. The dinner hour approached and she still had to escape through the manor and across the lawn to the overlarge oak tree.

With Charlie's help, she crossed to the settee and sat. She felt her ankle. A bit tender, but once she had her ankle boots on perhaps it would ease.

Her sister perched beside her. "Are you sure you're all right?"

She forced a smile. "Of course I am. I fall all the time, you know that."

Once again, she reached down to finger that rip. It might be her most impressive yet—it was at least three inches long.

She feigned remorse. "You'll have to go down without me. I need to change my dress."

Charlie stood. "I'll send in Lisane."

"Don't!" Freddie regretted her high tone the moment it left her lips. She stumbled over her tongue trying to recover before Charlie guessed that she was trying to avoid dinner. "I mean, she'll be disappointed with me. You know how she hates when I rip my clothes. And she has so much work with you and Mama, too... It's only the net overdress. There aren't any laces. I can put it on by myself." She shut her mouth with a click and tilted her head up to offer her sister a smile.

How could she possibly hope to impersonate a French spy when she couldn't even lie to her sister about a dress?

Charlie looked dubious. "If you're certain..."

"I am."

Her sister narrowed her blue eyes. "I can help you dress."

"If you do, you'll be late. I'll be fine on my own." The corners of Freddie's mouth started to ache. She held her smile in place by will alone. "I can take care of myself."

As she sighed, a look of resignation crossed Charlie's face. "Very well. I'll see you down shortly."

"Of course."

The pain in Freddie's cheeks mounted as she continued to smile. Charlie hesitated by the door, glancing over her shoulder as she slowly pulled it shut. Only once she was alone did Freddie let the smile fall from her face. Her ankle stung with short, insistent bursts that faded slowly. She took a steadying breath.

Standing wasn't difficult. A little sore, but nothing she couldn't manage. Her ankle wasn't swollen and fit easily into her ankle boot, which provided additional support. In case she happened to come across Charlie afterward, she changed the thin muslin overdress for another. She had just settled it into place when the door opened behind her.

Her muscles tensed. She forced a smile. "I don't need your help. I managed fine on my own." When she turned, she stopped short, her jaw hanging open.

Tristan shut the door behind him as he slipped into the room.

She stepped closer. "What are you doing here?" Her voice was the barest hiss, in case someone was nearby to overhear.

"I'm stopping you from making the worst mistake of your life."

His gaze lingered on her. He stepped closer, almost coming within arm's reach. She hadn't seen him since she'd snuck out of his room this morning. She hadn't expected the encounter to feel so...natural. She'd expected pain, torture at knowing the pleasure he'd evoked between them. Instead, it felt as though she'd been missing one shoe all day and the moment he arrived she'd finally slipped her foot into it and was whole again.

She swallowed hard. Did he know the specifics of what she was about to do or was he only guessing? He looked so earnest, so adamant, that she couldn't know for sure.

She cocked up her chin. "How do you know what I'm about to do?"

He shoved his hands into the pockets of his beige waistcoat. "At a guess, I would say that you're planning on interrupting the meeting my brother is having with his contact." Tristan's gaze sharpened. His eyes never left her face. "Please, Freddie, I implore you. Don't do it. Don't go."

How could he know? She must have been a little too good at avoiding him today. He must have gotten suspicious. She opened her mouth, but her throat tightened. Her chest burned. She couldn't bear to lie to him.

"I have to. If I don't, Harker will..."

Tristan's eyes narrow. "He'll do what?" His voice was edged with steel.

She averted her gaze. "He'll force himself on my sister."

"He said that?" Tristan's sharp, brusque tone punched through the air. He reached out to frame her shoulders with his big palms, preventing her from moving away.

She pressed her lips together, trying to collect herself. The sting in her eyes told her that she wasn't far away from becoming a watering pot. Her voice was small when she answered, "Not in so many words, but he hasn't hidden his wandering eye of late. I know it will happen if I don't do something to stop it. That's why I struck the deal with him."

"What deal?"

He already knew. Why not tell him the specifics? "I have to bring him the book. The code book."

Tristan said nothing at all. His silence was as ominous as storm clouds.

She nibbled on her lower lip. She still couldn't look him in the eye. "I have to stop Harker. I can't let him hurt my sister."

"You don't understand." Tristan's voice was every bit as soft. Almost pained. "You can't do this. It's too dangerous."

"I don't care." She lifted her head. Her show of strength evaporated as she met his gaze. His brown eyes were soft, pleading. She shook her head, trying to shake of the effect he had on her. "I'll do anything to keep my sister safe."

His hand tightened on her shoulder, pulling her marginally closer. Not quite into his embrace, but far enough that the heat of his body lured her. How good would it feel to press her cheek against his shoulder and let him hold her up for a moment or two? She was so tired of all this spying.

But the end was in sight. She had to stay strong.

"Are you willing to risk your life?" he asked.

"Of course I am." The words flew out of her mouth without thought. "Wouldn't you, for your sister?"

Dropping his hands, he turned with a muttered curse. When he turned back, running his hands through his hair, he admitted, "Yes, I would." He lowered his arms to his side. His gaze turned pleading. "If I can't stop you from doing this, then let me come with you. I can't let you go alone."

She frowned. Was he offering to change his allegiance? Slowly, she said, "We're on opposite sides, Tristan."

He caught her hand. His grip was firm, but not painful. "We don't have to be."

She pulled away. "Yes, we do. Even if Harker wasn't involved, I would never betray my country."

A look of bewilderment crossed Tristan's face. "How can you say that while you're working for our enemies?"

"What are you talking about?"

"You're working for Harker. He's a French—"

Freddie's stomach threatening to turn itself inside out at the word *French*.

"—spy." Tristan took a small step forward, hands outstretched, though he didn't touch her. "Didn't you know that?"

Her head swam. Her knees turned to gruel. She sank onto the nearest flat surface, the bed. She lowered her head into her hands as her ears roared, for a moment drowning out all other sound.

When sound returned, and her spotty vision cleared, she heard herself say, "That can't be."

But it could be. In her heart, she'd known Harker was a villain all along. She stared at the toes of her ankle boots.

Gingerly, Tristan lowered himself beside her. He reached out to caress her knee. She raised her head to look him in the eye.

"Harker told me *you* were..."

Tristan sighed. "I don't know why I didn't consider that he might twist my allegiance. No, Freddie. I work for England. Morgan, too."

"Can you offer any proof?"

His lips thinned as he pressed them together. After a moment, he ventured, "No. I'm a covert spy, remember? Any proof I have I am forbidden to show you."

He might be lying. After all the time she'd spent with him, she didn't believe so. She hadn't been able to reconcile the man she knew with the traitor Harker painted. Her relief at not having mistaken Tristan's character was palpable.

But it presented an entirely new horror.

She lowered her head into her hands. "Oh, God. What am I going to do?" If she didn't bring Harker the code book, he might do unthinkable things to her mother and sister. If she did... she would be betraying her country, and the man she loved, too. Her stomach swished as she contemplated her options. There was no way to win.

"I have an idea," Tristan said. He sidled closer, slipping his hand into hers.

In wonder, she lifted her gaze to his. He still wanted to help her? She leaned forward, capturing his lips in a fleeting kiss. She poured all her gratitude, all her love into that kiss.

"I have to save my family. I'll do anything."

When she pulled away, he smiled and tucked a wayward strand of her hair behind her ear. He didn't relinquish his hold on her hand. "Then hear me out," he said. "I think there's a way we can trick Harker into exposing himself, but you're better at thinking ahead than I am. I'll need your input. Freddie, I love you. I know nobody stronger or smarter. If we work together, I'm sure we can do this. We can do anything."

I love you. Her heart sang at the words. *We can do anything.* Yes. At that moment, she'd never felt like any words contained more truth. She didn't feel diminished by his help. If anything, he lifted her up. As much as she needed him, he needed her, too.

Was this what marriage was supposed to be about?

She tightened her hand on his. "I love you, too. You're right. We can do anything. What's your idea?"

Chapter Twenty-Four

This is a bad idea. You're a horrible liar.

Unfortunately, Freddie and Tristan's plan relied on her being able to lie to Harker's face. If she didn't convince him, her family would be in an even worse position than they were now. She would die before she let that happen.

She hovered in the doorway to the drawing room, praying that no one would notice her as she scanned the interior for her prey. There, standing off from everyone else with a glass of amontillado in his hand. His posture was stiff and hostile, a marked contrast from when he entertained in London. His squirrelly friends doted on him, making him the toast of the night. Harker usually soaked up the attention, telling lewd jokes and laughing at his friends' expense.

Now, Freddie had to wonder if his friends weren't all traitors as well. After tonight, she would never have to cross paths with them again. That brought some measure of relief. It had been getting progressively harder to keep Charlie's presence in the townhouse from being known, now that she'd made her bows.

She caught Harker's eye. He frowned, his hairy eyebrows uniting over his eyes. She jerked her chin toward the hall then stepped back before someone else saw her.

At the moment, the corridor appeared deserted. The servants had recently lit the candles to create their magical effect, even though the sun had not yet kissed the horizon. It would before supper was through.

Although her nerves jangled in her stomach like discordant bells, Freddie thrust her shoulders back and clasped her hands in front of her waist, the picture of serenity. Down the corridor, in an unused closet, Tristan waited with the door cracked open. If she looked to be about to fail, he would rescue her. Even though she wanted to perform her task without his help, knowing that his support was nearby and unwavering lent her strength.

Her chest warmed at the idea that soon, this debacle would be over, and they would never be enemies again. She didn't want to examine what the future held too closely, aside from that.

Harker squeezed his bulk through the door and stepped away, joining her. "What is this about?" His voice was low, but sharp all the same.

Her nerves erupted again. She pressed her palms against her abdomen to quell the sensation.

"I've discovered the rendezvous location to hand off the book you seek. I've also gleaned the signal the agent will provide to assure the Graylockes of his identity."

Was her voice too high pitched? Was the lie written on her face? Once Tristan had confessed the truth of the situation—that the hand-off was designed to catch a French spy—she couldn't believe she'd been so naïve as to think that the duke would leave vital information around for her to find. Even if that information had appeared to be dropped during his hasty departure.

Harker's lip curled. She nearly flinched. She held herself steady by biting into her inner cheek.

"Why are you telling me about it? Go get it."

She swallowed twice before she could speak. "I can't."

His expression darkened.

Her heartbeat sped, quickening the words falling out of her mouth. "They're expecting a man. It has to be you."

"The Graylockes already know I'm working for England."

You lying fiend. Freddie's stomach seethed with hatred. She tried not to let it show on her face. "Pretend your allegiances have changed, if you must. So long as you have the signal, they'll have to accept you. They don't know who their contact is, only that he is in Tenwick Abbey.

You're the only person who can make the exchange."

Although it made the hairs on the back of her neck stand at attention, she held his gaze. He raked it over her skin, leaving her feeling as if she were coated in slime.

"Very well," he spat. "I'll go. Where is the meeting and when?"

"It's to be held while the guests are at supper, beneath the big gnarled oak tree on the grounds. The signal is mockingbird, but you must make the hand signal as well." She demonstrated, hooking her thumbs together and flapping her hands as if they were wings.

With a disgruntled oath, he turned on his heel and marched down the corridor, hopefully on his way outside. When he turned into another hall, she looked toward the door where Tristan hid.

Did I succeed—or was I too transparent? For some reason, she wanted his reassurance that she hadn't blundered.

The door began to open, granting Freddie the glimpse of his profile. As she smiled in welcome, he shut the door again in haste. Why...

"Freddie, dear, was that Lord Harker?"

Freddie's heart kicked into a gallop at her mother's voice. She turned, though her smile felt wan. "Indeed it was. I, um, thought it best to let someone know that I wasn't feeling quite the thing and intended to take my supper in my room."

The worried lines in Mama's forehead deepened. She reached forward to press the back of her hand against Freddie's cheek. "You don't feel hot."

"I don't have a fever, Mama. I'm just feeling a trifle out of sorts. A night's rest will do wonders, I'm sure. Will you be able to give my regrets to the Graylockes? And to Charlie, too, of course."

Mama frowned, but she murmured, "Of course."

Freddie kissed her on the cheek and bid her goodnight. She watched as Mama slipped back into the room, then breathed a sigh of relief. This time when she turned to the closet door, Tristan had already slipped through.

Did he look a touch worried? He held out his hand. "Come. We don't have much time. I need to oversee the exchange, in case something goes awry."

"I thought you said the duke will be lying in wait."

"He will be, if he can slip away from the gathering in time. But I haven't had the opportunity to inform him about the change in plan."

The lines near his eyes deepened. He took hold of her hand, threading his fingers through hers.

As he turned to lead her down the deserted corridor, she whispered, "Are you afraid this won't turn out as we'd planned?"

The smile he bestowed upon her was blinding. It was also fake. His eyes didn't twinkle the same way they did when he usually smiled at her.

"I will turn out fine. It must."

She tightened her fingers on his, propriety be damned, and let him lead her through the abbey.

When they reached the open twilight, he reluctantly let her slip her hand away and follow him instead. His hand flexed on the empty air before he thrust it into his pocket. He didn't speak until they reached the bottom of the low rise leading to the tree. A portly figure paced beneath the shadow of the branches, too far away to make out his features.

Harker. It has to be.

The constriction of worry around Freddie's chest loosened somewhat. At least until Tristan turned to her.

"I'll have to leave you here."

"What?" She reached out, hoping to grasp his hand and keep him nearby, but he was too far away. "Why?"

"I have to meet with my brother and explain. He'll be on the north side of the hill." Tristan's dark gaze latched onto Freddie's face, his expression etched with concern. "There's a deer trail almost hidden in the brush on the south side. Take that to the fallen branch at the top and hide there. That will be close enough for you to witness the proceedings."

She opened her mouth to protest, but shut it without a word. She nodded. He could easily have insisted she wait out the debacle elsewhere. At least this way, she got to see this through.

To what end, she didn't yet know.

She swallowed hard and nibbled on her lower lip. "Goodbye, then."

He grinned. "Don't make it sound like you're off to the gallows. I'll see you again shortly."

Her heart leapt as he captured her hand and laid his lips against her knuckles. She warmed. She would rather have his lips elsewhere, but now wasn't the time. She and Tristan had to save her family.

As he slipped away to the north, she turned south. It didn't take long to find the trail he spoke of, wedged between the thorny bushes climbing the south side of the rise. They shielded her approach, at least, so long as she crouched.

It took entirely too long to navigate that trail. After ripping one of her few netted over-gowns, Freddie didn't want to ruin another. Waddling from bush to bush didn't help. She must have looked ridiculous if anyone spotted her climbing the hill. Luckily, the south side faced away from Tenwick Abbey.

Eventually, she met the fallen branch. At least a foot in diameter, she would have called it a tree, rather than a branch. It must have parted ways from the tree overhead quite some time ago, because there were no gaps in the nearly-leafless canopy overhead. Moss crept up its sides. She laid flat on her belly behind the earthy-smelling branch and peeked her head over to see the proceedings. It was a good thing her hair was brown, unlikely to be noticed.

Harker paused in his pacing at someone else's approach. A needle-thin man with a weak chin, utterly forgettable in his modest attire and meek deportment, crested the rise to stand in front of the tree.

"You." The man's nasal voice sounded surprised. Likely he had been expecting someone else —Freddie.

She scanned the far side of the tree. Where was Tristan? Unlike the south side, the north side had no cover to shield him. Harker's back was turned to him, but if he had been there, Freddie should have seen him. Had he been delayed? Did Harker have another agent left behind to do harm to anyone who approached?

Freddie's stomach lurched at the notion. Perhaps she was wrong. Perhaps Tristan was still engaged in relaying the situation to his brother. If so, he'd best hurry, or he would miss the exchange.

The thin man—who must be in the duke's employ, if not a spy for England—said in a timid voice, "My lord, I believe all the guests are to be seated at supper shortly. You'll have to hurry, if you don't want your gracious hosts to take offense."

Freddie marveled over the tone of his voice, coupled with his demeanor. His shoulders hunched forward, as if to make himself smaller. In a few words and a gesture of his hand, he made his idea sound like the best in the world, almost as though Harker had suggested it himself. Could Freddie learn to do that?

Fortunately, Harker was unmoved. He smiled, showing his teeth. "I'm not merely a guest. Trust me when I say you'll want to meet with me." With an almost comical rendition of the hand signal, he spoke the code word.

The spy's mien changed immediately. He drew himself up and said in a commanding tone, "Lord Elias Harker, you are hereby arrested in the name of Britain for the impersonation of a royal spy."

"No," Harker said, though his voice was strained. "I assure you, my allegiances have changed. I've been passing along information for Britain for some months—"

The spy paid his tirade no mind. His voice laden with sarcasm as he stepped forward, he said, "Then I'd love to know why you passed along a fake signal left for an enemy spy."

"There's been a mistake!"

The man snorted. He dug into the pocket of his coat.

Harker was quicker. He pulled a pistol from his pocket and shot the spy. As the man crumpled to the ground, clutching his shoulder, Freddie's ears rang. She didn't immediately realize that she'd screamed until Harker turned in her direction, gun still raised.

Tristan and his brother erupted from behind the five-foot-wide tree trunk. Freddie scrambled to get her feet under her, only to trip over her hem and collapse on top of the half-rotted, mossy branch. Harker's expression morphed into fiery outrage.

And then the shot went off.

Chapter Twenty-Five

Red bloomed on Harker's chest like the morbid unfurling of a flower's petals. His eyes glazed over as he collapsed face first onto the ground. Tristan and the duke fumbled to get their pistols out of their pockets and raised. If they hadn't shot him, then who…

Freddie rolled her back to the log to find her mother lowering a smoking pistol. Mama's face was set, her chin stubborn. Tendrils of her gray-and-blond hair escaped her coif, lending her a feral look. Freddie had never seen her looking so hard.

Tristan skidded to a stop beside Harker's gurgling corpse, his brother on his heels. Both raised their weapons at Mama.

No. Freddie had to stop this. She lurched to her feet, intending to throw herself between both parties if need be. Before she caught her balance, her mother dropped the pistol. It landed on the ground with a thud. Mama raised her hand, touching her forehead, then her lips, then her chest.

"A rose plucked unwillingly houses the sharpest thorns."

What?

The Graylocke brothers looked equally baffled. The duke's jaw dropped. "*You're* our contact?"

Wait, what? Mama was a spy? No. It couldn't be true. Freddie had been the only thing holding her family together upon Papa's death. Mama was too weak and malleable to spy.

"I was."

Mama stepped forward. She barely glanced at Freddie. Instead, she hiked her mauve skirt to her knees as she stepped over the branch. She skirted the growing red stain on the grass and crouched to lay her fingers at Harker's neck, beneath his cravat.

Her mouth twisted into an expression of disgust as she stood. "I'm not sure what good I'll do you, now. My value to the Crown rested in my ability to spy on Harker and report his movements."

Freddie's ears rang. Her breath gushed from her chest. When her knees weakened, she sat heavily on the log. It groaned, but held her weight.

"Mama? You're a spy?" The roar in her ears drowned out her words, but her mother must have heard, because she turned away from the Graylocke brothers.

The duke said something about a book and Tenwick Abbey, but Mama waved him off to attend to his spy. Until then, in her shock Freddie had forgotten there was another casualty. Her breath caught and she prayed the man was still alive.

Tristan caught her gaze and held it. He looked like he wanted to say something, but his brother called for his attention and he turned to attend the fallen man. The duke pressed his hand to the man's shoulder. He must still be alive.

Freddie half-expected Mama to follow after them and offer her assistance. Instead, she hiked her skirts and crossed over the log to sit beside Freddie.

Freddie swallowed twice, trying to summon her voice. When she did, it emerged as a distant croak. "Don't you want to help them?"

She clutched Freddie's hand. The squeeze barely registered. Her hand felt numb. Was Freddie going to swoon? She had more mettle than that. Her mouth tasted metallic.

"I'm more worried about you."

"I wasn't shot."

Mama smirked. The weak expression faded immediately. "I'm glad for that, darling, but you don't look well. You've had a shock." She pressed her free hand against Freddie's cheeks and clucked her tongue. "Clammy."

When she tried to pull out of Freddie's grasp, she clutched Mama's hand tighter.

"Freddie, darling. I need the smelling salts in my reticule. I'm not leaving."

Mama spoke in soft, dulcet tones that brought to mind the lullabies she used to sing when Freddie was ill. Reluctantly, Freddie loosened her hold, letting Mama dig through the embroidered reticule hanging from her wrist. The embroidery was only haphazardly done, including what was either supposed to be a dog or a dragon. It was one of the first things Charlie had stitched as a child. Mama refused to part with it for one better made, despite Charlie's repeated entreaties. Mama said she cherished it, because it reminded her of the past.

When she pulled out the small vial containing the smelling salts, Freddie made a face. "I hate those."

"I know." Mama uncorked it. "Have a sniff. They'll make you feel better."

With a sigh, Freddie leaned forward to endure the noxious torture. If anything could make her wish for a head cold, it was smelling salts. They did help to grant her some clarity, though. She took a deep breath of the fresh, clean air once Mama put the horrid bottle away. What was supposed to be a cleansing breath turned into a cough at the ripe stench of Harker's body lying not far away.

Mama eased her hand beneath Freddie's elbow. "Perhaps we should go inside."

Freddie dug in her heels. There was no love lost between her and Harker. In fact, it was a relief to know that neither Charlie nor Mama would ever become the subject of his attentions again. That ordeal was over.

Even if Freddie didn't quite know how she would keep a roof over everyone's head. No doubt Harker's estates fell to some long-lost male relative, if not the Crown.

"No, Mama. Not until you explain. How long have you been a spy?"

Mama sighed. Her shoulders drooped. "Since we moved into Lord Harker's household." When Freddie opened her mouth, Mama held up her hand. "Wait a moment. Let me collect my thoughts and start at the beginning. I only want to tell the tale once."

"What about Charlie?"

Mama pursed her lips. "Twice, then."

Satisfied, Freddie clasped her hands on her lap and waited. She tried not to breathe through her nose, to minimize the stench. If she didn't turn around and look at Harker's corpse, she could pretend he wasn't even there.

"Your father had a gambling problem," Mama began.

Freddie swallowed, but didn't interrupt. She knew that already.

Mama wasn't looking at her face. Instead, her gaze was fixed on the scenery, the line of trees cropping up on the edge of Tenwick Abbey to the south. "The problem with gambling is that whenever he lost, he always thought he would be able to win it back. Even if he recouped some of the money, he kept trying, and eventually, he lost again. Sometimes, even worse. By the time you turned fifteen, he feared that he would be hauled away to debtor's prison at any moment. The Crown came to him with a proposal, instead."

Freddie opened her mouth, but her voice must have fled to the soles of her feet with the shock. She shut her mouth again.

Mama continued, "They offered to absolve his debt and set me up with a small annuity if I completed a task for them."

"If *you* did?"

Mama turned her head, catching Freddie's gaze. Her eyes were cloudy in the growing twilight. "Yes, Freddie. Me. They knew Lord Harker was a traitor, you see, and they needed someone to report on his movements. As your father was Harker's closest living relative, if something were to happen to him, I would be in a prime position to insert myself into Lord Harker's household. From there, I could report on his movements, his correspondence, his associates. Any number of things."

Freddie gasped. "So the Crown killed Papa?"

"What?" Mama barked out an incredulous laugh. "Heavens, no. Don't be silly! Your father entered the service as well."

Freddie groped for Mama's hand. She didn't realize how tight her grip was until pain flashed across Mama's face. Freddie licked her dry lips. "Are you...are you saying that Papa is alive?"

Mama nodded. "He is. He leads a secret life somewhere in France, to the best of my knowledge. Our communication has been limited ever since I took up position in Lord Harker's household. Maybe now..."

Freddie shook her head. "Why didn't you tell me?"

Tears glimmered in Mama's eyes. "You and Charlie were so young when it happened. I thought it better to keep you innocent of the endeavor. Then, as you got older... Can you blame me for not wanting this dangerous life for you? I wanted you to have a chance at a normal life."

Helpless, Freddie shrugged. "I was introduced to this life anyway, by Harker. If I'd known what he was from the beginning I might have been able to do things differently."

Mama clutched Freddie's hand tightly. Movement from the corner of her eye and an agonized groan from the base of the tree caught Freddie's attention. Tristan finished tying a makeshift bandage around the wounded man's shoulder. The

Graylocke brothers positioned themselves at the spy's head and feet in preparation of lifting him.

In a steely voice, Mama said, "It's over, now. That's the important thing."

His hands red with blood, Tristan lifted his arm as if to run his fingers through his hair. He stopped at the last minute and gripped the spy's ankles instead. When he glanced up, his gaze met Freddie's.

She was too far away to discern the expression in his eyes, but if they in any way mirrored the emotions in her heart, he must be battling an inner turmoil. Longing, relief, uncertainty. Love.

When Mama urged Freddie to stand and leave the hilltop, she turned her face away from Tristan's, unable to look at him any longer and contemplate a future she might never have. Mama was right, this ordeal with Harker was over. But where did that leave Freddie and Tristan?

Chapter Twenty-Six

The Graylocke ancestors stared at Freddie with varying degrees of disapproval, but at the very least, it was a respite from the chaos in the rest of the abbey. Even the duke's cleverness hadn't been able to hide the fact that someone had been shot and a guest killed during supper last night. The servants flitted from room to room, gathering in groups to speculate.

The guests were worse. Although they should be packing in preparation of leaving early this week, the entire east wing was filled with sobbing, bacon-brained women bewailing who would be next—as though the Graylockes would allow a rampaging killer to roam free! Those not sniveling spread gossip like the plague, speculating that Harker had been killed in an illegal duel over a woman; now every debutante's reputation was suspect. Packing was conducted with doors wide open and women strolling alongside the strong, fearsome men they browbeat into escorting them, lest they need protection. Although the dowager duchess roamed the halls, assuring everyone they were in no danger, the ninnies of the *ton* seemed determined to fear the worst.

Freddie wouldn't mind half so much if their agitation hadn't unsettled Charlie even further. Last night, as Freddie had listened to her mother recite the same tale to Charlie as she had to Freddie beneath the oak, Freddie had tried to muster some sort of relief that her father was alive. But no, even if he'd left at the crown's behest, he'd still abandoned his family and left Freddie to pick up the pieces. At the moment, she was feeling a little churlish at Mama, as well. Clearly, Mama wasn't nearly as weak a person as she'd pretended all these years, perhaps for Harker's benefit. If Mama had only taken responsibility for the family instead of seemingly fallen apart, Freddie wouldn't have had to grow up so quickly.

Maybe she might even have the same charm and polish to attract a husband as Charlie.

Therein lay the rub. Until she'd met Tristan, she'd never wanted or needed a marriage. But he made her feel beautiful, strong, and protected. With Tristan to support her, she felt as though she could take on the world.

Oh, blast. She didn't want any husband. She wanted Tristan Graylocke. A man she hadn't spoken to since the messy debacle yesterday. Granted, Freddie had been occupied for most of the night in dissuading Charlie from haring off to

France to find their father. And neither Tristan nor the duke had surfaced from the west wing of the house, where the physician had rushed to tend Mr. Keeling, the man who had been shot. In a few short hours, she would depart Tenwick Abbey. She might never see him again.

She didn't quite know where her family would go, now that Harker was dead. But Freddie was resourceful. She would take care of her family. The thought of doing it alone, without Tristan, made her weary. He'd said he loved her...but he'd been trying to sway her to his side. Which, admittedly, she should have been on all along.

It all worked out for the best.

So she told herself, but Tristan hadn't proposed. He hadn't sought her out. Perhaps he didn't care for her as much as she did for him.

She eyed the door leading to the passage ending in the west wing. A swarm of butterflies took wing in her stomach. If she wanted to know for sure, maybe she had to seek him out.

She rose from her makeshift seat of a sturdy pedestal, leaving the ugly bronze statue she'd moved on the floor next to it. Squaring her shoulders, she stepped toward that ominous door.

"You're a difficult woman to find, Freddie."

Her heart somersaulted as Tristan's voice echoed in the cavernous chamber. She turned. He leaned against the frame of the door. The daylight pouring in from the high windows illuminated the chiseled planes of his face, but cast his eyes in shadow.

Freddie licked her lips. She dropped her gaze to her feet as she traversed the length of the hall, determined not to trip. When his boot steps rang on the stone floor, she raised her gaze to meet his. There was something fierce and determined in his eyes. It stole her breath. Did he mean to kiss her?

She stumbled and collided against his chest as he leaped to catch her. His firm muscles rippled beneath his clothes. His arm slipped around her waist, pressing her against him as she found her feet once more. She raised her gaze. The desire to kiss him mounted. She stepped away, instead.

"I didn't know you were looking for me. I needed a moment away from...everyone. It's difficult to think up there."

Tristan took a small step forward. His gaze was locked on her mouth. Absently, he said, "Do you have something pressing on your mind?"

You.

Freddie swallowed. "With Harker dead, I'm not sure where we'll go. We won't have a home much longer." Not that Harker's townhouse had ever felt like home to her.

Reaching out, Tristan caught one of her hands. He held it between them, over his pounding heart. Could he be half as nervous to see her as she was to see him? He studied every inch of her face, from her eyelashes to the freckles on her cheeks.

When his gaze met hers squarely once more, he murmured, "You can stay here."

She licked her lips. "That's very kind, but—"

"No." His hand tightened on hers. "It isn't kind. It's selfish. I don't want to be parted from you, Freddie. I want you to stay here…as my wife."

Her breath caught. "Are you proposing to me?"

He nodded, a short, curt thrust of his head. He opened his mouth, but it took him a moment to speak again. "If you'll have me. You've seen what my life is like. It involves danger and secrets. I'll have to continue my cover as a gambler and carouser. That'll mean late nights in London." His grip lightened on her hand as he shifted to examine her fingers, tracing them with his. "I'm probably not the kind of husband any woman would want."

"Will you be faithful to me?"

His hand clenched on hers. He met her gaze, his eyes sharp. "Always. I love you. My God, Freddie, you have to ask?"

She covered their joined hands with hers and leaned closer. "I love you, too. Don't make yourself out to sound like you'll be a monster. Don't all men drink and gamble?"

He hesitated. "Most. Some don't stay out as late after marriage."

"I'd wager that's because they have beautiful wives awaiting them at home."

A smile teased at the corners of his mouth. When he leaned closer, she tilted her face up, hoping for a kiss. Instead, he whispered, "I would certainly have that. What do you say, Freddie? Will you be my beautiful wife?"

A thrill ran through her at the thought that he found her beautiful, born in part because she knew he did. With him, she felt wanton, seductive. It was a powerful feeling, one she looked forward to feeling for the rest of her life.

"Yes." Worry constricted her chest as she thought of her father. "Promise that you won't gamble us into debt, though."

He laid a chaste kiss on her knuckles. "I gamble at the crown's behest, with Crown funds. You don't have to worry."

Gambling could be addictive, an urge a man couldn't shake, but Tristan didn't seem to have that urge. He would have made good on it while she was here if he had. If he developed that addiction in the future... They would face the future together. Living without him wasn't an option.

She leaned closer, pressing her body against his. "I believe now is the time for you to kiss me."

He cocked an eyebrow. "Is it?" He obliged, pressing his mouth to hers in a sweet, lingering kiss.

Passion ignited between them and that kiss grew fierce. Freddie threaded the fingers of her free hand into his hair. Her other hand was still trapped between them alongside his.

When he broke the kiss, they both panted. They parted for only an instant before Freddie swayed closer, needing him to hold her up as her knees weakened. Their lips met again, then parted. Quick, butterfly kisses that she couldn't get enough of.

Tristan drew away. "I'll leave for London posthaste."

She tightened her hand on his, keeping him near. "Why?"

One side of his mouth raised in a rueful grin. "My dear, we'll need a special license if we're to have any hope of not anticipating our wedding vows."

Her cheeks flamed and she bit her lower lip, as much in expectation as modesty. "Perhaps we ought to announce our engagement first."

"More delays," he bemoaned, but he offered his arm to her nonetheless to escort her from the room.

She rested her cheek against his shoulder. "The reward will be that much sweeter."

He raised his hand to cover hers where it perched on his sleeve. His presence beside her was soothing and strengthening. They walked in companionable silence, the noise of the abbey mounting the closer they came to the guest wing. This time, instead of feeling overwhelming, it was a storm she could brave. No doubt they were about to give the rabble something else to squawk about, in any case.

She canted her head to admire the line of his jaw as she asked a question that had much weighed on her mind over the past week. "Where did you hide the book, by the way?"

He grinned at her. Butterflies batted at her stomach. He had no right to be so handsome.

Then again, considering she would be the sole object of his affections, perhaps he had every right.

"I can't tell you, or I'll never be able to hide anything from you!"

She turned her face to press her lips into his shoulder. "You won't need to hide anything from me, remember? We aren't enemies anymore. We're on the same side."

"So we are." His gaze softened. "In that case, I would be more than happy to show you my every hiding place, my dear. *After* the wedding."

Freddie had the feeling that that would be a rather wicked exploration, indeed. She couldn't wait.

Epilogue

Morgan Graylocke had never been so happy for a moment alone. With a sigh, he abandoned the candle-lit corridor in favor of his study.

He stopped short as the candle he held shed light on a man by the sideboard. His hand reached automatically for the butt of the pistol he didn't carry while in Tenwick Abbey.

Perhaps, given the events of the last few weeks, he should start.

As the man turned, granting Morgan the knowledge of his identity, Morgan relaxed somewhat. He shut the door to his study and crossed to his desk.

"Tristan isn't here. He's on honeymoon touring the Lake District with his new wife."

A strange sensation enveloped Morgan's chest. Though he'd suspected some attachment between the pair, his brother's plunge into marriage had taken him by surprise. Not too long ago, Tristan had been adamant that he wouldn't marry. What had changed?

Frederica Vale. Or Frederica Graylocke, as she was now known. Did that mean Morgan would one day meet a woman who would spin his world on its axis?

That was a notion he didn't care to contemplate.

As he turned back toward the stout man by the mantle, the unexpected visitor said, "Yes, I know. You conveyed the news in the same letter you used to announce Elias Harker's death."

Morgan gritted his teeth and fought the urge to flinch. The man, Lord Clement Strickland, spoke in a tone designed to eviscerate. In person, the Lord Commander of the spy network wasn't very threatening. His hair thinned on top and he carried a bit of a paunch, though not enough to hamper his mobility. His eyes crinkled at the corners like a benevolent grandfather, though he couldn't be much older than Mother. When he offered a friendly, jovial mien, he could coerce enemies into becoming loyal friends overnight. When he was livid, like now, he had been known to reduce grown men to tears.

Strickland stepped closer, his face a mask of outrage. "Harker was our biggest link to the French intelligence network in London. Now we are operating blind!"

Clenching the corner of his desk to steady himself, Morgan answered calmly. "The situation was far from ideal. I almost lost a man. He may never recover the full mobility of his arm."

Strickland snapped, "You'll have to find us Harker's replacement. We need to know what the French know, and for that, we need to have eyes on their man inside the *ton*."

Frustration beat at Morgan's chest. "I just told you Tristan is in the Lake District. He isn't at liberty to accept a mission at the moment."

"I'm not talking to Tristan, am I?"

Morgan's breath fled. Something surged within him, something that felt uncomfortably like hope. Eagerness. Excitement. Surely Strickland couldn't mean...

He cleared his throat. "Are you...are you assigning me to field duty?"

Strickland's eyes flashed in the candlelight. "I am. We can't wait for your brother to return from his honeymoon. We need this information now."

Morgan opened his mouth. He didn't know what to say. *Thank you. I won't let you down.*

Strickland had already turned his back. "Get your noble arse to London. Your man can keep up with the paperwork until you return. It sounds as though he isn't fit for field duty, anyway." At the door, Strickland turned, his eyebrows raised. "I expect to see you at your townhouse within the week."

Morgan straightened. "Yes, sir."

This was it. He was finally going to get out from behind his desk and make a difference.

Maybe he ought to thank Tristan for falling head over heels in love and getting married. It seemed to be working out to everyone's advantage.

Also By Leighann Dobbs

Regency Romance

***

The Unexpected Series:

An Unexpected Proposal

Dobbs Fancytales:

Dobbs Fancytales Boxed Set Collection

———

Western Historical Romance

***

Goldwater Creek Mail Order Brides:

Faith

American Mail Order Brides Series:

Chevonne: Bride of Oklahoma

Contemporary Romance

***

Reluctant Romance

Sweetrock Cowboy Romance Series:

Some Like It Hot (Book 1)

Too Close For Comfort (Book 2)

Witches of Hawthorne Grove Series:

Something Magical (Book 1)

COZY MYSTERIES

Blackmoore Sisters

Cozy Mystery Series

* * *

Dead Wrong

Dead & Buried

Dead Tide

Buried Secrets

Deadly Intentions

A Grave Mistake

Spell Found

Mooseamuck Island Cozy Mystery Series

* * *

A Zen For Murder

A Crabby Killer

A Treacherous Treasure

Mystic Notch Cat Cozy Mystery Series

* * *

Ghostly Paws

A Spirited Tail

A Mew To A Kill

Paws and Effect

Lexy Baker

Cozy Mystery Series

* * *

Lexy Baker Cozy Mystery Series Boxed Set Vol 1
(Books 1-4)

Or buy the books separately:

Killer Cupcakes
Dying For Danish
Murder, Money and Marzipan
3 Bodies and a Biscotti
Brownies, Bodies & Bad Guys
Bake, Battle & Roll
Wedded Blintz
Scones, Skulls & Scams
Ice Cream Murder
Mummified Meringues
Brutal Brulee (Novella)

About Leighann Dobbs

USA Today Bestselling author Leighann Dobbs has had a passion for reading since she was old enough to hold a book, but she didn't put pen to paper until much later in life. After a twenty-year career as a software engineer with a few side trips into selling antiques and making jewelry, she realized you can't make a living reading books, so she tried her hand at writing them and discovered she had a passion for that, too! She lives in New Hampshire with her husband, Bruce, their trusty Chihuahua mix, Mojo, and beautiful rescue cat, Kitty.

Find out about her latest books and how to get discounts on them by signing up at:

http://www.leighanndobbs.com/news-letter-historical-romances

If you want to receive a text message alert on your cell phone for new releases, text ROMANCE to 88202 (sorry, this only works for US cell phones!)

Connect with Leighann on Facebook:

https://www.facebook.com/leighanndobb-shistoricalromance/

About Harmony Williams

Harmony Williams has always longed for the adventurous life of a spy. Unfortunately, she's even more clumsy than Freddie, so she's had to make do with writing out exciting tales instead of living them. She lives in rural Ontario, Canada with her 90-pound dog, who proves to her every time he squeezes himself onto her lap that all it takes to accomplish your goals is determination! Visit her online at *www.harmonywilliams.com* or subscribe to her newsletter at *http://eepurl.com/bUWUof*

Made in the USA
Las Vegas, NV
20 January 2023